D0007789

KISS AND TELL

KISS AND TELL

A Truth or Dare Novel

JACQUELINE GREEN

poppy

LITTLE, BROWN AND COMPANY
NEW YORK BOSTON

Copyright © 2015 by Paper Lantern Lit

Poppy

Hachette Book Group
1290 Avenue of the Americas, New York, NY 10104
Visit us at lb-teens.com

Poppy is an imprint of Little, Brown and Company.
The Poppy name and logo are trademarks of Hachette Book Group, Inc.

The publisher is not responsible for websites
(or their content) that are not owned by the publisher.

First Edition: February 2015

Library of Congress Cataloging-in-Publication Data

Green, Jacqueline, 1983–
    Kiss and tell : a Truth or dare novel / Jacqueline Green.—First edition.
        pages cm
    Summary: "High school seniors Tenley Reed, Sydney Morgan, and Emerson Cunningham follow clues that lead them to the killer behind a twisted game of truth or dare set in the isolated beach town of Echo Bay, Massachusetts"—Provided by publisher.
    ISBN 978-0-316-22033-0 (hardback)—ISBN 978-0-316-22032-3 (ebook)—ISBN 978-0-316-36506-2 (library edition ebook) [1. Murder—Fiction. 2. Conduct of life—Fiction. 3. Massachusetts—Fiction. 4. Mystery and detective stories.] I. Title.
    PZ7.G8228Kis 2015
    [Fic]—dc23
                                                        2014024951

10 9 8 7 6 5 4 3 2 1

RRD-C

Printed in the United States of America

For Lauren, Rachel, and Meryl—three girls I'd be lost without

PROLOGUE

THE CLIFFS WERE SLICK WITH SNOW, AND SHE SLIPPED as she climbed higher, slamming hard onto her knees. Pain reeled through her, but she refused to stop. In the distance, a round beam of light broke through the snow. *A flashlight.*

The killer was here.

She pushed herself further. One foot, then the next, then—*ice.*

Her foot slid out from under her. Suddenly she was careening forward, the edge of the cliff much too close. She cried out as she caught herself on a jagged rock. She stretched a toe out, searching for a safe pathway, but at every angle she was met with ice. This high up, it coated everything.

Behind her, the flashlight burned brighter. She was trapped.

She looked out over the cliff. The storm was colorless: stark white brushstrokes against a black sky. Down below she could hear the ocean roaring and crashing. She wrenched the sapphire ring off her finger. She was breathing hard as she threw it over the cliff.

She was nearly at the edge now. Just a few more inches and, like the ring, she, too, would fall into nothingness.

The icy crunch of footsteps rang out through the night.

There was nowhere left to run. Nowhere left to hide.

CHAPTER ONE
Sunday, 11:37 PM

SYDNEY WAS DRIVING MUCH TOO FAST. THE SCENERY blurred outside her window, but it didn't matter; she could dredge up every inch of it from memory. The sprawling Cape Cod–style homes. The paved walking path that wound alongside the ocean. The taut stretches of golden sand, dotted with seagulls. On the surface, Echo Bay looked like a picture-perfect beach town. But things weren't always what they seemed. Sydney had learned that the hard way.

Her phone buzzed from inside the car's cup holder. Instantly, her muscles tensed, but she forced herself to relax. *It can't be from the darer*, she reminded herself. Earlier that morning, she, Tenley, and Emerson had destroyed their cells, running over them with Tenley's car. Sydney was now using an ancient, beat-up phone that had once belonged to her mom—probably back when smartphones were first invented. The upside was that no one but her parents, Emerson, and Tenley had her new number.

She grabbed for her cell at a red light. *23 minutes till MOT*, Tenley had texted.

MOT: Moment of Truth. It was what Tenley had taken to calling tonight ever since they'd sent a threat to the darer on Facebook that morning: *It's over. There's no more tracker, no more phones. If you want us, you're going to have to come get us. The pier, tonight at midnight. It's show and tell, remember? And it's finally time you show.*

Sydney slammed on the gas as soon as the light changed, making her car lurch forward. She was sick of being played and tortured, taunted and teased. She was ready to catch whoever was sending the dares.

Dares. The word made rage boil under her skin. Every time her focus slipped, the memory would assault her: Delancey's lifeless body dangling from the beam last night. She'd looked so young up there in her homecoming dress, and so scared, her eyes frozen wide with horror. Bile rose in Sydney's throat. Delancey would never be in school again. She'd never run another Purity Club meeting or choose another photo for the yearbook or spend another lunch period whispering with Abby Wilkins. She would never graduate from high school or go to college, leave Echo Bay or get married. She would be a high school senior forever, just like Caitlin and Tricia—and it was all because of one person's sick, twisted game.

For over a month now, someone had been after them: sending them threatening notes and punishing them when they disobeyed.

Caitlin had paid the ultimate price, dying out on the ocean, and now Sydney, Emerson, and Tenley had been promised a similar fate. They'd blamed Tricia, then Delancey. But it turned out that those two were just puppets. There was a mastermind behind them both, pulling their strings.

Sydney screeched to a stop on Hillworth Drive. Tenley was already there. She wore black jeans and a black sweater under her dark coat, her long chestnut waves swept back in a ponytail. With Sydney's own all-black ensemble and ponytail, they almost matched: a spying uniform. "You drove?" Sydney asked. Tenley lived a short walk away, in one of the oceanfront mansions that lined Dune Way.

"Leg's sore." Tenley gestured to her left leg. Her pants covered the injury, but Sydney had seen it before it was bandaged: an angry red burn slicing across Tenley's calf. Last night at the homecoming dance, the darer had lured Tenley onto the auditorium's catwalk, where a spotlight had been rigged to fall on her. Tenley had been lucky to walk away with just that burn.

Tenley lifted up a long-lens camera. Sydney recognized it as one of Guinness's, but she quickly pushed the thought away. She couldn't let anything distract her right now. "You have yours?" Tenley asked.

Sydney responded by crawling into the backseat of her car. Her hand brushed against her RISD scholarship application, making her jaw clench up. It was due tomorrow. "My two best," she said as she climbed out with the cameras she'd brought. Their lenses glinted under the beam of her car's headlights.

"You should probably…" Tenley nodded toward the lights.

Their plan was contingent on the darer never seeing them. It was why they'd parked five blocks from the pier. Sydney switched off the headlights, and darkness spilled in, making the hair on her arms stand on end. "Do you really think this will work?"

"It has to," Tenley said softly, and again Sydney saw it: Delancey's crooked neck, her feet swinging in her high heels. "If we can get a photo of the darer—actual, hard evidence of who this person is—then we'll finally have something we can lord over him or her."

Sydney nodded. Earlier that day, they'd taken a small step in figuring out more about the darer. So many crimes had plagued Echo Bay over the past ten years—the deaths of the Lost Girls, Caitlin's kidnapping in sixth grade, and now their own stalker—and each incident seemed tied to one another. It had made them wonder: What if the same person had been tormenting Echo Bay residents for all these years?

But how could they go to the cops? Last night, when the police came for Delancey's body, Tenley had blurted out that it was murder, even though they'd been warned against it. The cops had explained that wasn't possible: Delancey had left behind a suicide note. Immediately after, the darer had texted Tenley. *Tsk, tsk, Ten. Looks like I have another girl to silence.*

Even if they could convince the police, it would take the cops weeks to hunt down the culprit—plenty of time for the darer to exact retribution. But if the girls took in a photo of their stalker, then the police would have a real lead, which meant they wouldn't have to waste time searching.

A pair of headlights flashed in the distance. The car flew toward them without slowing, its lights blinding. Sydney shielded her eyes, her brain frozen on a single thought: *Darer.* Next to her, Tenley grabbed Sydney's arm, her hand cold and clammy.

The car skidded to a stop a few feet away. The headlights switched off, and Emerson Cunningham climbed out. She, too, wore all black, but in her leather jacket and cashmere scarf, she still managed to look photo-shoot ready.

Sydney sagged with relief as she handed Emerson a camera. "Phones on vibrate?" Emerson asked. Sydney nodded. So did Tenley. "Okay, then." There was a tremor in Emerson's voice. "Let's do this."

They were silent as they walked the five blocks to the pier. Sydney's pulse raced faster with each step. "I guess it's time to split up," she said hesitantly. None of them moved. Sydney felt for Tenley's hand in the dim light of the pier. "*M-O-T,*" she said.

They all turned away at once. They'd chosen their individual stakeout spots during a run-through earlier that day; they were each to cover one section of the pier. Soon the darkness swallowed up the others, leaving Sydney all alone. It was cold by the water, and she wrapped her coat tighter around her as she located the boat she'd chosen earlier. Small and tethered close to the pier. A perfect hiding spot.

She clutched her camera to her chest as she climbed into the boat. It rocked under her feet, making her stomach flip as she knelt beneath its rim and dropped her purse next to her. Minutes crept past, the only sound the shriek of a seagull overhead. The ocean slapped against the docks, punctuating the silence.

A clock on the boat glowed. *11:56.* What if no one showed?

Sydney's chest hitched. Or what if someone did—and her hiding spot wasn't good enough?

Her grip tightened on the camera as time ticked by.

11:59.

There was a sound.

Sydney froze, every nerve suddenly on high alert. There it was again—a footstep! It came from above. Sydney lifted her camera, her gaze landing on the country club's pool deck, which jutted out over the ocean at the end of the pier. Her hands shook as she trained her camera on the deck. But the darkness formed a barricade; she couldn't see past it.

Her finger rested on the camera's shutter button. She could press it—set off a flash and clear the cobweb of darkness. But what if it wasn't the darer? Or what if it was and the flash scared him or her away before she could get a clear shot?

A loud scuffle up on the pool deck gave her a start. Her finger slammed against the button before she could catch her balance.

Flash.

For a single instant, the sky lit up. The light caught something tumbling over the railing of the pool deck. Arms and legs and—*oh god.*

Her camera slipped from her hands. The world seemed to stop as Sydney watched the body plummet through the air. She heard it hit the water with a sickening splash. She was moving before she could fully process what had happened, grabbing her flashlight and sprinting off the boat and down the pier.

Was it the darer?

No. The darer didn't lose, didn't make mistakes. Which could mean only one thing: It was another victim.

Panic clutched at Sydney's chest. If this was retribution...If someone else had died because of the threat they'd sent the darer...

Tenley and Emerson must have seen the fall, too, because Sydney heard them running behind her, their footsteps breaking open the silence. It didn't matter. None of it mattered anymore, not their plan, not the photo. All that mattered was getting to the victim. Could someone survive that fall?

Sydney reached the shore at the end of the pier first. She scrambled to turn on her flashlight, shining its thin beam over the ocean. Body parts caught the light as they tossed on the waves. A leg. An arm. A flash of long blond hair. It was a girl. "We need to get her out!" she heard Tenley scream.

Instinct took over as Sydney dropped the flashlight and launched herself into the ocean. She gasped as the cold water stabbed at her. Her limbs screamed in resistance, but she ordered them to move, kicking and paddling toward the body. *Please don't be dead.* The thought crashed into her with each wave, again and again.

Two splashes sounded behind her. She could hear Tenley and Emerson in the water now, but she kept her eyes locked on the body. The girl was bobbing facedown, her hair floating in a halo around her.

Paddle. Kick. *Please don't be dead.* Paddle. Kick. *Please don't be dead.*

"Who is it?" Tenley screamed. Sydney shook her head soundlessly. It was too dark to tell. The darkness made everything seem mercurial, as if at any moment she could blink and this would all disappear.

Another stroke and Sydney was at the girl's side. She hooked her arm around the body, but the girl was slippery and heavy—soaked with water—and when a wave hit, she couldn't hold on. Sydney paddled desperately, trying to stay afloat. "I need help!" She tried again, but a fresh wave hit, pulling her under instead.

She came up gasping for air. Emerson was there, wrapping her arms around the body. "Let's get her to shore." Tenley reached them, too, and together they towed the body to the sandy beach at the end of the pier.

"On three!" Tenley said. "One, two—"

Together, they crawled onto shore, dragging the girl's body with them. Sydney's teeth were chattering violently, but all she could focus on was the girl. "Is she—?" Tenley began.

She stopped short.

The girl was on her back, blond hair splayed around her. Except she wasn't a girl at all.

Sydney collapsed onto her knees next to the body. A red clown nose and black beady eyes stared up at her. "A doll," she choked out. "It's a clown doll." Scrawled across the clown's face in thick red marker was a message.

This is no joke.

Sydney couldn't breathe. Once again their tormentor had bested them. He or she had been there—had fooled them—and then had vanished again without a trace.

Unless...

Her camera. She raced down to the pier, panting as she snatched her camera off the boat. She jabbed at the screen. There it was: the photo that had lit up the night. The pool deck was too tiny to make out any details. She zoomed in, and then zoomed in again. A doll came into focus, hoisted on top of the deck's railing. Behind it, a shadowy figure ducked low.

She zoomed in again and again, as close as the camera would let her. But the figure on the deck remained nothing more than a dark outline, impossible even to tell if it was male or female.

Buzz!

The noise made Sydney jump. It was coming from the boat. From inside her purse.

Buzz!

There it was again, this time from behind her. Emerson joined her on the pier, then Tenley. They were both holding their phones.

Buzz! Buzz!

"How?" Emerson whispered. "We have new cells, new numbers!"

No one replied. Terror became a noose as, with a single click, the text message popped up on Sydney's phone.

Mutiny leads to war—and I fight dirty.

CHAPTER TWO
Monday, 7:50 AM

TENLEY IGNORED THE ACHE IN HER LEG AS SHE
sprinted toward Winslow's red double doors. She'd overslept, and
now she was ten minutes late to school. Which would look just
great alongside the math test she'd recently bombed and the classes
she'd recently skipped. For a while the "my best friend died" excuse
had allowed these things to slide, but she could tell it was starting
to wear thin. What was she supposed to tell the attendance office
today? *Sorry I'm late, but I was awake half the night thanks to a clown
doll haunting my dreams.*

Tenley felt sick at the memory of what had happened last
night. At first, she'd been sure it was a person—another casualty
in this cruel game. As she'd watched the body fall, the possibilities
of who it could be had curled around her like smog, until she was
choking on them. *Mom. Marta. Tim.* But the whole thing was just

a sick joke, the darer's way of showing them that they weren't in control.

Mutiny leads to war—and I fight dirty.

The darer had already tried to kill Tenley twice—in her hot tub and on the catwalk in the auditorium. What was dirtier than that?

She was halfway to her locker when two large hands grabbed her from behind. The scream that slipped out of her was so high-pitched it sounded like it belonged to a little girl.

"Whoa there." The voice was low and lazy. And familiar. Tenley spun around to find Tim Holland staring down at her, an amused look in his dark blue eyes. "You being chased?"

Tenley tried to speak, but her voice was trapped somewhere beneath her still-pounding heart. She forced herself to focus on Tim: his messy, damp blond waves; his beat-up hemp necklace that he never took off; his calm, easy smile. "I overslept," she managed, finally.

"I oversurfed. It happens." Tim pushed a strand of hair off her cheek, and Tenley had to fight the urge to bury her head in his chest and not lift it again until Christmas. "Did you get my messages, Tenley? I've called you, like, ten times since you disappeared on me Saturday night."

Tenley tried not to wince. Tim had shown up at the homecoming dance Saturday night just for her. They'd kissed, and it had been amazing. But then everything had spiraled out of control and she hadn't spoken to him for the rest of the weekend. "I got a new phone number yesterday. I'm sorry. I meant to call and tell you, but it was a pretty rough day."

"Delancey, I know. The whole town's been talking about it." Tim entwined his fingers through hers. "How are you doing?"

Tenley sighed. "Honestly, I'm just trying really hard not to think about it."

"Maybe I can help with that." Tim pulled her into a hug. She closed her eyes, letting herself melt against him. His arms were strong and warm, and he smelled faintly of the ocean. She could feel the muscles in her neck unclenching, just a little.

"Miss Reed and Mr. Holland!"

Tenley drew away from Tim with a start. Mr. Lozano, the art teacher, crossed his arms against his chest as he strode toward them. "May I ask why you two are not at the assembly?"

Tim fiddled with the tangled mess of string bracelets tied around his wrist. "Assembly?"

"The suicide-prevention assembly that was announced just before homeroom?" Mr. Lozano arched an eyebrow. "It's mandatory."

"Oh *that* assembly," Tenley backtracked. "We're on our way right now. Tim was just helping me out." She gestured down to her left leg, which was thicker than her right thanks to the bandage underneath her jeans. "I hurt my leg, so I'm moving more slowly."

"Oh." Mr. Lozano nodded, looking placated. "Take your time, then."

Tenley gave the art teacher her sweetest smile before limping off toward the auditorium. "Impressive," Tim murmured as he made a big show of assisting her. "I should keep you around to get me out of detentions."

Normally, Tenley would have been quick with a retort. *You*

should keep me around for more than that. But her thoughts were stuck at a standstill on the assembly. *Suicide prevention.*

Everyone in town, cops included, believed Delancey's death was a suicide. Besides the darer, only Tenley, Sydney, and Emerson knew the truth. Their tormentor had hunted Delancey, torturing and toying with her before going in for the kill.

Tenley's eyes went immediately to the front of the room as she and Tim entered the auditorium. The same person had tried to kill her on that very stage. In the two days since, the stage had been mended and scrubbed clean. If it weren't for a few cracked planks on the catwalk above, you'd never know anything had happened.

"Looks like your fan club saved you a seat." Tim nodded toward the back of the auditorium, where Emerson and Sydney were waving her over. Between Sydney's rat nest of a ponytail and Emerson's unusually drab outfit, they looked as terrible as Tenley felt.

"I should probably—"

"Go," Tim agreed. "Find me later." He gave her a quick smile before sauntering over to the exit row, where his best friends, Tray Macintyre and Sam Spencer, were seated.

"Did you show up with Tim Holland?" Emerson whispered as Tenley dropped into the empty seat next to her. Emerson's brown sweater dress might have been unusually plain for her, but her cocoa-latte skin glowed as always. "What were you talking to him about?"

Tenley hesitated. She hadn't told anyone she'd kissed Tim at the homecoming dance. Caitlin had dated Tim before she died, and Tenley knew how touchy that made this situation. But Tenley and Tim had bonded over missing Cait, and she'd been surprised by how much she liked him.

"I bumped into him in the hall," Tenley answered vaguely. Her gaze fell on the thick manila envelope Sydney was clutching. "What's that?" she asked, hoping to change the subject.

"My scholarship application for RISD." Sydney tugged at the red flannel shirt she was wearing, looking nervous. "It has to be postmarked by today, so I'm taking it to the office."

"I can't believe you're already doing applications," Tenley murmured. "I can't even *think* about applying to college until all this is over."

"I don't have a choice." Sydney gripped the folder more tightly. "Scholarship applications are due earlier in the year." She didn't say it accusingly, but, still, Tenley felt her face flush. She busied herself by pulling out her new phone. She'd splurged on the nicest case in the store: matte gold, with white polka dots.

Emerson pulled her own phone out with a smirk. It was identical to Tenley's. "Nice case."

"Better than mine." Sydney held up her phone, which had a hideous orange case on it, imprinted with the letter *S*. She gave them a wry smile. "It was the only one I could find that was old enough to fit."

"No phones, girls," Miss Hilbrook called out sternly. Her lips were pursed as she patrolled the aisles of the auditorium. "Eyes up front."

Tenley turned obediently to the stage, where Mrs. Shuman, the school counselor, was standing with Principal Howard. "Delancey Crane was a beloved student at Winslow," Mrs. Shuman said, her voice trembling as it poured through the auditorium's speakers. "She was cofounder of the Purity Club, head of the yearbook committee, and enrolled in all honors classes. She was a kind person and a dedicated student, and now, because of a tough time, she's gone."

Mrs. Shuman teetered on her heels. Her eyes flitted across the auditorium, wide and dismayed, and suddenly Tenley got the feeling that she knew something—knew the truth. But then she cleared her throat, and her lips curled down at the corners, and she was just naive Mrs. Shuman again, the counselor who passed out lollipops to high school students.

"Delancey was just like the rest of you," Mrs. Shuman continued. "And I think she'd want us to take a lesson away from this. Depression and suicidal thoughts can happen to anyone. If you notice a friend who's down or acting strange, it's your responsibility to talk to them, to ask a question." A motto flashed across the screen behind her as she spoke: ASK A QUESTION, SAVE A LIFE. "We'll be passing out information packets on suicide prevention at the end of the assembly, but first, Abby Wilkins has put together a touching slide show to help us honor Delancey's life. I hope it reminds you all what's at stake here. We're at this school together, and that makes us responsible for one another's well-being."

As classical music played, photographs faded in and out on the screen. Delancey running into the ocean, curls flying in the wind. Delancey volunteering with the Red Cross, her porcelain skin reddened by the sun. Delancey posing with her parents, her arms draped around their shoulders. As a photo of Delancey wearing this year's homecoming crown filled the screen, someone began to cry nearby. Soon the auditorium was filled with muffled sobs and sniffles.

On the screen, a photo of Delancey playing with her cat faded out, replaced by an image of Delancey and Abby. Delancey was smiling widely as she leaned against her best friend, and suddenly it wasn't Delancey that Tenley saw, but Caitlin. Caitlin squinting as she hung on to Tenley's every word. Caitlin brushing Tenley's hair after Tenley sprained her wrist in gymnastics. Caitlin yelling, "Race you!" and sprinting down the beach, her blond hair whipping in her face as she looked back at Tenley, laughing.

Tenley bit down on her lip so hard she drew blood. Caitlin was gone, and Delancey was gone, and Tenley had no idea who would be next. The darer had swept through their lives like a tornado, leaving only wreckage behind. Tenley looked over at Emerson and Sydney. She saw her own fierce expression reflected back at her.

"We're going to end this," Sydney whispered grimly.

"We're going to make this person pay," Emerson added.

Tenley nodded. She wanted to agree, to *insist*, but, for the second time that morning, her words were trapped inside her, just out of reach.

A burst of static drew Tenley's attention back to the stage. The screen showing the slide show had gone black. "What's going on?" a voice called out. There was another burst of static as a video flickered onto the screen. In it, a girl stood inside Winslow's empty locker room. Tenley sucked in a breath. The girl in the video wasn't Delancey. It was Tenley.

"What is this?" someone screeched from several rows up. Tenley recognized the high-pitched voice immediately. Only Abby Wilkins could sound that whiny and indignant at the same time. "What happened to my slide show?"

On the screen, Tenley walked over to a locker and looked

19

around furtively before opening it. Tenley watched in horror as the video showed her pulling a water bottle out of the locker. Two large red initials were inked on its side. *JM*. Video-Tenley glanced hastily over her shoulder again. When she saw that no one was coming, she took a small pink pill out of her pocket and dropped it into the water bottle. Then she shoved the bottle back into the locker and slammed the door shut.

Scandalized gasps filled the auditorium. People were twisting around, gaping at Tenley. She ignored them, her eyes glued to the screen. The footage skipped ahead. The locker room door swung open, and the cheerleading squad jogged in. Jessie Morrow, the captain of the squad, was at the front of the group. "This routine is going to kick ass," she said with a grin over her shoulder. She stopped in front of her locker and pulled out her water bottle. Two red initials—*JM*—winked in the fluorescent light of the locker room. "I'm talking epic pep rally." She lifted the bottle to her lips, taking a long swig of water.

A time stamp flashed on the screen. It was the day Jessie had a seizure during the pep rally.

"Oh my god!" someone shrieked in the auditorium.

"Did she drug her?" someone else cried.

The world darkened around Tenley. Voices lifted, swirling around her in a tunnel. *Insane . . . Criminal . . . Evil . . .* And then Principal Howard, screaming, "Quiet, everyone! Order!"

In her own head, the words from their text: *I fight dirty.*

"Ten—" Emerson began.

Tenley didn't stick around to hear the rest. Faces spun around her as she raced out of the auditorium. She flew down the hallway, searching for a place to be alone. She could still hear the voices behind her, in an uproar. There was a bathroom, but that was too public. An unmarked door caught her eye at the end of the hallway. *The janitor's closet.* She squeezed inside it. Tears clogged her vision as she slid to the ground on top of a mop head.

Everyone knew.

Everyone knew.

How could she ever leave this closet?

Beep!

The sound reached down through her thoughts, shaking her into awareness.

Beep!

Her hand clamped around her phone. The number was blocked, just as she'd expected.

Like I said: I fight dirty.

CHAPTER THREE
Monday, 8:29 AM

TENLEY WASN'T ANSWERING HER PHONE.

Any luck? Emerson texted Sydney. They'd split up to find Tenley after she fled from the auditorium. *Still MIA,* Sydney wrote back. Emerson tugged at the horseshoe necklace she'd dug out of her jewelry box that morning, desperate for any semblance of luck. Where *was* Tenley?

She jogged up Winslow's back stairwell, taking the steps two at a time. She had to find her. She knew what it felt like to have the darer flaunt your biggest mistake. But it was more than that, too. Because what no one knew, not even Tenley, was that this whole disaster was Emerson's fault. Tenley might have drugged Jessie, but it was Emerson—not the darer—who, in an awful, weak moment, had sent the note daring Tenley to slip the antianxiety pill into Jessie's water bottle. The memory made Emerson's stomach turn. It was one of the lowest moments of her life, and the darer must have watched her do it—watched the whole thing unfold as if it were some kind of television show. And then videotaped the result for good measure.

A noise from the art studio grabbed Emerson's attention. A muffled sob. "Tenley?" she called out. But when she burst into the room, it was Abby Wilkins she found. Abby was sitting at a desk in the back, her head buried in her arms. Her shoulders heaved up and down with sobs. Behind her, the mural that last year's senior class had painted shone on the wall: bright, happy splotches of color. Emerson started to turn away. She really had to find Tenley. But Abby's cries made her waver. The sound tugged at something deep in her chest.

The day she found out Caitlin had died, Emerson had cried so hard, and so long, she'd barely had the strength left to stand. She'd really thought it was over after that—how could she have anything more left inside her? But the pain kept striking, relentless. She'd see a blond girl in the bleachers at cheerleading practice, or hear an actress in a commercial who sounded just like Cait, and all at once, the tears would return.

She turned back. "You okay, Abby?"

Abby sat up. She was wearing an ugly ribbed sweater and an even uglier patterned skirt. Normally, Emerson would jump at the chance to mentally edit clothing like that, but Abby's face was so red and blotchy that Emerson quickly forgot her atrocity of an outfit. "I just miss her so much." A sob accompanied Abby's words, and the sound stabbed at Emerson's chest.

Abby pushed a sweaty strand of hair off her forehead. "You know who I wanted to talk to about that ruined video? Delancey.

She would have told me to take a deep chakra breath, probably. Or maybe she would have known who was behind it, because she always knew gossip like that. I'll never know, though, because I can't talk to her." Abby's shoulders heaved with another sob, and Emerson was taken by an urge to hug her, wrap her up in her arms the way her mom always did. But she and Abby weren't friends; they barely even knew each other. So, instead, she took the seat next to her, tracing a heart that had been graffitied on the desk.

"I do that all the time," she admitted. "Last night, I was halfway through dialing Caitlin's number before I remembered." The realization had been like a truck slamming into her chest at a hundred miles per hour. "Every time I start to think I'm okay, something happens that rips my heart open all over again."

"Do you ever feel like your memories are warping?" Abby wiped a tear off her chin. "I keep thinking there must have been *something* I could have done to help her, something I could have said or asked." Abby squeezed her eyes shut, then opened them again. "Delancey was so jumpy the week before she died. I just figured she was worried about the homecoming race or college applications...."

Fresh tears rolled down Abby's cheeks. "Then, before the homecoming dance, I got an e-mail from Nina, a freshman in Purity Club, saying she was worried about Delancey. Something about Delancey saying she was going to lose her virginity in the bio lab before the dance. When I showed up to talk Delancey out of it, I ended up locked in a supply closet for half the night. The whole thing was some weird setup. I talked to Nina after, and she never even sent that e-mail."

Emerson stared at a row of half-finished ceramic mugs. The

truth burned a hole inside her. She, Tenley, and Sydney had sent that e-mail, and locked Abby in the closet. It was back when they thought Abby was the darer. The truth rose inside her now, begging for release. But she couldn't tell Abby. Not with the darer still on the loose. No one else deserved to be dragged into this game.

"Did you ever figure out what happened?" she asked instead.

Abby shook her head. "I've gone through the whole thing a thousand times in my head. Maybe Delancey was secretly dating someone. Maybe he set it up, so he could have her to himself at the dance. Or maybe—maybe it was Delancey herself who did it." She choked on the last sentence. "How could I have been so in the dark about my own best friend? How could I not have known she was planning her *suicide*?"

Guilt squeezed painfully at Emerson's chest. Abby couldn't have known—because Delancey hadn't killed herself. If the darer's taunts hadn't been enough proof of that, Delancey's suicide note would have been. Emerson had watched Delancey's mom show it on the news earlier that morning, in a segment about suicide prevention. It was a short tearjerker of a note—typed up on the darer's trademark typewriter. But once again she couldn't tell Abby any of this. Not without telling her about the darer. "It's not your fault, Abby." She said it firmly, but the words hung limply between them, not nearly strong enough.

"It just makes me wonder if I even knew her at all," Abby said sadly.

Emerson dug her nails into the soft wood of the desktop. She chose her words carefully. "Maybe it wasn't planned. Maybe it just sort of . . . happened. A moment of terrible weakness."

Abby shook her head. "She was planning it. She had to have been. Her mom told me she stopped at the Landing Spot diner the day before she died."

Emerson scrunched her forehead up in confusion.

"Delancey's cousin works there," Abby explained. "But she hated that place. Said it gave her major creeps. She never went there, not even when her cousin was working. And then the day before she dies, she just walks in on her own? She must have gone to see him one last time, to say some kind of good-bye."

Emerson looked up sharply. Delancey couldn't have gone to the Landing Spot to say good-bye, because Delancey *didn't kill herself.* So why had she been there?

She stood up, giving Abby a shaky smile. "I should go find Tenley." She started toward the door but paused halfway there. "Abby?" She turned around for a second time. Abby's eyes were wet and rimmed in red. "If you ever need to talk more, I'm here. I—I know what it's like."

Abby gave her a small smile. "Thanks, Emerson."

- - - - - - -

The rest of the day passed in a blur. Emerson finally found Tenley in a janitor's closet and managed to talk her out. She took a math test after that and ate lunch with Tenley in her car, and waited outside the principal's office while Tenley's stepdad pulled strings to keep her from being suspended. But she was so consumed by thoughts of the darer that she barely remembered any of it. Now, as Emerson headed to cheer practice, she braced herself. Cheer practice meant seeing Jessie.

She couldn't help but cringe when she saw the group gathered around Jessie on the field. They were standing in a circle, and from a distance they looked like a flock of birds, pecking and chirping at its leader. "Hey, Em," Jessie called out as Emerson rounded the bleachers. "We were just talking about Psycho-Ten."

"We're taking bets on how much Stepdaddy Reed is going to have to cough up to make this one disappear," Marisa Henley said with a giggle. "Apparently he's already donating a new auditorium just so she won't get suspended."

Emerson shifted uncomfortably. "Have you even talked to Tenley, Jessie?"

Jessie gave Emerson a weird look. "You want me to talk to the girl who almost killed me as a *prank*?"

"I really don't think she meant—"

"I don't care what she meant," Jessie said, cutting her off. "She drugged me and nearly ruined my life in the process. That's all I need to know."

Emerson opened her mouth. There were a thousand things she wanted to say, but everyone was watching her, their eyes like laser beams, and not a single word came out.

"Girls!" Coach's voice cut across the field. "Why aren't you warming up?"

"Just about to, Coach!" Jessie replied. Her voice was high and sugary again. She brushed past Emerson, knocking into her arm.

"Cunningham?" Coach called out. "You planning on joining the team?"

Emerson's stomach turned as she watched Jessie whisper something to Marisa. "I'm not feeling so great all of a sudden."

Emerson waited for Coach's okay before hurrying off the field. She headed straight to the locker room and dropped down on a bench, burying her head in her hands. This was all her fault. If she'd never sent that note to Tenley, then Tenley would never have slipped the pill into Jessie's water bottle, and the darer would never have found a way to film it. The guilt was like thorns, pricking at her insides.

She grabbed her bag out of her locker and rooted around for her phone. There was only one voice she wanted to hear right now: Josh's. But when she pulled out her phone, she paused.

She had seven missed calls and four texts. Three of the texts were from Marta.

Call me ASAP!!!

Check ur phone Em!

Have you seen Facebook??

A cold sense of dread crept into her chest. Her fingers moved clumsily as she jabbed at her phone to open Facebook. There was a new video up on her wall. It had been posted by someone named Jane Doe, whose profile picture was a bright red question mark. The dread slithered into Emerson's limbs, making it hard to move.

It took a few seconds for the video to sharpen into focus.

In it, Emerson was standing in front of a mirror at the Seagull Inn, wearing her cheerleading skirt and a red bra. She looked nervous, but at the sound of footsteps behind her, she brightened. A man walked into the camera frame. He was shirtless, and you could see his defined muscles as he walked toward Emerson. His face was blacked out, but the camera caught a clear shot of his salt-and-pepper hair. There was no doubt he was older.

It was a video of her and Matt Morgan—town fire chief and Sydney's father—from their night at the Seagull Inn.

In the video, the faceless man stopped in front of Emerson and ran his hands—big, rugged *man* hands—down her bare arms. And then they were kissing, tangling together, Emerson's skirt riding up and Matt's pants riding down and no music, no background noise, only the sound of their breathing growing heavier and heavier. Just as the man went to unclip her bra, the video went black.

Underneath there was already a slew of comments.

Slut it up, Emerson!

Is that someone's DAD?

OMG, he's ancient!!!!

At least he's hot...

Daddy complex much?

Emerson couldn't move. She couldn't even blink. By tonight the whole town would know. Maybe not Matt's name, but the act. She imagined her friends, her classmates, her teachers all watching this.... What if Josh saw it, just when things were finally getting back on track with them?

I fight dirty. It was exactly what the darer had promised.

CHAPTER FOUR
Tuesday, 7:30 AM

SYDNEY KNEW THE MINUTE SHE WALKED INTO SCHOOL. She knew from the darting looks, all squinty eyes and curled-up lips. She knew from the sound: that buzz that builds out of laughter and whispers, like a swarm of bees homing in on its victim. It had happened to Tenley and Emerson, and now it was happening to her.

Something small and round smacked her back. A crumpled-up photograph. As she knelt to pick it up, she was consumed by the urge to destroy it, tear it up. But she couldn't. She had to know.

The photo smoothed out easily in her hand. A younger version of herself stared up at her from the glossy page. It had been taken at the Sunrise Center. She was on a softball field during one of the games she played in. The bold yellow logo stood out on her black team shirt. SUNRISE CENTER FOR REHABILITATION.

Across the top of the photo, someone had scrawled a single word in all caps: *PYRO*.

The hallway had frozen, all eyes on her. "They gave a *pyro* a scholarship to Winslow?" someone said loudly, making laughter sprinkle through the hallway.

It was her best-concealed secret, and now it was out.

The photo slipped out of her fingers. For what felt like an eternity, she stood there frozen, watching it flutter to the ground. "Need a match?" someone called out. The voice shook her out of her stupor, and suddenly she was moving, down the hall, to anywhere else. She kept her eyes cast to the ground, but, still, on every side she heard them: the sneers, the whispers. She bumped into one person, then another, but she just kept going. Her feet carried her automatically to the darkroom. She didn't stop until its door slammed shut behind her, and there was darkness, and peace.

She slid to the floor in the dark, trying to catch her breath. She had no idea how the darer had gotten that photo. She certainly didn't have a copy of it. Then again, she had no idea how the darer had gotten that video of Tenley. Or the one of Emerson. She shuddered, trying to banish that last image from her mind. Everyone else might be wondering who the mystery man going at it with Emerson was, but she knew. It was Sydney's dad.

She rested against the wall, squeezing her eyes shut. The darer had done this to break her, but she'd been a pariah before. She could handle it again. Because she had her secret weapon: an escape plan. One day soon she'd be at RISD, and then Winslow would be nothing more than a speck in her past.

Slowly, her breathing returned to normal. With a sigh, she stood up and switched on the light. A red glow descended on the windowless room. The space was as messy and crowded as always, so it took her a second to register it.

Photos.

They were littered everywhere. And every single one was destroyed—burned to a crisp.

Sydney reached for one. The photo was so singed it was hard to make out the image. But one corner was intact, and Sydney recognized it instantly. It was a shot of the ocean taken from the Anaswan lighthouse. She'd spent hours developing that photo, again and again, until she got it just right. She grabbed the remains of several more photos. They were all hers, images she'd spent weeks perfecting. In the back of the room, shreds of a manila envelope were scattered on the floor. She dropped to her knees, gathering them up. Fragments of a familiar address flashed up at her. RHODE ISLAND SCHOOL OF DESIGN.

How? She'd left her scholarship application in the college counselor's outbox yesterday! Someone must have stolen it out of the box. Which meant it had never been mailed.

The handwritten pages of her application were strewn across the row of developing bins, big X's slashed through each one. Propped up against the last bin was a note.

You'll never escape.

A strangled noise slipped out of Sydney. RISD was her shot at leaving Echo Bay, at becoming something *more*. And now the darer wanted to take that from her, too.

She moved furiously through the room, gathering up the remaining photos. For years she'd felt like a misfit at Winslow, an extraterrestrial who'd touched down in a foreign colony. But RISD had always been this sparkling star, shining above her, beckoning her home. And now it was gone.

She lunged for the door. She had to get away: from this room and this building and everything the darer had soiled. She yanked the door open and threw herself into the hall.

"Syd!" She heard Calum's voice before she saw him. She spun around to find him jogging toward her, his blond curls winging into a halo around his head. He was holding one of the *PYRO* photos in his hand.

"Please get me out of here," she begged. She could feel the eyes lighting on her again from every side. "Anywhere."

"This way." Calum took her elbow and guided her out a side exit. The door opened into the wide corridor that connected Winslow's lower and upper schools. Sydney took a deep breath, drinking in the solitude.

"Thank you," she said after a moment. She slid to the ground and tucked her knees under her chin.

Calum dropped down cross-legged next to her, crumpling the photo in his grip. Shiny tiled walls stretched out on either side of them, blurring into a mosaic on the ceiling: a blue tile ocean arcing above them. "I've been looking for you ever since I saw this photo." He tugged at the zipper on his lime-green sweatshirt. "I can't believe someone would do that."

"I can." Sydney closed her eyes, reveling in the silence. There was a small echo in the corridor, and it amplified her breathing. "I used to believe that everyone had some goodness in them. But I'm starting to think I was wrong."

She opened her eyes. Calum was watching her intently. Tiny flecks of green floated in his brown eyes, catching the light. He scooted closer, putting a hand on her knee. The simple gesture made her want to cry. She hadn't spoken to Calum since he'd tried to kiss her at the homecoming dance on Saturday. She knew he'd been hurt when she pulled away. But now here he was, putting that aside to comfort her. It made her wonder if she'd made the wrong choice that night.

"Thank you," she said softly. "I needed this. A friend." She met his gaze. There was a fierceness in his eyes she couldn't quite read. Protectiveness, she thought.

"It's going to be okay, Syd." His voice was gentle and sure. "Gossip like this always passes eventually. If anyone can vouch for that, it's the computer nerd." He gave her a small smile, and she couldn't help but smile back. A curl slipped onto Calum's forehead, and Sydney pushed it off without thinking.

They were so close. She could smell the fresh scent of his clothes, as if he'd just pulled them out of the laundry. One more inch and they'd be kissing, and suddenly she wanted it—wanted to let it sweep her away, carry her off to oblivion. But before she could act on the urge, the door on the other end of the corridor swung open. A high-pitched voice spilled in, followed by the distant drone of construction drifting in from the lower school's field.

"Mr. Michaels is sooo cute!" The voice belonged to a small, bony girl. Her long-legged friend tripped into the corridor after her.

Sydney pulled back, blinking hard. As the girls hurried past them, Calum glanced at his watch. It was digital, with a dozen flashing symbols and numbers, and several tiny buttons protruding from each side. Knowing Calum, Sydney suspected that it was the highest-tech watch money could buy. Calum didn't flaunt his wealth, but when it came to technology, Sydney knew, he couldn't resist. "We should probably get to class," he said.

"You go," Sydney told him. "I can't have you tarnishing your valedictorian status." She managed a tiny grin in his direction. "I'm going to stay and think awhile."

"I can skip class and keep you company," Calum protested. "It wouldn't exactly be cataclysmic."

"Now that you used an SAT word on me, it would be." She waved him toward the school. "Really, go ahead. I'll follow soon."

Calum started toward the school, then paused, turning back. "I'm here if you need me, Syd. I will *even* refrain from using four-syllable words if that's preferable."

This time, Sydney's grin was a little easier to call up. "I'll keep that in mind."

A half hour later, Calum was long gone, and Sydney was still sitting in the corridor. She'd checked her phone five times already, expecting to find a gloating text from the darer. But so far, nothing. She'd called the RISD admissions office, too, and left a message begging for an emergency extension on her application. Now all she could do was wait. Wait to hear from RISD. Wait to hear from the person who was ruining her life.

She rubbed her eyes with the palms of her hands as the words from that text ran through her mind for the thousandth time. *I fight dirty.* Now that she, Emerson, and Tenley had all been hit in this latest blitz, she couldn't help but wonder: What next? It made her feel as if a sledgehammer were hanging over her head, and she was just waiting for it to fall.

She pulled out her phone yet again. Still no callback from RISD. She had one new e-mail, though. When she saw who it was from, she nearly dropped her phone in surprise. *Joey Bakersfield.*

When they were younger, Joey and Sydney had been close friends. They'd grown apart over the years, but then the darer had pulled Joey into this twisted game: first forcing Sydney to kiss him, then framing Joey for everything. Until Tricia came forward claiming to be the darer, Sydney had actually believed Joey was responsible. She and Tenley had gone so far as to report it to the police. They'd dropped the charges after Tricia revealed herself, but the damage had already been done. Joey had left Winslow and enrolled at Danford, a fancy boarding school an hour away in Boston. Sydney had sent Joey two e-mails apologizing for everything, but she'd never heard back. Until now.

Sydney,

I know this e-mail comes late. To be honest, I hadn't planned on responding at all. Not because of the accusation; that I could get over. It was what happened before that... and how horrified you seemed after. For a second, I thought something was happening between us. But then you'd acted like I'd done something wrong.

Sydney gnawed on her lower lip. She knew he was talking about the kiss. After Tricia had dared her to kiss Joey, Sydney had gone through with it in a haze of emotion: anger and confusion and, worst of all, terror. Joey clearly hadn't known what hit him. Swallowing hard, she forced herself to keep reading.

But then today I heard about what happened with Delancey Crane. It must have been awful to witness a suicide like that. I know what the Winslow clones can be like: dead set on acting like the whole town is perfect, like nothing is wrong even when something so clearly is. I used to feel like such a freak for refusing to drink the Echo Bay Kool-Aid. But coming to Danford helped me see everything more clearly. Before I left, Echo Bay felt so haunted with memories. I can only imagine how it feels for you now. I just wanted you to know that there IS a nonbrainwashed Echo Bay-er out there, if you ever need one to talk to.

–Joey

Sydney stared at the e-mail for a long time after reading it. She couldn't believe how different Joey sounded. At Winslow, he'd always been so quiet and miserable. But in this e-mail he actually sounded happy. And sweet, too. Maybe Winslow had been what was poisoning him all along.

A second e-mail popped up in her in-box from Joey. *PS. Did you hear about this?* He'd included a link. It took Sydney to a page on RISD's website. *Prospective Students Fair*, the page read. Sydney scanned it over.

Sydney jumped to her feet. She had to be at that fair on Friday. Which meant she had to somehow redo and resubmit her entire scholarship application before then. Maybe then RISD would still consider her. It was a long shot…but it was her only shot. She took off through the lower-school entrance, hurrying out to her car. She'd earned a day off from school.

Ten minutes later she made a quick stop inside her apartment building to get the mail, something her mom was always forgetting to do. As she scooped up the pile of junk and bills, she noticed a large white envelope sticking out from amid the smaller ones. She gasped when she saw the handwriting on the front of it. When had *Guinness* sent her a package?

Guinness, her ex-more-than-friend-but-not-quite-boyfriend, and also Tenley's stepbrother, had been found passed out from an overdose on Friday. He'd been rushed to the hospital and then straight to rehab. But not before Sydney learned the truth. The darer had set Guinness up—laced his weed and tried to kill him. All because he "knew too much." About what, Sydney wasn't sure.

She glanced at the postmark on the envelope as she hurried up to her apartment. *Friday.* Guinness must have mailed this the day he accidentally ODed. The thought gave her the strangest feeling, as if she were about to come face-to-face with a ghost.

She waited until she was safely locked inside her apartment to open the envelope. A stack of papers was shoved inside. She felt jittery as she pulled it out. On top was a note, scribbled in Guinness's messy handwriting.

Blue—

I need you to see this, but I don't think it's safe for us to talk right now. I'm being watched, followed...I can feel it. Remember how you were asking me about Kyla Kern? I wasn't completely honest. I do know something more. I think Kyla was being harassed before her death. Proof is in this envelope. Promise me you'll be careful. Don't let anyone see you. I've been getting notes—threats—and I don't want them to start for you, too.

~G

The page wobbled in Sydney's grip. Kyla Kern, along with Meryl Bauer and Nicole Mayor, were Echo Bay's original Lost Girls: three beautiful local girls who, over the years, had each died in the ocean during Echo Bay's historic Fall Festival. Meryl Bauer—Calum's

40

older sister—was the very first Lost Girl. She died in a boating accident ten years ago. Nicole Mayor's death had come during the Fall Festival four years later, and Kyla Kern's the year after that.

With their deaths arrived the ghost lights—three lights flickering mysteriously over the Phantom Rock—as well as talk of a curse. The Fall Festival was banned. But five years later, it was back. This fall, Echo Bay had once again celebrated. On the last day of the festival, Tricia had taken them all out on the yacht, and both she and Caitlin had died. Many in town believed the curse was alive once more, but Sydney knew it was something else—something far worse—at work.

Last week Sydney had tracked down a photo that had been missing from Kyla Kern's accident report. The report named an electrical fire as the cause of Kyla's death, but the missing photo showed a crater in the float that could never have been made by fire. Instead, it looked as if someone had thrown an explosive at Kyla's float—and then hidden the photo to cover it up.

Was Guinness's package further proof that her hunch was right, that Kyla's death was no accident? Sydney sank down on the couch, flipping through the first few pages of the packet. They were phone records that belonged to a local number, labeled *Kyla Kern*. The same unlisted number appeared in them over and over again. Guinness had highlighted their call times. He'd scribbled in the margin: *2 seconds. 1 second. 3 seconds. Hang-ups?* Then: *STALKER???*

Sydney shuffled to the next page. Behind the phone records were two folded slips of paper. The first was old and worn, crumpled around the edges. A Post-it was affixed to the front of it. *Found in Kyla's belongings*, Guinness had written on it. Gingerly, she unfolded it.

Glaring up at her was an all-too-familiar typewriter font.

Some secrets are never safe.

The paper dropped soundlessly onto her lap as realizations slammed into her, one after another. Kyla had a stalker. Kyla had received notes in a typewriter font. The darer had been after Kyla. *Five years ago.*

It only solidified the awful suspicion that she, Tenley, and Emerson shared: The same person had been haunting Echo Bay all these years.

Sydney's heart was pounding as she turned to the next note. This one was newer, crisper. Guinness had scribbled two lines on the Post-it on the front: *Left on my car. Same person???* Sydney opened the paper to find a line of identical typewriter font.

You know what happens when you keep digging? You fall down a hole.

Kyla was what Guinness had known too much about. Kyla was what had almost gotten him killed. She'd wondered it before, but seeing the proof right in front of her...She stood up, pacing restlessly through the apartment.

This was a lead. A solid one. The darer clearly wanted to keep the truth about Kyla's death buried. Maybe if she found out what *really* happened to Kyla, it would be enough to force their stalker out of the shadows.

CHAPTER FIVE
Tuesday, 2:30 PM

PULLING INTO THE PARKING LOT OF THE ECHO BAY police station made Tenley's stomach hurt. She'd hoped her next trip to the station would be to see the darer in handcuffs. Instead, she was the one being questioned.

"Ten Ten!" Her mom was already there, leaning against her huge SUV. The wind ruffled the bottom of her very short, very pink skirt.

"You didn't want to go with pants?" Tenley eyed the thin white sweater and shiny stiletto booties that accompanied her mom's barely-there skirt. "Maybe a suit?" She herself had worn the drabbest outfit she could find in her closet. A black skirt that nearly reached her knees, black tights, and a striped blazer.

Her mom tossed her expertly curled hair. "Someone has to win over our cop! Just doing my motherly duty to keep my little girl out of jail."

Tenley fought the urge to roll her eyes. When the police had called the night before to tell her she was needed at the station after school the next day for questioning about the video, Tenley had asked if she could go alone. But in true Trudy fashion, her mom had ignored the request. "You're still a minor, Tenley!" she'd trilled. "You need your mommy!"

"Tell me the story again, Ten Ten," her mom ordered now.

"To the best of my knowledge, it was a caffeine pill," Tenley recited. Lanson, Tenley's CEO stepfather, had a whole team of lawyers on retainer. After the call came from the police, he assigned every one of them to the "Tenley situation" until they could concoct an acceptable legal explanation for her very illegal behavior. "I was just trying to help Jessie out," Tenley continued. "It was something I did for my best friend, Caitlin, sometimes."

"Perfect." Her mom's Botox-smooth face broke into a creaseless smile. "The lawyers said that without any evidence proving what the pill was, it's unlikely anyone will press charges. But we can always stop the questioning at any point and return with a lawyer if we feel the need."

Tenley nodded. She knew her mom would have preferred to have a lawyer with them now, but Lanson's team was in court this afternoon, and the whole family wanted this over with. The sooner the better.

"Remember," her mom added as they crossed the parking lot. "Don't be afraid to bring up Caitlin's death. A little pity never hurt anybody." She paused outside the door to tug up Tenley's skirt. "Neither did a little skin."

"Hello!" Her mom threw open the door as if they were arriving at a party instead of a police station. "Tenley Reed is—"

"Three minutes late," a woman barked. Or at least Tenley *thought* it was a woman. With her broad face, frizzy hair, and standard-issue cop uniform, it was hard to be sure. Tenley read her name tag. Officer Funley. *Doubtful*. "Come with me."

Tenley's leg was aching, but she refused to limp as Officer Funley led them through the police station and down a long, winding set of stairs to a small, windowless room in the basement. "Our questioning room is full," the officer explained. "But this will be fine for our purposes." Harsh fluorescent lights bore down on Tenley as she took a seat next to her mom. Officer Funley glared in the direction of her mom's skirt, which was riding up to a nearly indecent level. Her mom's win-over-the-cop plan was clearly off to a great start.

"Thanks for seeing us, Officer," her mom chirped. She leaned forward in her seat, allowing Officer Funley a front-row view of her ample cleavage. Tenley shot her a warning look, but she didn't seem to notice. "I'm Trudy Reed, Tenley's mom, and I just want to start by thanking you for your honorable, brave service to our beloved town." She curled her lips down in a serious expression. "I'm so sorry if this little episode has caused any inconvenience in your busy day, but as you'll soon see, this is all just a big misunderstand—"

"I'll have to ask that you let your daughter do the talking, Mrs. Reed," Officer Funley interjected.

Trudy snapped her mouth shut, looking miffed. Before Tenley

could mouth a warning at her, her mom's phone rang from inside her oversize purse. Officer Funley let out an irritated cough.

"Sorry about that!" Her mom fumbled through her bag. "Let me just find...where is that...ah, got it." The ringing cut out.

"If we're all done receiving personal calls, we can get started." Office Funley went over to a computer in the back of the room. "Tenley, please start by stating your full name and birth date." As she spoke, she logged on to the computer and opened a new file. Tenley watched as she titled it *Reed, Tenley*. Seeing her name on the screen made Tenley's stomach twist. How had she ended up here, with a police file of her own? The more the darer toyed with her life, the less she recognized it.

"Thank you," Funley said once Tenley had choked out her information. "Now, please state for the record what occurred in the video played at Winslow Academy's assembly yesterday."

"I just wanted to help Jessie out—"

Before Tenley could continue with her story, her mom's phone rang again. "Sorry, sorry," Trudy trilled. "I guess I'm popular this afternoon!" Officer Funley's face hardened as her mom dug into her bag once again. "Let me just...here we go...." The ringing stopped. "I'll turn it on vibrate," she said graciously.

"How kind of you," Officer Funley grunted. She turned back to Tenley. "Please proceed."

Tenley had just opened her mouth to launch back into her story when a loud buzzing penetrated the room.

"Oh, just answer it!" Officer Funley snapped.

Trudy extracted her phone from her purse. "Hello? Yes. Uh-huh.

I see." Across the room, Officer Funley coughed pointedly. "Can you hold on for a second?" Trudy asked. "It's about Guinness," she whispered to Tenley. "I should—"

"Go take it. I'll be fine. Really." Tenley gave her mom a pointed look. They'd practiced her story at least fifteen times. There was no messing this up.

"Okay. But just shout if you need me." Trudy already had the phone pressed back to her ear as she slipped out of the room.

"Now," Officer Funley said wearily. "Let's try this again."

Tenley went carefully through her story. As she spoke, Officer Funley typed notes into her file. "And you're sure it was a caffeine pill?" she asked when Tenley finished.

"To the best of my knowledge," Tenley repeated.

Funley sighed. "So then it's possible it *wasn't* a caffeine pill?"

"I guess anything's possible," Tenley said carefully. "To the best of my knowledge it was a caffeine pill; but believe me, the whole thing has haunted me every day since." That part, at least, was the truth. Tenley looked up, meeting Officer Funley's eyes. She remembered her mom's advice. *A little pity never hurt anybody.*

"And then my best friend, Caitlin, died so soon after," Tenley continued. "Now it's like I have no break from my own thoughts." A surprise tear worked its way down her cheek, and she angrily swiped it away. Pity was one thing, but losing control in front of some random cop? That wasn't in the playbook. But as Tenley watched Officer Funley shift in her seat, looking supremely uncomfortable at the sight of a tear, an idea crept its way into her mind.

She could use this.

Here she was at the one place in all of Echo Bay that held information about Caitlin's kidnapper. It was probably right there on that computer—in a file labeled *Thomas, Caitlin*.

Back when Caitlin was in sixth grade, the police had concluded that a local man named Jack Hudson had been responsible for her kidnapping. But according to Caitlin's diary, her real kidnapper hadn't been Jack at all, but a woman. A woman who, as far as Tenley could tell, was now also their darer. What if there was something in that file that could lead Tenley to her?

"I have nightmares every night," she continued, talking a little faster now. "Just last night I dreamed about Caitlin." This time, when a fresh tear fell, she didn't try to hide it.

Officer Funley cleared her throat, looking more and more uncomfortable. Tenley let tears gather in her eyes. They were surprisingly easy to call up, as if they'd been just waiting under the surface all this time. Soon her shoulders were shaking with soft sobs.

"I just miss Caitlin so much," she blubbered. "S-sometimes I wonder if losing her was a punishment for what I accidentally did to Jessie. Like maybe I deserved it." Her voice rose to a fever pitch. The tears were coming fast and furious now, rising from the darkest part of her. "I—I'm sorry," she choked out. "I'll try to pull myself together so we can finish. May I just have some tissues first?"

"Sure. Of course." Officer Funley leaped out of her chair, clearly relieved to escape Tenley's sobs. "I'll go get some from upstairs."

Bingo.

Tenley waited for the door to click shut before hurrying over to the computer. She was suddenly grateful for the lack of windows in the room. Funley had left the computer logged on. Thanks to its search feature, it didn't take long to find the file she was looking for.

There were too many documents to read before Funley got back. She glanced over her shoulder. The door was still firmly shut. Officer Funley had to go all the way upstairs, probably to the bathroom in the very front of the building. Biting down on her lip, she hit Print.

She glanced at the door again as the printer began spitting out the file. On the screen, the computer counted out the pages. Halfway there... Now more than half...

Through the door, she heard her mom wrap up her phone call. "Oh, hello, Officer Funley!" Trudy called out. "Sorry again for the interruption. What are the tissues for?"

Tenley glanced nervously at the screen. Still six pages to go. "Come on," she whispered. She clicked out of the file, ready to grab the papers and bolt. Out in the hall, two sets of footsteps made their way toward the door.

The printer spit out one more page, then another.

The door handle turned. The door creaked open a crack.

"Are you in there for questioning, Funley?" At the sound of an unfamiliar voice, the door halted in its path.

"Yeah," Tenley heard Officer Funley reply. At that moment, the printer shuddered, then fell silent. "Shouldn't be much longer, though."

Tenley grabbed the papers and dove back into her seat. She'd just jammed the stack into her purse when Officer Funley strode into the room, followed by her mom.

"Thank you," Tenley said when Funley handed her the tissues. Her heart was hammering wildly as she wiped at her eyes.

"What happened in here?" Trudy huffed. She went over to Tenley and put a protective hand on her shoulder. "In the few minutes I was gone, you managed to reduce my daughter to tears?" She squeezed Tenley's shoulder, hard. "I will not have that, Officer. We're leaving. If you'd like to continue this line of questioning, you can do so in the presence of our lawyer!"

"I don't think—" Officer Funley began.

"Come on, Tenley." Trudy tossed her hair. "We're going home."

Tenley made a big show of dabbing at her eyes as she followed her mom out of the station. "Of all the nerve," her mom was muttering. "Making my baby cry! Are you okay, Ten Ten?"

Tenley nodded absently. There were a million explanations she could give her mom, but she was too busy thinking about the stolen pages inside her purse.

"Do you want me to drive you home?" Her mom patted Tenley on the head, the Trudy version of a hug. "I can come back later with Lanson to get your car."

"No," Tenley said quickly. "I'll be okay. I actually have an errand to run for school, so I'll just meet you at home." She hurried to her car before her mom could protest. She couldn't wait a second longer to get her hands on those pages. She sped away from the station, driving to the first place with a parking lot. Alone outside the minimart, she dug the file out of her bag.

The first few pages were nothing interesting: photos and notes documenting the DNA on Caitlin's coat, which had been discovered abandoned on the beach not long after her return home. The evidence had been all over the news back in sixth grade. The DNA belonged to Jack Hudson. It was the evidence the police had used to name Jack as the prime suspect in the case. Tenley shuffled through more pages. There was a police report, some official-looking documents about Jack's suicide, and—*oh my god.*

Tenley froze, the pages shaking in her hands.

She was looking at Jack Hudson's suicide note. It held just five words: *I can't be this man.* But it wasn't the words that struck Tenley; it was their shape. They were typewriter letters: boxy but curved and slightly faded. Just like in all the notes she'd received.

Delancey's suicide letter had been typed in the same way—because the darer had faked it.

The air in the car suddenly felt much too thin. There was no way this was a coincidence. Which left only one logical conclusion.

Jack Hudson didn't commit suicide. He was killed by their darer, too.

CHAPTER SIX
Tuesday, 3:15 PM

THEY'D ALL SEEN THE VIDEO. AS EMERSON STRETCHED with the cheerleading squad and sweat her way through warm-up laps, not a single person met her eye. She wasn't sure which was worse: the silence or the insults. Because there had been those, too: catcalls and so many comments on her Facebook wall that she'd had to take down her profile.

Years ago, when she lived in Florida and still had gangly legs and frizzy hair, Emerson had been an outcast at her school. But that was nothing compared with this. It wasn't an outcast the darer had turned her into; it was a leper.

As the squad went through the last rounds of warm-up, Coach gestured for Emerson to join her. A pit formed in Emerson's stomach as she jogged across the field. She could feel Jessie and the others watching her, making her cheeks burn. She was panting a little as she stopped in front of Coach. "You wanted me?" she asked, her voice coming out much too high-pitched.

Coach gave her a brisk nod. "I want to talk to you before we start practice, Emerson." Her gaze dropped to her white sneakers. "I'd like to think this goes without saying, but maybe we all need a reminder sometimes." Her eyes flitted up briefly to meet Emerson's, then dropped down again. "When you wear the Winslow Lions cheerleading skirt, you're not only representing our squad, but our whole school. You and the team are the face of Winslow, and with that comes responsibility." This time, when Coach lifted her gaze, she didn't look away. Emerson flinched at the unmasked disappointment in her eyes. "Wearing this skirt is a privilege. I'm going to need you to think long and hard about whether you can live up to that privilege." She paused. "If you can't, I think it's best you turn in your uniform."

Emerson's heart plummeted to her shoes. Coach had obviously seen the video.

Emerson opened her mouth. She closed it. She opened it again. "I..." she began. But the words wouldn't come. A giggle drifted over from across the field. Jessie, probably. She was sure they were all watching her right now, guessing exactly what Coach was saying. She wanted to close her eyes and disappear, vanish into nothingness. "I..." she tried again. Once again words failed her. "I—I still don't feel well," she finally choked out.

She didn't wait for Coach's response. She didn't wait for anything. She just ran, away from the field and away from her life.

Tears blurred Emerson's vision as she changed out of her uniform and drove home. Caitlin was gone. Everyone at school hated her. Now, even Coach wanted her off the squad.

She inhaled deeply as she headed into her house, breathing in the familiar home smell. Maybe she'd tell her mom she was sick. She'd curl up on the couch and let her mom feed her chicken soup and stroke her hair. She could stay home all week, wrapped in the blanket knitted by her grandmother, a cocoon from the outside world. "Mom?" she called out wearily. She wandered into the kitchen. "You home?"

"In the living room, Emerson." The voice that replied wasn't her mom's, but her dad's. What was her dad doing home in the middle of the afternoon?

"Dad? Is everything okay?" She hurried into the living room to find her parents on the sofa, matching frowns on their faces. "What is it?" Emerson asked. "Is someone hurt?"

"Everyone's fine." Her dad studied his hands as he wrung them together, and for the briefest of seconds, Emerson was relieved.

Then all at once, reality hit her. A tidal wave dragging her down.

Her parents had seen the video.

"Someone sent a video to my work e-mail," her dad continued, confirming her suspicions. His voice cracked slightly as he said it.

Emerson's thoughts were caving in on her. *Bare skin. Heavy breathing. Matt's salt-and-pepper hair.* "Who?" she whispered. "Who sent it to you?"

"It was anonymous," her dad said. "Though that's not what matters right now."

Her dad shoved a hand through his mess of blond hair, where

it was starting to gray at the roots. He looked up, and Emerson was shocked to see tears in his eyes. She'd seen her dad cry only twice in her life, both times at funerals. She dropped her head as an awful thought pounded through her.

This was *her* funeral.

"I thought we raised you better than that," her dad said.

Shame swept through her. "It was a mistake, I swear. I didn't mean for it to happen and I didn't film it! I don't know who did." The words were tumbling out of her, one after another, but they weren't enough. "I'm sorry," she whimpered.

Her mom gripped her dad's shoulder. "We're worried about you, honey. You have to tell us who this man is. You might be eighteen, but you're still in high school; he took advantage of you! We need to make sure he can never come near you again."

Emerson looked wildly between her parents. She'd promised Matt she'd keep his secret. He could lose his job as fire chief if she didn't; and then Sydney would lose her Civic Service Scholarship to Winslow. The room spiraled around Emerson, family photographs flashing in the corners of her vision. If she told, she'd be as bad as the darer. "I can't," she whispered. "It wasn't his fault."

"You're just a child, Emerson!" her dad exploded. "He's the adult. That means it's always his fault."

"I'm not a child," Emerson shot back. "Like you said, I'm eighteen. It was a terrible mistake, but it was *my* mistake to make." Emerson looked pleadingly at her mom, but her face was grim, her lips pressed in a tight line.

"We need you to tell us, Emerson," she said. "Right now."

"I—he..." The room spiraled faster, floor morphing to ceiling back to floor. She felt the day closing in on her—school and Coach and now this. "I can't," she gasped. She took off for the door. Her parents were still calling after her as she threw herself into her car and sped out of the driveway.

Tears rolled down her cheeks as she pulled to a stop on Ocean Drive. Outside, the ocean unspooled toward the horizon, all open space and wide blue expanse, and all of a sudden, Emerson had never felt so small. The darer had turned her whole world against her. *No.* There was still one person on her side. And she wasn't about to let the darer take him, too.

She opened a new text. *Can we meet up?*

Josh's response came quickly. *I was hoping you'd ask. :) Anaswan lighthouse in an hour?*

Emerson blew out a shaky sigh of relief as she typed back a quick yes. When Emerson had called Josh the night before, it was clear he hadn't seen the video yet. He wasn't on Facebook, but she knew the darer would make sure he saw it eventually. Which was why she had to tell him first.

Emerson had met Josh a little over a year ago, during the summer she'd modeled in New York. He was a native New Yorker, and he'd introduced her to all his favorite places in the city. After just a few weeks together, they were inseparable. She'd never had someone look at her like that before, as if she were a gift. She kept waiting for it to wear off, for Josh to peel back her layers only to discover that he didn't like what was wrapped inside. But it just kept getting better.

She'd never given all of herself to someone before. It made her feel like he was carrying her heart in his hands. All it would take was one drop, and he'd break it. So, of course, she'd sabotaged things instead.

She'd made the worst mistake of her life, sleeping with Remsen, a popular photographer. Afterward, she hadn't been able to face Josh. So she'd left New York without a good-bye—just a note posted to his door—and she'd ignored every phone call and e-mail he'd sent. There was nothing to say. She'd fallen into her own trap and ruined everything. If she couldn't forgive herself, how could he? But then last week, after a year of no contact, Josh had shown up in Echo Bay, and all their old feelings had resurfaced.

Now, Emerson drummed her fingers nervously against the wheel. Soon she'd have to tell Josh about the video of her and Matt. The thought of Josh looking at her differently afterward made her chest squeeze painfully. She put her car back into gear. She had to do something to keep herself busy for the next hour or the nerves would eat her alive.

She was subconsciously driving toward the Landing Spot diner before she realized where she was headed. Delancey had gone there the day before she died, even though she had despised the place. It could mean nothing at all. Or it could mean something important. If there was any connection between the Landing Spot and their darer, Emerson was going to find it.

The smell of grease and stale coffee bombarded her as she walked into the diner a few minutes later. The place was a steel box, with fluorescent lights that made the waitresses' orange polyester uniforms glow. She grabbed one of the cracked vinyl stools along the bar and pretended to study the menu.

"What can I getcha?" Emerson looked up to find a bleached-blond woman standing over her. Her plastic name tag read KARRIE.

"I'll have a decaf coffee," Emerson said, choosing the first thing she saw on the menu.

"That all?"

"For now." Emerson pulled out her phone as Karrie went over to the coffeepot. Her stomach turned as she opened Winslow's website and clicked to the memorial page dedicated to Delancey. Delancey's big blue eyes smiled up at her, and suddenly the image twisted before her vision: those same eyes, now wide and glassy.

Karrie placed a chipped mug in front of her, making some of the coffee slosh over the edge. "Cream or sugar?"

Emerson shook her head. "Actually, I was wondering if you've seen this girl before? I think she came in here to see her cousin." She held up her phone, and Karrie crouched down to get a better look.

"That's the girl who hung herself, right?"

Emerson nodded. "Do you happen to know her cousin who works here?"

Karrie shrugged, making her gold snake pendant slide across her collarbone. "No, but I only work Tuesdays. Helen, on the other hand, practically lives here. She'd be the one to ask." She waved a white-haired waitress over. "This girl has a question for ya, Helen."

Emerson held up her phone once more. "I'm looking for this girl's cousin. Her name's Delancey Crane?"

Helen leaned heavily against the green Formica bar. "Poor girl. Was she a friend of yours?"

"Yeah." Guilt flashed through Emerson at the lie, but she pushed past it. "It was just so sudden." She hadn't had time to plan out a story, but one just came spilling out. "My therapist thinks the best way for me to move on is to try to relive her last few days, feel what she was feeling, you know? And someone told me she came by here to see her cousin." She looked up at Helen with her most innocent expression.

"Marcus," Helen said. Emerson's heart leaped as Helen twisted a short strand of white hair around her finger. "He's one of our line chefs. Pretty beat-up about her death. He's in today. You think talking to him would help, honey?"

Emerson nodded eagerly. "Definitely."

Helen pointed toward a swinging door behind the bar. "Kitchen's through there. Just go on back."

Emerson glanced nervously over her shoulder as she went behind the bar, but no one seemed to notice, or care, that a customer was strolling toward the kitchen. She squared her shoulders and pushed through the swinging door. "You lost?" A guy with hairnet-covered cornrows stopped in front of her. He made no attempt at hiding the once-over he was giving her.

"Are you Marcus?" Emerson asked, shifting uncomfortably under his gaze.

"I could be," the guy said appreciatively.

"Ignore him," a voice called out from across the kitchen. "What's up?"

Emerson followed the voice with her eyes. When they landed on its owner, her jaw practically hit the floor. The guy was young, probably only a few years older than she was. He was medium height and a little gangly. But it was his face she couldn't stop staring at.

The resemblance was uncanny; he could easily have been Delancey Crane's brother.

"You're Marcus?" she choked out.

The guy nodded. "And you are…?" he asked, coming over to Emerson.

"I'm Emerson. I was a friend of Delancey's." Emerson's eyes bounced between Marcus's brown curls and big blue eyes. "You were her cousin, right?"

Marcus's smile faltered. "I still can't believe you have to say *were*."

"I know," Emerson said quietly. "Delancey came by to see you, didn't she? Right before…?" She trailed off, unable to finish.

"Oh, are you here for the key?" Marcus asked. "I was wondering what to do with it now."

"The key," Emerson repeated. Instantly, her pulse began to race. "Yeah," she said quickly. "I thought I'd come get it." She paused, praying she got the next question right. "When did she leave it with you?"

"The day before she died. She said she was playing this big game of truth or dare with her friends and asked if I would hold on to it, hide it for her. Girls and their games," Marcus added, with a rueful smile. "I just wish I'd known that it would be the last time I saw her."

Emerson nodded mutely. Her thoughts began to tailspin at the mention of truth or dare. Delancey wouldn't have chosen that phrase at random; it *had* to mean something.

"Yeah." Her voice croaked and she quickly cleared her throat. "I know the feeling."

Marcus went over to the line of cabinets in the back of the kitchen and pulled a key off the top shelf. "Here." He held it out to Emerson. It was gold and plain-looking, like a regular house key. "Good luck with your game."

Nerves shot through Emerson as she left the diner. This key had something to do with the darer; she was sure of it. Why else would Delancey have gone to such lengths to hide it?

Whatever it was that Delancey had learned, this key was going to lead Emerson to it.

— — — — — — —

As Emerson drove the winding roads to Anaswan, she forced her thoughts off the key and back onto Josh. He'd shocked her last week when he'd arrived in Echo Bay. He'd gotten a publishing deal for the book he'd been working on for as long as she'd known him, and he had put off college to work on revisions. He'd come to town looking for inspiration for the ending, but what he'd found instead was Emerson. Over the weekend, they'd finally kissed again. Emerson smiled at the memory. Kissing Josh had been like coming home after a long trip away. In some ways it had been the same, familiar and comforting. But it had been different, too, like finding a new bend in a road you'd traveled all your life.

A heavy silence wrapped around Emerson as she climbed the long stairwell to the top of the lighthouse. It was dark, half of the lightbulbs burned out, and a shivery feeling crept under her skin. For a second, she could swear she heard the soft patter of footsteps behind her, but when she froze, the noise faded into nothingness.

Just my imagination, she told herself. Still, she jogged up the last bend, emerging slightly out of breath into the lantern room.

"Whoa." She stopped short. The usually bare lantern room had been transformed. Strings of lights twinkled along the circular wall of windows. In the back of the room, a blue blanket had been laid out. It was covered in food: a box of Wheat Thins, a bottle of spray cheese, a tub of mint-chocolate-chip ice cream, a pile of York Peppermint Patties, and a bowl of Cheez-Its. A laugh bubbled out of Emerson. They were all her favorite snacks. Candles in small votives glowed next to the blanket, sending shadows dancing across the lighthouse ceiling.

Josh was leaning against one of the windowed walls, his eyes a swirl of green and brown under the flickering lights. "I thought we were due an official second first date." He grinned, and the sight of him was so familiar: the slight gap in his teeth and the crook in his nose, his hair combed into its half Mohawk, his frame almost too tall for the room. Something swelled deep inside Emerson's chest.

"I don't know what to say." She took a seat on the blanket and popped several Cheez-Its into her mouth.

"A smile would suffice," Josh replied. He sat down next to her, tucking his long legs beneath him. "You've been so down lately, Em. I thought you needed some cheering up." Josh touched her hand, making a tingle shoot up her arm.

"Thank you," she said softly. "This is perfect."

Josh watched as she spooned up some mint-chocolate-chip ice cream, then crumbled several Cheez-Its over it. She added a spritz of cheese before sticking the whole spoonful into her mouth. "You do know that's disgusting, right?" Josh asked, looking amused.

"You mean *delicious*," she replied, sending crumbs dribbling down her chin.

Josh shook his head. "There's the model I know and love."

Emerson started at the sound of that word. Josh was busy spraying cheese onto a Wheat Thin, completely oblivious to his word choice. But Emerson had heard it. The word rang through her head like an echo. *Love. Love. Love.*

It was the one word they'd never said, the one word she'd never said to any guy. It made her squirm with a mixture of exhilaration and fear. She *had* to tell him about the video. Before someone else did.

"Josh, there's something I need to talk to you about." She stood up abruptly, walking over to one of the windowed walls. Down below, the ocean rolled steadily toward the shore, waves rising and falling, rising and falling, as sure as breath. "I started seeing someone. After we broke up. It's over now, but somehow someone got hold of a video of us and—"

"Whoa, Em. Hold on." Josh came up behind her and wrapped his arms around her waist. He pulled her close, letting her head rest against the crook of his neck. "Were we broken up when this happened?"

"Yes," Emerson said quietly. She let herself rest against him, loving how solid he felt behind her. Not many guys were taller than she was, but Josh had a good three inches on her.

"Then let's not worry about it, okay? All that matters is that we're honest with each other now that we're back together. Right?"

"Right!" It came out more forcefully than she'd intended, and she heard Josh chuckle.

"Good." Josh kissed the top of her head. "You know how things were with my parents after my mom cheated on my dad. If it taught me anything, it's how important honesty is in a relationship. More important than anything."

"Honesty," Emerson repeated. She kept her eyes on the waves below. Rising, falling, rising, falling.

She should tell him. Not just about the video, but the real reason she'd left New York that summer, the real reason she'd spent a year avoiding his calls and texts and e-mails.

She'd cheated. And then she'd run. And, worst of all, she'd lied.

But Josh's arms were still around her waist, and he was kissing her neck now, and he smelled so good, new and familiar at the same time. And it really was in the past. It had taken her a year, but she'd finally put it behind her. There was no reason to dredge it back up. Josh was right: Now was what mattered.

"Should we go back to the blanket?" Josh whispered.

It was her last chance. She could grab him by the shoulders. She could force him to listen. But then he kissed her again, and it was so sweet, and so *here*, and suddenly the rest of it—the darer and all her mistakes—seemed miles away, a ghost from another life. When Josh lifted her up and carried her to the blanket, she didn't say a word at all.

CHAPTER SEVEN
Tuesday, 4:30 PM

RELIEF FLOODED SYDNEY AS SHE STOPPED OUTSIDE the Fishing Hole Gallery & Bakery. She'd just spent an hour on the phone with Winslow's college counselor, convincing her that the office had lost her scholarship application. It had taken about a thousand promises that Sydney really *had* handed the application in—and confirmation that the secretary had seen her do so—but, finally, the college counselor had agreed to call RISD tomorrow to work out an extension. For the first time since walking into school that morning, Sydney felt as if she could finally breathe.

She still had to finish redoing her application, of course. She'd spent the whole day working frantically to duplicate it. She'd dropped her digital memory cards off at the photo shop for a rush printing. She'd spent hours in her makeshift darkroom, redeveloping her nondigital images. And she'd redone her written application from memory. There was still more to do, but first she needed some fuel.

She grabbed a coffee and muffin at the bakery counter and took a seat in the back of the gallery. She plugged her phone in to charge. It was down to 10 percent battery for the third time that day, confirming her suspicion that her used phone was as old as cavemen.

She clicked on her e-mail, chugging down some coffee while her phone took a full minute to process the request. Finally, Joey's message popped up, still unanswered. She took another sip before opening a reply.

Hey Joey,
It's been crazy here to say the least. Maybe everyone drank the Kool-Aid, like you said. Do you ever actually miss it here? I used to think I wouldn't, but then the other day, I was shooting photos down at Willow Pond, and I started thinking about how you and I used to play there when we were little. Standing there, hearing a breeze rustle the willow trees and smelling that unmistakable Echo Bay smell of salt air and concrete, I actually kind of felt . . . affection. It's weird how a place can beat you down again and again, leave you bruised and battered, and still you can feel this unbreakable tie to it. One of the great mysteries of life. Or a sign I have attachment issues.

Anyway, thanks again for writing. For what it's worth, I'm sorry every day for what happened.

Sydney

Sydney stared down at her words in surprise. They'd poured right out, as if they'd been inside her all along, just waiting for an escape. But she couldn't actually *send* that. Could she? Joey barely knew her anymore, and she was pretty sure he didn't like what he did know. Her finger skimmed the Delete button. It had felt so good to write it, to unclog her brain. She didn't want to banish it to oblivion. Before she could change her mind, she hit Send.

She chugged more coffee before dumping the contents of her bag onto the table. Guinness's packet was on top. She took a nervous scan of the gallery. The bakery counter was empty except for a lone employee. Watercolors of local settings sprinkled the walls, but the only viewers were a couple of tourists in matching Brooks Brothers outfits and the kind of canvas hats that screamed *we're not from here.* There were no prying eyes, no one to watch her.

Satisfied, she began to pore through the packet again, hoping something new would jump out at her, a clue she'd missed the first time. But no matter how carefully she read, nothing more slunk out from between the lines. Kyla was being stalked, that much was clear. But the *by whom* was still a big question mark.

Sydney dropped her forehead onto the table with a soft bang. If only she could talk to Guinness. But he was still on lockdown in rehab: no phone, no computer. With a groan, she sat back up and returned the packet to her bag. Two photos were left on the table, the same two photos she'd been carrying around for days. Sydney laid them out side by side.

The first was the photo she'd stolen of Kyla's destroyed boat float—the photo that had been missing from the file at the firehouse.

The shot showed the solitary crater at the center of the float. Sydney had spent hours researching accidents, and over and over she'd drawn the same conclusion. There was only one thing that could create a clean, single hole like that: an explosive.

Kyla's float had been in the middle of the ocean when it went up in flames. Which meant if the darer had thrown an explosive, it would have to have been from up on Dead Man's Falls, Echo Bay's expanse of cliffs.

Sydney turned to the second photo on the table. It was a stunning shot she'd captured of Echo Bay's ghost lights. In the corner of the photo, right where the lights originated, there was a shadow—a shadow that looked a lot like a person. The shadow was standing on Dead Man's Falls.

What if that shadow belonged to the darer? What if he or she had not only thrown an explosive at Kyla's boat, but had been faking the ghost lights all along, too?

Sydney scraped her chair back. Adrenaline was suddenly pumping through her veins. She had to see the sight for herself. Maybe there was some kind of clue there. If she could just figure out who had been after Kyla, it could be the answer to all their questions.

Fifteen minutes later she was winding her car up the twisty, steep roads that lead to Dead Man's Falls. She parked in the flattest area she could find. She'd have to make the rest of the trip on foot. She tucked the small bottle of pepper spray Tenley had bought each of them into her purse. Then she started up one of the narrow, bouldered paths that forked and crisscrossed as they ascended to the top of the cliffs. Sydney wavered as the path grew narrower. She could hear the ocean roaring at the edge of the cliff, and it struck her how easy it would be to just disappear up here. She shoved the thought away. She'd made it too far to turn back now.

The path twisted several more times before she reached the top. Down below, the ocean was a velvety blanket, silky and dark as it flapped in the breeze. Sydney breathed in the cool, salty air. She was standing in the very spot where she'd seen the shadow in her picture—the very spot where someone might have launched an explosive at Kyla's float.

There was just one problem. Sydney's gaze landed on a rock that jutted out in the distance. It was wide and crooked, and it stretched straight out over the ocean, like a bridge to nowhere. That rock would have served as a barricade. An explosive would have crashed into it long before it reached the ocean.

Sydney crept closer to the edge, searching for another place that could have served as a launching spot. She stopped in front of a patch of rock that sloped sharply downward. At the bottom was a tiny, flat, cave-like area. It would be the perfect vantage point to launch something toward the ocean. Except that it was barely large enough to hold a raccoon, let alone a killer.

Sydney groaned, frustrated. Every time she thought she was getting somewhere, a brand-new roadblock sprang up. It was like being trapped inside a never-ending maze. The wind picked up, howling through the rocks. It was time to get out of there.

She'd just started back down one of the bouldered paths when a strange pattering made her stop. Were those *footsteps*? She froze, her breath narrowing into soft, raspy pulls.

There they were again. They were definitely footsteps—but animal or human, she couldn't tell. Where were they coming from? She looked frantically around, but the sound was echoing off the rocks, making it impossible to locate its origin.

She pressed her back against a rock, feeling quietly for the pepper spray in her purse. It was all she had to protect herself. Her eyes flickered toward the edge of the cliff, where rock met air. All it would take was one push backward.... She shuddered, imagining it. For a second there would be free fall, the wind a tunnel around her. Then, just like the explosive, she, too, would hit that plank.

The footsteps sharpened. There was no doubt: They were two feet, not four. A person—maybe the darer—was up here.

Instinct took over as Sydney crouched down. The sound echoed all around her, making it seem as if the person were everywhere at once. The ocean roared behind her, a warning. She had no choice. She had to move.

She took off down the path, keeping her head low. She could hear the intruder drawing closer. She hurried right, her heart in her throat. There were the footsteps again. The noise circled around her, dizzying. The edge of the cliff was just feet away, and her eyes went to the drop as she kept climbing down. One wrong step, and it would all be over.

Sydney broke into a run. When she finally reached her parking spot, she gasped in relief. She'd never been so happy to see her reject of a car before. She threw herself into the front seat and locked the doors. As she fumbled with her key, she could swear she caught a glimpse of a shadow, darting swiftly behind a rock. She jammed her key into the ignition, turning hard. But before she could slam on the gas, she saw it.

A delicate gold chain was draped over her steering wheel. A pendant swung from the bottom of it: four swirly gold letters. *KYLA.*

The air in the car seemed to thin as Sydney shoved the necklace into her bag. The darer really had been there: on the cliffs, in her car. Whoever it was had been watching her, trailing her. There was no need for a note; the necklace screamed the message loud and clear.

The darer had killed Kyla. And one by one, they would be next.

CHAPTER EIGHT
Wednesday, 12:00 PM

FOR A FEW BLISSFUL SECONDS, TENLEY HAD FORgotten. She headed straight for her table in the cafeteria as if everything were normal. But the faces around it were cold and hard. Jessie glared at her as she muttered something under her breath, making everyone laugh. Tenley looked beseechingly at Hunter, but he averted his eyes, guilt written across his face. Next to him, Marta did the same.

The cafeteria seemed to swirl around Tenley as she backed away. Her lunch bag slipped out of her grip, its contents scattering everywhere. Her cheeks flushed red as she crouched down to collect them.

"Need help?"

Tenley looked up sharply. Tim was standing over her, a wrinkle forming between his eyebrows. "Here." He handed her her yogurt, which had slid several feet.

Tenley took it gratefully. Just seeing Tim made the thorns inside her retract a little. She'd barely talked to him since the video was shown at the assembly. He'd been reassuring when he saw her in the hall on Monday, but thanks to Lanson's lawyer-story boot camp, she hadn't even had time to call him that night. Then yesterday he'd texted to say he was skipping school for a "mental surf day."

She shoved the yogurt into her lunch bag as she stood up. "You don't know how happy I am that you're here." Nearby, the hot-food line erupted in whispers, multiple pairs of eyes flickering in her direction. She forced her focus on Tim. "Want some company for lunch?"

Tim fiddled with a loose string on his hemp necklace. "I'm not sure that's the best idea right now." He'd been looking over her head, at something in the distance, but he finally lowered his gaze. The guarded look in his eyes took her aback.

"I spent a lot of time thinking yesterday, Tenley. I like you. I have since that night you first tripped over my surfboard. But these games you and your friends play..." He shook his head, looking bewildered. "They're really messed up. First you're playing with fireworks out on the water, and Caitlin ends up dead. And now you're drugging your friend's water bottle for fun?"

"It wasn't for fun!" The words slipped out before Tenley could stop them. She recoiled, regretting them instantly.

Tim raised his eyebrows. "Then what was it for?"

"I..." she began. But every sentence led to the same unspeakable conclusion. "It was a mistake," she finished weakly.

"That's just not enough of a reason for me." Tim pulled harder at his necklace. It snapped off, coming away in his hand. He closed his fingers around it, his expression hardening into resolution. "I need some time to sort out my head." In the dim roar of the cafeteria, his voice was quiet. But there was no mistaking his words.

"Time," Tenley repeated dully. First Caitlin, then her other friends, and now Tim. The darer was snipping away at her life, person by person. Soon only tattered scraps would be left. Her anger returned hard and fast. This wasn't supposed to be her life. "I have to go," she mumbled. She didn't look at Tim as she tore out of the cafeteria.

She headed straight to the computer lab. Last night she'd spent hours rereading the dream journal she'd taken from Caitlin's bedroom. Before Caitlin died, she'd been recording in that journal her dreams about her kidnapping. It was where she described in detail the room where she'd been held: a basement with red walls and red carpet and red curtains. It was also where Tenley had learned that Caitlin had finally seen her kidnapper's face in a dream: not Jack Hudson at all, but a woman.

Now that Tenley had proof that the darer—this mystery woman—had set Jack Hudson up, she was desperate to find another clue about the real kidnapper. But no matter how many rereads she did, all she took away from Cait's journal were the same basic facts. The kidnapper was a woman with a red basement, who owned an antique toy circus train and a sapphire ring. It wasn't much to go on. She couldn't exactly search all the basements in Echo Bay, and she'd already tried to track down the train to no avail. Which left her with the ring.

The darer had recently given Sydney a sapphire ring—presumably the very one she'd worn when she'd kidnapped Caitlin. It made Tenley wonder: What would happen if the ring suddenly and publicly changed hands? Would the darer panic enough to get sloppy?

She'd talked it over with Sydney and Emerson the night before, after they'd caught up one another on all the recent darer developments. They'd all agreed: It was worth a shot. So in the middle of the night, with sleep eluding her, Tenley took action. Ever since the ring accidentally ended up in Guinness's belongings at their house, Tenley had been storing it for safekeeping. At 3:00 AM she dug it out from the bottom of her dresser and took a few photos of it. Then she listed it on North Shore Sales, a popular local resale site. Each morning, Channel 4 News did a short feature on the site's best new listings, and, just as Tenley had hoped, that morning the feature had been on the ring. She knew it was a long shot, but if the killer saw the ring on TV and tried to buy it back, they'd finally have a solid lead.

Now, Tenley took a seat in the back of the computer lab and logged on to North Shore Sales's website. The description she'd listed popped up onto the screen. *Gorgeous sapphire ring for sale! Top quality!* Tenley's eyes went to the two blue envelopes at the top of the page. It looked as if she had messages.

The first one was spam. But the second one looked legitimate. *I'm interested in purchasing this ring,* a user named Computerlover2 had written. *Would you be able to meet at 4:30 today so I can take a look at it through a jeweler's loupe? I'll be at 331 Hillside Drive in Echo Bay.*

Tenley's heart rate spiked instantly. It probably wasn't their darer. But there was always a chance.

I'll be there, she wrote back.

- - - - - - -

At four twenty that afternoon, Tenley was on her way to 331 Hillside Drive. She had the radio on a smooth-rock station, something she did only when she drove alone, and she let the piano-dominated song calm her nerves. In just ten minutes she would find out who Computerlover2 was.

The song ended, replaced by the DJ's low, smooth voice. "Marlin Coby here with a North Shore weather update. Eight states are likely to be hit by a blizzard building off the Gulf of Mexico, including our great state of Massachusetts."

"Snow in October *again*?" Tenley muttered. "Why do I live in Massachusetts?" She reached forward to turn up the volume.

"The storm has already been dubbed Octo-storm," Marlin continued. "You might want to put away your pumpkins and take out your sleds, because we're talking a full nor'easter: closed roads, power outages, downed phone lines. We still have almost a week before it hits, though, so don't wait until the last minute to stock up on essentials and put up those storm shutters."

A new song started, but Tenley wasn't listening anymore. She kept hearing those words: *closed roads, downed phone lines.* Maybe snow in October wasn't such a bad thing. There was a lot the darer could control, but *no one* could operate in those conditions, not unless he or she was superhuman.

A few minutes later Tenley pulled up to a huge, industrial-looking building. Confused, she double-checked the address on her phone's map. *331 Hillside Drive.* She'd been expecting a jeweler's office, since the buyer had mentioned a loupe, but this looked more like a factory. She peeked into her purse. Her pepper spray was tucked safely next to the ring box.

A long, wooded pathway led up to the building. As Tenley rounded a bend, a sign came into view. BAUER INDUSTRIES.

Wait, wasn't that—

"Tenley!" Calum Bauer emerged from the building's steel doors, waving energetically. He was wearing a zip-up sweatshirt over a T-shirt that illustrated the step-by-step evolution of a human into a robot. "I didn't realize that you were the seller until you e-mailed me back." He flashed a lopsided grin as he ambled toward her. "How fortuitous!"

Tenley swallowed a groan. In her opinion, Calum Bauer was the worst kind of tragedy. He'd been born to one of the richest men in the country, only to grow into a ghostly pale, computer-loving supernerd. The bidder's handle, *Computerlover2*, suddenly made complete sense. "You're looking to buy a ring?" she asked dubiously. "For a female?"

Calum nodded, oblivious to her sarcasm. "I've been on a quest to find a gift for a special someone, and your ring seems like it could be perfect."

Tenley averted her gaze. She wondered if he was talking about Sydney. She'd seen the way he'd looked at her at the homecoming dance: One word from Sydney and he'd morphed from computer nerd into slobbering puppy. She winced at the thought of his regifting Sydney with the darer's ring. Not exactly the way to her heart. Then again, neither was his penchant for talking like a grandfather.

"I just want to take a quick inspection through a loupe," Calum continued. "If it's as perfect as I think, I'll proffer whatever price you're asking."

Proffer? It took all of Tenley's willpower not to roll her eyes. "The thing is, Calum, I, um, actually changed my mind on the drive over." She cleared her throat, thinking fast. "The ring is more sentimental to me than I realized. I don't think I can part with it after all." *Not unless it's to a kidnapping darer.* "I hope you understand."

Calum nodded, looking disappointed. "Of course. Would you mind if I still take a quick look at it, though? If there's a brand name on it somewhere, I might be able to replicate it. Then you won't have come all the way out to my dad's offices for nothing."

Tenley hesitated. She didn't love the idea of letting the ring out of her possession. But the hopeful look on Calum's face was so sweetly pathetic that she found herself agreeing.

Calum led her into the building and down a long hallway. Huge computer screens filled every room they passed. Tenley caught sight of several young guys hunched over their keyboards. With the thick glasses and scrawny arms, they managed to make Calum look like a movie star. He, at least, was actually pretty built, thanks to a summer of lifeguarding at the Club.

She followed Calum to a room in the back of the building. Floor-to-ceiling windows lined one wall, offering an unobstructed view of the bay behind the building. "Conference room," Calum explained. He pulled a small jeweler's loupe out of his pocket.

Tenley handed him the ring and dropped down at the table. She kicked her foot absently as she watched Calum. He was holding the loupe over the stone, turning it left and then right so the facets caught the light. She was pretty sure she'd never seen a male under the age of thirty look that closely at jewelry in her life. She shifted a little in her seat. Why *was* Calum so interested in the ring? A warning bell rang in her head.

"I don't think you're going to find a brand name inside the stone," Tenley said tightly.

Calum looked up, blinking hard. "Sorry, I just got caught up." He paused, turning the ring between his fingers. "My mom taught me. She used to be somewhat of a connoisseur when it came to jewelry." He dropped his gaze to the table. "Old habits," he said with a shrug.

Tenley's chest squeezed. This was what the darer had done to her: filled her with paranoia, turned everyone into a suspect. "My dad used to love to walk along Dune Way and analyze all the waterfront houses," she said quietly. "I still do it to this day."

"Habit," Calum confirmed. He looked over at her. "Is that what that locker-room video was all about? Old habits?"

Tenley tensed at the mention of the video. She could feel her eyes blazing as she met Calum's gaze. But there wasn't any judgment on his face. Just an open curiosity.

"In a way," she said carefully. "It got more out of control than I meant for it to."

Calum nodded knowingly. "I understand."

Once again Tenley gave him a dubious look.

"Really!" he insisted. "You know how I attended Danford Academy for a few years?" Tenley nodded. She remembered Calum going away to boarding school in seventh grade, but she'd forgotten it was Danford. "Well, your prank pales in comparison with some of the senior pranks I witnessed there," he said.

"From the sidelines, I'm sure," Tenley couldn't resist teasing.

"Except for one time," Calum said proudly. "I assisted with one prank at the end of my sophomore year. It involved strawberry jelly squirting out of showerheads...." He grinned. "Suffice it to say that I know how easily things can go awry."

Tenley laughed. "I'm surprisingly impressed, Calum."

Calum took one more look at the ring before handing it back to Tenley. "No clues to the brand," he said with a sigh. "Guess I'm back to square numero uno."

"Have you thought about artwork?" Tenley straightened up in her seat, surprised to find she actually wanted to help him. "Some girls"—*avid photographers*, she added silently—"might prefer that to jewelry."

Calum nodded, looking thoughtful. "A painting of a computer could be nice."

"No, it could definitely not," Tenley groaned.

Calum broke back into his goofy grin. "Just joshing."

Tenley stood up, her nice streak wearing thin at the use of the word *joshing*. "Or you could buy yourself a new vocabulary instead," she offered. "By the way you talk, I'd think you were turning eighty any day now."

"Nope," Calum said cheerfully. He stood up, too. "Just eighteen. This Saturday in fact."

"A word of advice," Tenley said. "If you throw a party, don't give dentures as favors."

"How about flasks?" Calum offered. "Would that meet with your approval?"

Tenley laughed despite herself. "Are you really having a party?"

A wistful expression crossed Calum's face. "I'm not exactly adept at gathering the masses. Unlike you." A smirk tugged at Calum's lips, and Tenley had a feeling he was thinking about the last party she threw—where she'd been dared to kiss him during a game of truth or dare.

"I was born with the party-throwing gene," she acknowledged. She stopped in the doorway. *Of course.* It was what her mom had always taught her. The one solution to every problem? A party.

"You know what," she said slowly. "You *should* have a party." She wove her hands together as the idea took shape. "And I'm going to help you. You provide the house and the drinks, and I'll take care of getting everyone to come." This was her chance to get back in her grade's good graces. Everyone was dying to check out Neddles Island, the private island where Calum and his rich Einstein of a dad lived. A party there was the perfect way to erase the Jessie incident from everyone's mind. It also, she realized, would be perfect darer bait. Whoever was tormenting them seemed to love big scenes. A party could be just the thing to lure their stalker out of hiding.

"Do you really think people would come?" Calum asked doubtfully. "Would you, if you weren't doing the inviting?"

Tenley studied her shoes. The question gave her a squirmy feeling in her stomach. She'd spent so long clinging to the top of Winslow's social ladder that she'd never bothered to look down. But now she was on the ground, too, and the view was worse than she'd imagined.

"You're having a party," she said firmly. "I'll take care of the invites if you do the rest." She put her hands on her hips, fixing him with her fiercest stare. "I'm not good at taking no for an answer."

"Okay, okay." Calum held his hands up in surrender. "I acquiesce. We'll party on Saturday like it's 1999."

This time, Tenley couldn't help but roll her eyes. "Just as long as you never say that again."

Calum gave her a salute. "Come on, I'll take you out the back way. Just be careful of wires. There's some construction going on."

Tenley picked her way around a few stray wires as she followed Calum toward the exit. "Careful," a construction worker grunted as they passed. "Some of the areas are—"

He didn't get to finish his sentence. As Tenley stepped past him, several wires suddenly broke loose from a clump in the ceiling. Sparks flew as the wires tore away, bringing metal piping with them. "Watch out!" someone yelled.

Adrenaline surged through Tenley as she hurtled herself out of the way. She landed on the floor only inches out of the piping's path.

"Ow!" The howl made her whip around. Calum, who'd been a few steps behind her, had caught some of the falling piping on his arm. It left an open gash behind. Calum's already pale face grew several shades paler as he stared down at the blood pooling out of it.

One of the construction workers rushed over. "We've got a first aid kit in the truck," he assured Calum. He glanced over at Tenley, sweat pooling on his upper lip. "You okay over there?"

Tenley nodded mutely. She shook out her arms, then her legs. She was in one piece, but the burn on her leg ached, and her skin was clammy all over. It was the accident at the homecoming dance all over again, the very worst kind of déjà vu. She could picture the light crashing down next to her, could almost feel the heat searing into her....

"You sure, Tenley?"

Calum's voice pulled her back to the present. "Yeah," she said, her voice trembling slightly. "You go take care of your arm."

As one of the construction workers hustled Calum off to get first aid, another came over to help her up. "You're lucky you're so spry," he commented.

Tenley stood up carefully, regaining her balance. "Who knew being a gymnast would save—"

She was interrupted by an angry shout. "What the *hell*?" someone yelled.

Tenley looked toward the source of the voice. A construction worker stood at the top of a ladder. He was holding a chunk of loose wires in his hand. The bottoms had been sliced neatly across. "No wonder that fell. Someone clipped the wires!"

Tenley shrank back, bumping her shoulder into the wall.

Someone had planned this.

No, not someone. The darer.

A beep rose from inside Tenley's bag. Her body went numb as she reached for her phone. *Blocked.*

I just kicked things into high gear. Who knew doing my own dirty work could be so much fun?

CHAPTER NINE
Wednesday, 7:00 PM

EMERSON SAT IN HER CAR, TRYING TO MUSTER UP
the energy to drive home. It had been a terrible day: The only people
to utter a single word to her were Tenley and her teachers. Even
Marta had successfully avoided her. It had made Emerson feel like
a magic act: Just one blink and she could disappear forever. Unable
to take the silent treatment any longer, she'd skipped cheer practice
and spent the afternoon trying to figure out what Delancey's key
unlocked.

She'd tried every avenue she could think of. She'd e-mailed
Abby to ask if she knew about it. She'd taken the key to the hard-
ware store to see if anyone there had suggestions. She'd made sure
it wasn't a fit for a local PO Box. She'd even ransacked Delancey's
bedroom, on the fabricated excuse that Delancey had borrowed
one of her textbooks. But after all that, she was left with only one
possible lead: a scribbled, balled-up note she'd found in the trash

can next to Delancey's desk. It had just two words on it, written in Delancey's perfect cursive: *Purple door.*

Was it possible Delancey's key led to a purple door? And, if so, what did that door have to do with the darer?

Despite the dead ends, racing around town and actually *doing something* about their situation had Emerson feeling the most like herself all week. With a sigh, Emerson put her car in gear. When she slipped into her house a few minutes later, she could hear the buzz of a TV drifting out of her parents' bedroom. She crept quietly up the stairs, hoping they wouldn't hear her. She couldn't take another lecture, not tonight. She made it safely into her bedroom, closing the door behind her with a soft click before she turned on the light. That was when she noticed it.

Her underwear drawer.

It was hanging open, underwear and bras a tangled mess inside. Emerson walked toward it in a daze. When she'd opened the drawer that morning, it had been neat and orderly, underwear on one side, bras on the other. Now straps were hanging out and her underwear was jumbled in haphazard piles.

She inched closer, fear thrumming through her. It wasn't until she was right there, close enough to touch, that she saw the invitation.

She lifted it up. It was printed on thick pink card stock and lined with a silver ribbon. YOU'RE INVITED! it screamed at the top. Underneath, in the same typewriter font, were the details.

What: A tryst

Where: The Bones

When: Tonight

Why: Disobey, and Tenley finally dies

Dress Code: Your underwear...and

nothing else

Emerson squeezed her eyes shut, shaking all over. She had no choice but to obey. As strange as it was, Tenley was the only real friend she had right now. She couldn't risk losing her, too.

She knew the whole thing could be a setup. But if it wasn't, and Tenley ended up paying the price, she'd never be able to live with herself.

Emerson sneaked back out to her car in a daze. The drive to the Bones barely felt real. But then it appeared in the distance: a tower of boxes stacked to the sky. This far away, it reminded her of concrete LEGOs. Officially, the building was called the Tides Condominiums, but in the three years that it stood unfinished, the local news stations had coined it the Bones: as in a skeleton of a building. One day, it would be all glass and gleam, luxury apartments that would draw the rich in from Boston. But for now it was just a shell.

Emerson tried to quell the shaking in her hands as she parked in the Bones' abandoned lot. She touched a finger to the horseshoe necklace she was still wearing. She could use all the luck she could get tonight.

Emerson had just turned off her car when her phone buzzed. Fear spiked inside her, making the temperature in the car suddenly feel like a hundred degrees. But the text was from Josh. *You around?*

Emerson stared grimly down at her phone. *Running a quick errand. Call u after!* The false cheeriness made her stomach turn as she climbed into the dimly lit parking lot. She gave her pocket a quick pat. Her pepper spray was there.

It was dark inside the building, but someone had lined up two rows of tea candles. Their tiny fingers of light created a pathway through the building. Blood pounded in Emerson's ears as she followed it. The path wound past steel beams and concrete walls and bags of cement before stopping abruptly in a wide-open space.

"Whoa." Emerson's palms grew wet as she looked around. Red rose petals were everywhere. They lined the room, bathing the space in red. In the center of the floor, the silky petals had been delicately arranged into the shape of an *X*.

Emerson moved closer, the pounding in her ears now a full-on roar. The message was clear. *X marks the spot.* Or maybe it meant something else. X'd out—*done*.

Her instructions flashed though her mind. *Dress Code: Your underwear... and nothing else.*

Closing her eyes, she slipped out of her jeans, then her top. The clothes fell to the floor, leaving Emerson in her underwear.

"Okay," she called out angrily. She opened her eyes, wrapping her arms around herself. "I'm half naked! What now? Are there cameras? Video?"

Outside, the wind howled, lifting goose bumps on her bare skin. From the distance came a faint creak. Every muscle in her body tightened. "Hello?" she yelled out. "Who's there?"

Nothing.

But she could sense it. Her neck prickled. Someone was there. "Hello?" she tried again. "Show your face!"

A creak rang out in the distance, and then something else. Was that a *snicker*?

Fear choked her. Someone was waiting. Watching.

A shadow flickered in the corner of her vision. She spun around, but there was no one. Another breeze tickled her arms, and suddenly she was furious. "If you're here, come out!" she yelled. Her voice bounced off the distant walls, circling around her. But the space was eerily still again, the kind of quiet that came from being truly alone. If someone had been there, they were gone now.

"You know what? Fine!" She grabbed desperately for her shirt. "I followed your orders! I'm out of here."

Her shirt was dangling above her head when she heard them. *Footsteps.*

The fabric slipped out of Emerson's hands. The footsteps drew closer, the sound drumming through the wide-open structure. Emerson stood paralyzed, her limbs like stone.

A person emerged. Tall build. Broad shoulders. Mohawked hair. *"Josh?"*

"Emerson!" Josh took a step forward as his eyes darted from Emerson's underwear to the rose petals and back. "What—what is this?" Confusion and horror flitted across Josh's face. And then— anger. "This was your errand? Were you *meeting* someone here?"

"No!" Emerson swore. "I wasn't—"

"Really?" Josh cut in. "Because you're half naked, and I'm not sure what else I'm supposed to think." Suddenly Josh slapped his forehead. "Oh my god. Was this what you were trying to tell me in the lighthouse? That guy you mentioned—are you still seeing him?"

"No!" Emerson went over to Josh and tried to take his hand, but he shook her off. "I swear, Josh, I'm done with him. This...this was just a dare! That's all, I promise." She gazed pleadingly up at him. "I wouldn't lie."

"Really?" Josh pulled out his phone. "Because it seems like that's all you've been doing." His expression was steely as he handed her his phone.

The instant Emerson saw the name on the screen, any last bit of hope leaked out of her. *Blocked.*

Liar, liar, pants on fire...Oh wait, Emerson isn't wearing any pants! Go to the Bones for proof she hasn't changed.

A photo was attached. It was a screenshot from Twitter, posted two Julys ago by RemsenPhotog.

SCORE! Model Tally = 4, it declared over a fuzzy selfie shot of two scantily clad figures embracing.

Emerson swallowed hard, tears welling in her eyes. The photo was of her with Remsen, the photographer with whom she'd made the worst mistake of her life. A girl she'd modeled with in New York had found the image on Twitter last year and e-mailed her a screen shot. The darer must have dug it out of her old e-mails.

Emerson crumpled over, gagging. The darer wanted to take everything from her, strip her bare until she had nothing at all.

"So it's true, then," Josh whispered.

She wrenched herself back up. Josh was staring at her in disgust, a tear working its way down his cheek. The candlelight cast shadows across his face, darkening his eyes.

"In New York, yes," Emerson choked out. "But not now. I swear, Josh. It was the worst mistake of my life and I would never, ever make it again. I—I love you."

As soon as the words slipped out, she wished she could take them back. But they were words you couldn't reverse, words you couldn't misunderstand. They hung in the air between them, tainted and unreturned.

"I don't know what to do, Em." Another tear slid down Josh's cheek. "I don't know what to believe." He kicked at a pile of rose petals, shaking his head. "Every time I let my guard down with you, I end up getting hurt."

Emerson felt as if her chest were splitting in two. He was right. As long as Josh dated her, he was in danger. No one was safe when it came to her stalker. There was only one way to protect Josh. Only one way to make sure she never hurt him again.

"I know." Her voice broke. "I'm not good for you right now. I'm not good for *anyone* right now." Each word felt like a nail jabbing at her insides. She forced herself to keep going. "I do love you, Josh. I have for a long time. But I think I need some time apart. Some time alone."

Josh's eyes shone green-brown behind a film of tears. "You're ending things?"

"I'm sorry," Emerson whispered.

For a long moment, Josh just stared at her. "I really thought we could make it this time," he said at last. "But I guess that only happens in fiction." He didn't hug her or say good-bye. He didn't beg or try to sway her. He just gave her one last look, as if he was memorizing her face. Then he turned and walked out.

Emerson sank to the floor, a sob racking through her. She could hear Josh's car revving up and screeching off. She ripped her horseshoe necklace off and threw it across the room. Luck couldn't do anything for her anymore.

Ding!

The noise made her leap to her feet. It took her a minute to locate her phone in the pile of clothes.

They say that breaking up is hard to do. At least we still have each other.

CHAPTER TEN
Thursday, 7:40 Am

SYDNEY FELT A STAB OF GUILT AS SHE WATCHED
Echo Bay recede in her rearview mirror. Right now, she should be
taking her seat in homeroom, listening as Abby Wilkins droned on
over the loudspeaker. Instead, she was headed toward Moorhead,
Massachusetts, population three hundred. Well, three hundred, and
one rehab center.

At 6:23 that morning, Guinness had called. He'd been granted
visitor privileges for the day, and he wanted to see only her. Guinness had asked her to drive out after school, but there was no way
she could wait that long. Sydney kept the windows down as she
drove, hoping the rush of wind might drown out her thoughts. No
such luck. Ten minutes into the drive and her brain was already a
fun house of theories, twisting and contorting at every turn.

They all agreed that the kidnapper theory made sense. The

same woman who had kidnapped Caitlin, and set up Jack Hudson to take the fall, was now torturing them. But how did it all connect to Kyla? And how did this adult woman know so much about their lives?

It had always felt to Sydney as if the darer was someone their age—someone they *knew*. Then again, it could be a woman who worked at Winslow. Sydney tried to imagine Principal Howard or Miss Hilbrook hiding in the hallways, shadowing their every move. A snort slipped out of her. The image would almost be funny if the reality wasn't so horrible.

By the time Sydney turned into Moorhead an hour and a half later, she'd talked herself in circles so many times she could barely see straight. At least there was one thing in her life that the darer hadn't destroyed. Thanks to the Winslow counselor's wheedling, RISD had granted her an extension on her scholarship application. She'd overnighted the application herself, which meant it should be arriving safely at RISD today.

Sydney tried to clear her head as she passed a shut-down post office, a tiny diner with a half-lit sign, and a one-pump gas station. At the end of the road, a sign for Roseview Drug & Alcohol Rehabilitation Center came into view. 2 MILES DOWN THE ROAD! it read in big, cheery letters.

She followed the sign to a fancy, wrought-iron fence that stood at least eight feet tall. It encircled an ornate stone building that looked more like a castle than a rehab center. Sydney pulled up to the entranceway and pushed the buzzer on a high-tech security system. A video screen flickered to life. "Sydney Morgan, here to visit Guinness Reed," she said into the screen. She squeezed the steering wheel, right where Kyla's necklace had been left when she was on the cliffs Tuesday. Just the memory was enough to set her heart pounding again, and she sighed with relief when a man in a suit appeared on the video screen.

The man was sitting behind a huge wooden desk. "One moment, please," he said in a formal voice. With a ring of a bell, the door to the fence swung open. "Please park in Lot A," the man said, sounding disturbingly like a robot. "Then proceed to the visitors' desk in the lobby."

Lot A, it turned out, was a field lined with flawlessly manicured bushes. A flagstone path led to the center's stained glass front door. Only the Reeds would find a rehab center that was *nicer* than their beachfront mansion.

It took Sydney fifteen minutes to make it through the center's rigorous sign-in regimen. (ID: deposited. Bag: examined. Clothes: patted down. Four-page release form: signed.) Finally, a tiny, wrinkled nurse guided her to an expansive rec room, lined with shelves of board games, books, and instruments. "Your friend's in the back," she informed Sydney, nodding in the direction of a small chess table. "He's a charmer, isn't he?" She gave Sydney a wink before leaving.

"That he is," Sydney murmured to no one in particular. She lifted her hand in a hesitant wave to Guinness. Now that she was actually here, waves of nerves were suddenly rolling through her.

It wasn't as if she hadn't seen Guinness in rehab before. She'd first met him at the Sunrise Center, when they were both patients. They'd connected immediately back then, even though Sydney was several years younger. She'd never met someone who understood her like he did; someone who didn't shy away from the anger brewing inside her, but met it head-on. At Sunrise, she and Guinness were on the same plane; they shared the same world. It had tied them together with a knot so tight she was still working to loosen it.

She'd thought seeing him here would bring back a rush of memories—tighten that knot once again. But it felt different this time. They weren't on the same plane anymore. This time, Guinness was on the inside, and she was on the outside. It made her feel as if they'd been tossed around in a snow globe, and only she was left standing.

Guinness waved her over. She studied him as she crossed the room. He had a few days' worth of stubble on his cheeks, and his dark hair hung in tousled waves. She was surprised by how good he looked, more relaxed than she'd seen him in a long time.

"So have you prepared for the impending weather doom?" Guinness asked as she dropped down across from him.

"I can barely fit inside my apartment with all the canned goods my mom's stockpiling," she confirmed.

"Octo-storm is all anyone here can talk about," Guinness said. "The nurses are freaking that we'll lose power. Addicts without electricity," he said with a laugh.

"Sounds like a reality show," Sydney mused.

Guinness's dark brown eyes met hers, holding her gaze for several seconds. He was usually so hard to read, a book written in a different language, but right now his expression was surprisingly unguarded. "It's good to see you." He put his hand on hers and an old, familiar tingle worked its way through her.

"It's good to see you, too, Guinness. You look great. Better."

"I am." Guinness glanced around the mostly empty room. In

the corner, two women were playing chess, both bent low over the board. A few tables up, a gangly guy who looked as if he couldn't be more than thirteen was absorbed in a book. No one was paying any attention to them. "I actually kind of like it here. They have fancy cameras that I'm allowed to play around with, and as long as I follow my treatment plan, people leave me alone. There's no one following me, no one leaving me notes." He leaned back, resting his hands on his stomach. "I feel like I can breathe again."

Sydney twisted at her ring. She let herself imagine what that would be like: to slip out of Echo Bay's chains and just walk away. But she wasn't in rehab. Unlike Guinness, she had to go home at the end of the day. "I was hoping we could talk about that package you sent me," she said.

A muscle clenched in Guinness's jaw. "I figured as much." He scraped his chair back, standing up. "Let's take a walk. As of today, I'm allowed on the grounds unsupervised." He pressed his hands to his chest in a fake swoon. "It's like Christmas and my birthday all wrapped into one!"

Sydney laughed as Guinness began the long process of signing them out. Finally, he led her outside and onto a wooded path. The iron fence rose on either side in the distance, but inside the property, tree branches threaded into an awning of gold and orange. Sydney breathed in deeply. The air smelled strongly of fall, that fresh, blank-page smell.

"So, Kyla," Guinness sighed.

"Kyla," she repeated. A bright red leaf fluttered down, and Sydney reached up, letting it land in her palm. "When I brought her up last week, you said you barely knew her, Guinness. But you don't hunt down a stalker of some girl you barely knew." She glanced over at him. "Why did you lie to me?"

Guinness kicked at a rock on the ground, watching it skitter ahead into the grass. "I was getting those notes, Syd. Not just the one I sent you, but others, too. I was freaked out. And I didn't want you getting dragged into it. But then things started to get really weird, and I just—I *had* to tell someone. You'd been asking all those questions, so…" He looked over at her, squinting in the morning sun. "At the time, that package seemed like the safest way to do it." He shook his head. "If I'd known what this person was capable of, I would never have sent it. The last thing I want is for you to get involved with this."

Sydney hesitated. She wanted so badly to tell him that she already *was* involved, but what would that accomplish? Guinness was finally doing well. How could she ruin that for him? Besides, it wasn't as if he could help her from inside rehab. "How close were you with Kyla?" she asked instead. She knew Guinness had once had a thing for Kyla. He'd even dated her sister, Lacey, like some kind of consolation prize. She tried not to let the memory sting. She and Guinness were over; whom he'd dated in the past shouldn't have a bearing on her.

"She was Kyla Kern," Guinness said with a shrug. "She was the hottest waitress at the Club. Every guy who summered in Echo Bay was into her. It drove me crazy that she wouldn't give me the time of day." He gave her a sheepish grin. "I wasn't used to hearing no."

Sydney made a face at him. "You don't say."

"But Kyla never seemed to be dating anyone," Guinness continued. He kicked at another rock, and Sydney watched it leap ahead. "Or at least that's what I thought."

"What changed?"

"The summer before she died, I was at a party at her house, and, being my usual drunken asshole self, I decided it was a great idea to sneak into her room. I was going through her underwear drawer—I *know*," he groaned when Sydney gave him a horrified look. "Like I said, drunken asshole. How do you think I ended up here?" He waved broadly at the grounds surrounding them. "Anyway, that's where I found a hidden note. It was this whole love poem, written to 'Lion.'" He air-quoted on *Lion*. "At the time, I figured that was why she wasn't into me—because she had some secret boyfriend."

Sydney twisted her ring. "And now? Do you think it could have been from the person who was stalking her?"

"It's hard to know. I've been trying to remember what the note looked like, but I can't." He gave his head a frustrated shake. "It was a while ago, and I was drunk. The only thing that really stuck with me was that name—Lion—because it was such a strange nickname for a girl as sweet as Kyla." He guided Sydney toward a long, gurgling brook. "It would make sense, though, wouldn't it?"

"It would." Except that it didn't fit with their kidnapper theory. Caitlin's kidnapper had been a woman. "You definitely think the note was from a guy?"

"Unless Kyla had a lady love." Guinness gave her a rakish grin.

"Was there anything else you found?" Sydney pressed, ignoring the comment. "Maybe something about the night she died?"

"No." Guinness pushed a strand of dark hair out of his eyes. "I ended up here before I could dig any further."

"And nothing else you remember about that first note?" Sydney was walking faster now, and Guinness picked up his speed to match hers.

"No, and listen, Blue." Guinness grabbed her arm, pulling her to a stop. Despite everything, her heart swelled at his use of his old nickname for her. "I want you to drop this when you leave here today, okay? Someone clearly wants to keep this information buried—enough to have my weed laced so I almost *died*. I finally feel safe now that I'm out of Echo Bay, but you . . ." He swallowed hard. "I couldn't live with myself if something happened to you." Guinness's eyes searched hers. "Promise me you'll let it go, okay?"

Sydney clamped her lips together. There was no way she could do that, but she wasn't about to tell Guinness that. Not when he was doing so well. "Sure," she lied. "Whatever you want."

"Good." Guinness looked relieved. "So," he said, taking off down the path again. "Tell me about you, Syd." He stopped next to a wide rock at the edge of the brook. He sat down, gesturing for Sydney to join him. "Have you stayed . . . in control?"

Sydney knew what he was asking. "I'm fire-free," she informed him.

Guinness broke into a huge smile. "That's great, Blue. I'm so proud of you." Sydney's chest squeezed. For so long, she'd wanted Guinness to look at her like that: as if she were the only thing in the world that mattered. But most desires had an expiration date, and as she turned away, focusing on the water foaming over the rocks, she wondered if she'd finally hit hers.

Next year she'd hopefully be leaving Echo Bay behind. There would be new teachers and new roommates and probably new guys. But none of them would ever understand her like Guinness did.

"I'm so sorry, Guinness." She reached out and took his hand. "You needed me last week, and I had blinders on. I was too caught up in my own problems. I should have been there, like you've always been for me."

Guinness shook his head. "You were there, Syd. You're always there. I think I just forgot where to look." Then he was leaning in, pressing his lips against hers, and, for a minute, Sydney was fifteen again and this was the moment she'd been waiting for. She felt it all—the hope and exhilaration and desire and love—but the emotions were softer this time, muted somehow. It reminded her of how, on a sunny day, even after you looked away from the sky, you could still see spots of color behind your lids. The light lingered, even after the sun was gone.

Gently, she pushed Guinness away. "I can't," she said softly. "Not anymore."

Guinness looked down. "So it's not just fire you're done with."

Sydney touched his cheek, not sure what to say. She and Guinness had stopped and started so many times over the past few years. But this time, she could feel something shifting. It felt less like turning a page and more like closing a book. Guinness looked back up at her. It was written across his face: He knew it, too. So she said nothing, just wrapped her arms around him and hugged him tight.

CHAPTER ELEVEN
Thursday, 12:22 PM

TENLEY LEANED OVER THE DESK SHE'D CLAIMED IN the back of the computer lab. She'd skipped the cafeteria, unable to face another freeze-out during lunch. Right now she preferred the peaceful quiet of the computer lab anyway. After the near-disaster at Bauer Industries yesterday, she'd been jumping at every little sound. Here, among the rows of computers, with just two freshmen geeking out over computer games up front, she could almost relax.

She'd planned to use the period to finish an essay, but twenty-two minutes later, all she'd done was Google Jack Hudson's name. Posting the sapphire ring online had turned out to be a dead end, which left only one lead: Jack himself.

The darer had set Jack up to take the fall for Cait's kidnapping, then orchestrated his suicide. It didn't just feel convenient; it felt *personal*. Which got Tenley wondering: If she could find Jack's enemies, would it lead her to her own?

She took a bite of a granola bar as she scanned over the list of facts she'd compiled.

JACK HUDSON

1. Grew up in Boston

2. Attended BU, dropped out after sophomore year

3. Started and sold several businesses—including website paying cash for gold

4. Prior conviction for a bar fight, attended anger-management classes as punishment

5. Never married

At the bottom of the list, Tenley had pasted the few photos she'd found of Jack, each one showing him with a woman more gorgeous than the last. Most were at events: him in a tux, a (usually blond) woman at his side in a jaw-dropping gown. Jack Hudson might never have married, but he didn't seem to have a problem with the ladies. Could the kidnapper have been a scorned ex? A lover desperate for revenge?

The bell rang and Tenley quickly deleted the document before logging out of the computer. She'd already erased any trace of her search. She wasn't taking chances anymore. She'd just pushed her way into the crowded hallway when she heard her name. "Tenley!"

She tensed, bracing for the insult to follow as they had all week. But none came. She looked over to find Calum leaning against a trophy case in Winslow's Hall of Fame, waving his bandaged arm at her. She smiled, relieved for the first time in her life to run into Calum Bauer. She quickly crossed over to him. "How's the arm?"

"Vexatious, more than anything." Calum's backpack hung from his good arm. It was so full that it strained at the sides, the zippered pockets bulging. "I'm just sorry you had to witness that malfunction yesterday," Calum continued. "I promise, Bauer Industries isn't usually a death trap."

Only when I'm there, Tenley replied silently. Guilt wormed its way through her. She'd been targeted, and Calum had gotten caught in the cross fire. The beginning of a headache pulsed at her temples. "At least I got a party out of it," she said, changing the subject.

"As long as Octo-storm doesn't interfere," Calum pointed out.

"They're saying it won't hit until Tuesday or Wednesday, so your party should be safe. Which reminds me." Tenley dug into her bag and removed a sheet of paper. "For the party."

"'Tenley Reed's Guide to Planning the Perfect Party,'" Calum read off the sheet. His brow furrowed as he looked over the list of friendly tips Tenley had thrown together the night before. "Wow. This is very, uh... detailed."

Tenley gave him a reassuring smile. "Just follow that guide and it will be a killer party, I promise."

"Killer," Calum repeated. He looked down at the list again. "If you say so."

"I do." Out of the corner of her eye, Tenley caught sight of a familiar pair of broad shoulders. "I've got to run. Party inviting to do." She pointed a finger at Calum as she backed away. Her leg was still aching, but she fought the urge to limp. "Follow the guide!"

She caught up with Hunter Bailey at the other end of the hall.

"Thanks for sticking up for me at lunch yesterday," she said sarcastically. She hugged her arms over her chest. "I thought you owed me, Hunter." Recently, Tenley had discovered what very few people knew: that Hunter Bailey was gay. She'd promised to keep his secret for him—at least until he was out of his house and away from his monster of a father. She'd even campaigned with him for the homecoming court, leading most of the school to believe they were a couple.

"I do." Hunter peered down at her with icy-blue eyes. "I'm sorry, Ten. Everyone's really pissed."

"Yeah, I got that."

"Jessie's our friend. Tyler's *girlfriend*. What you did—"

"I know," Tenley cut in. "Believe me, I've regretted it every day since. But I really thought it was a caffeine pill!" She'd already repeated the story a dozen times into her friends' voice mail. "I keep trying to apologize, but no one will call me back!" She grabbed his arm, causing a freckly girl with big eyes and bony arms to gape jealously as she passed. "I need your help, Hunter."

Hunter gave her a wary look. "What am I supposed to do?"

"I need you to get everyone to go to a party I'm throwing Saturday night. It's going to be at Calum's mansion on Neddles Island." She bounced nervously on her toes as she spoke. The night before, when nightmares about the darer had kept her awake once again, writing Calum's party-planning guide had been the only thing to soothe her. Parties and popularity: Those were what she knew. The darer could strip everything else away, but she refused to lose that, too.

She gave Hunter a pleading look. "It's going to be amazing. A private party, just for our grade, on the island that everyone's been dying to visit. This party is my big gesture, Hunter. My way of showing everyone how sorry I am."

Hunter went to his locker, and Tenley followed. "I'll go, Tenley, but, honestly, I don't know that anyone else will."

"Then convince them!" She threw her arms up in frustration. "Do whatever you need to."

Hunter pressed his lips together, looking frustrated. "All right," he relented. "I'll take care of it."

"Thank you," she said gratefully. "You won't regret it."

"And my thing...?" Worry showed in his eyes.

"My lips are still sealed," she assured him. "Party or no party." She knew what it was like to have to protect yourself. Sometimes the armor got so heavy it felt as if it were crushing you.

She kept her head down as she ducked into her next class. She was early, but Emerson was already there, staring out the window in the back. Tenley's shoulders loosened up at the sight of her. At least there was still someone who didn't despise her.

"Hey." She joined Emerson at the window. "Your day been as lovely as mine?"

"Better, I bet." Emerson's dark skin was almost always perfect, but today it looked pale and blotchy. Her hair frizzed at the crown, where she'd pulled it into a messy ponytail.

"Any luck with the purple door?" Tenley asked hopefully.

Emerson pressed her fingers into her temples. "None." She lowered her voice. "I've spent hours researching, but I can't find anything about a purple door anywhere on the North Shore. I'll keep at it, but I think this key might be another dead end."

Tenley groaned. Before she could say anything else, the warning bell rang. She was halfway to her seat when she saw it: a small, gift-wrapped box sitting atop her desk. Every nerve in her body went on high alert.

"What...?" Emerson murmured.

"I have no idea." She thought of the last gift she'd received. It had been a trap from the darer: another attempt at killing her. Tenley crept closer to her desk. People were streaming into the classroom now, chatter and laughter swirling around her. Next to her, Emerson said something. But Tenley heard none of it.

Slowly, she lifted the box. It was small and featherlight. Its silver ribbon glittered under the classroom's bright lights.

She spun around, her eyes flitting from person to person. But no one was watching her. No one looked suspicious.

"Ten—" Emerson began.

Blood pounded in Tenley's ears. Who had delivered this?

"Be right back." She sprinted out of the classroom, the box clutched tightly in her grip. The hallway was emptying out, only a few stragglers left behind. She jogged to one end, then the other. *Who left me this?* she wanted to scream. But there was no one to listen.

She was breathing hard as she leaned against a locker, turning her attention back to the box. There were no attachments, no flashing lights, nothing that might trigger a falling beam or splinter a window. Still... she really didn't want to be the one to open it.

She took another quick scan of the hallway. A boy was on his way to the bathroom. A teacher Tenley didn't recognize disappeared around the corner. "You!" Her eyes landed on the freckly girl she'd seen gaping at Hunter earlier. She was headed toward the band room, clutching a flute in her left hand. "Hold up!"

The girl stopped so fast she nearly tripped over her own feet. "Yes?" she squeaked.

"Open this," Tenley commanded, shoving the box at the girl.

The girl clumsily took the box in her free hand, looking shell-shocked. "I...uh...why?" she stammered.

"Just do it," Tenley snapped. "And I'll get you a date with Hunter Bailey."

The girl brightened. "Will you get him to talk to me at lunch, too? In front of my friends?"

"Sure, whatever." Tenley waved her hand dismissively. "Just open the box. And no questions."

Tenley took a subtle step backward as the girl ripped the wrapping paper off and removed the box's lid. Her body tensed, ready to bolt at the first sign of exploding foam or a loud horn blasting. But nothing happened. No crashes, no noise, no frights.

"Ew!" the girl cried. "Why would someone give you this?"

Tenley snatched the box back. Nestled inside was a small lock of shiny chestnut hair. The girl's gaze went from the box to Tenley and back again. "Is that *yours?*"

"I...uh..." The ground swam up to meet Tenley, and for a second she thought she might pass out. She put a hand on a locker to steady herself. It was definitely her hair. But how did the darer have it? She was just about to slam the lid back on the box when she noticed a folded piece of paper at the bottom.

"Seriously," the girl went on. "That's so creepy!"

"It's for a...uh...science project," Tenley lied hastily. "Thanks for your help!" She took off down the hallway at a sprint, clutching the box to her chest.

"Wait!" the girl called after her. "How are you going to set me up with Hunter if you don't know my...?"

The girl's voice faded away as Tenley flew through the doors, emerging into the afternoon sunlight. The wind whipped her hair into her face as she threw herself into her car. Only when all four doors were locked did she flip open the lid and yank out the note.

```
Think what else could happen while
           you're sleeping.
```

Tenley sagged dizzily against the seat. At some point, this person had crept into her room, stood over her bed, touched her hair.... She let out a cry. The darer didn't just want her to die. No, first she had to be toyed with. And the message was clear: It could happen anytime, anywhere.

She forced herself to move, to grab her phone. *Reed Park*, she texted Sydney and Emerson, her fingers flying across the keys. *ASAP! 911!!!!* Then she threw her phone down and sped out of the lot.

— — — — — — —

A half hour later, Emerson and Tenley were jammed inside Reed Park's kid-sized tree house. "Do we really have to do this here?"

Emerson grumbled, trying unsuccessfully to make room for her long legs. The box of Tenley's hair sat open between them, and Emerson flinched as her knee bumped into it. "We're not all the size of garden gnomes, you know." She shot Tenley an accusatory look as Tenley easily crossed her legs underneath her.

Tenley opened her mouth, but before she could formulate a comeback, Sydney climbed into the tree house. "Sorry, sorry." She was panting a little as she forced herself into the tiny slot of space that was left. "Is there maybe a larger place we could do this?"

"Finally, someone with sense!" Emerson threw her arms up in the air for emphasis. Her knuckles smacked against the wooden ceiling, eliciting another grumble.

"This is the closest park to school, and I scouted out the whole place," Tenley said firmly. It was what she'd done as she waited for Sydney and Emerson to show up, after she'd sent them a dozen texts about the lock of hair. "This is the only area that's unexposed. We need privacy to talk."

"Let's just get this over with." Emerson wiggled in place, looking uncomfortable. "I want to get back to school before the end of the period."

Tenley looked over at Sydney, who was pink-cheeked and panting. "Where were you this morning, anyway? Why weren't you at school?"

Sydney picked at her fingernail. "I went to visit Guinness."

Tenley's eyebrows shot up, but she didn't say anything.

"He wasn't ready for family to visit yet," Sydney continued hastily. "But he told me something kind of interesting. You know how

Kyla was getting notes and phone calls before she died?" Tenley nodded. Sydney had already filled her and Emerson in on everything she'd found in the package Guinness had sent her. "Well, Guinness said that the summer before Kyla died, he found a note in her room. He can't remember what it looked like exactly, but it was a love poem. What if the same person stalking Kyla also wrote her that love poem—calling her *Lion* like it was some special nickname? It almost makes it sound like a guy, doesn't it? Maybe even—"

"Wait," Emerson cut in. Tenley glanced over at her. She looked uneasy all of a sudden. "What did you just say?"

"A guy," Sydney repeated.

"No, before that. The nickname."

"Oh, Lion," Sydney said. "That was the nickname that the guy—or whoever—used in the love poem. Guinness remembered it because he thought it was a strange nickname."

"Maybe she was quick to extract her claws," Tenley offered.

"Cheerleader," Emerson burst out, making them both turn toward her. Her face was now an alarming shade of puke green. "Kyla was a Winslow cheerleader, right?"

Sydney nodded. "Yeah, I think so. Why?"

"Winslow Lions." Emerson's voice cracked. "The cheerleaders. That's why the nickname."

"Could be," Tenley agreed. She cocked her head, studying Emerson. Her face was scrunched up, and she was squeezing her legs so tightly her knuckles had turned white. "What is it, Em?"

Emerson fidgeted, knocking against the box of hair again. "The guy I was seeing... You know, the one in that video? He—he used to call me that."

"*What?*" Tenley blanched. "Well, who was it, Em?" She scooted closer to Emerson, until she was practically sitting on top of her. Still, Emerson avoided eye contact. "I know you're trying to protect your privacy, but this could be what we've been waiting for—a clue that actually *leads* us somewhere!"

"I..." Emerson looked frantically between Tenley and Sydney. "I don't... I can't..."

"My dad." Sydney said it flatly, not a drop of emotion.

"Excuse me?" Tenley cried at the same time Emerson yelped, "You *know?*"

Sydney leaned back against the wall. "I've known for a while now," she said quietly. "But it doesn't make my dad a stalker, Emerson. Or someone after his own *daughter*."

Tenley's gaze flipped from Sydney to Emerson and back again. One looked grimmer than the next. "You're probably right, Sydney," she said quickly. "Besides, we really think the darer is the same woman who kidnapped Caitlin." She glanced at Emerson for backup, but Emerson was looking down, tugging at a loose strand on her jeans.

"There's something else I haven't told you," Emerson said quietly. "Last week, the darer made me sneak into Matt's apartment. I found something under his bed. Kind of a trophy box. With my stuff in it, and other girls', too. Other Winslow girls." She closed her eyes, looking sick. "I'm sorry, Sydney," she whispered.

Sydney's dad had a *Winslow trophy box*? Tenley gnawed on

117

her lower lip, her thoughts launching into overdrive. "Where's the box now?"

"The darer made me take it," Emerson muttered. "It's under my bed."

Tenley bit so hard on her lip that she drew blood. "So you're saying the darer had you remove proof from Matt's apartment that would tie him to any girls from Winslow?"

Emerson nodded miserably.

"Then the darer outed you in that video, but covered up Matt's face. Protecting Matt."

Emerson nodded again. Tenley kept her gaze on her, unable to look at Sydney. "Let's say Kyla did hook up with Matt. She ended up stalked and dead. Then Emerson hooked up with him, and now her best friend is dead and she's being stalked—"

"Enough!" Sydney jumped up, bumping her head against the tree house's ceiling. "I'm not going to sit here and listen to this. You might have pissed off the darer by hooking up with a guy twice your age, Emerson, but that does not make this tormentor my *dad*. We don't even know for sure that Kyla dated him! Anyone could have called her Lion." She climbed over Emerson's legs, pushing angrily toward the exit. "All you're doing is spinning conspiracy theories. One minute it's the kidnapper, the next it's my dad. Next it will probably be me!" She clambered onto the stairs. "You guys play Nancy Drew all you want. I'm out of here. I've got an *actual* murderer to find."

Tenley shifted restlessly as Sydney's footsteps pounded down the stairs. She'd been so sure that the darer was the woman

Caitlin had mentioned in her diary. Could she really have been so off? She felt queasy as she turned back to Emerson. "What do you think, Em?"

Emerson closed her eyes. When she spoke, her voice was barely a whisper. "I think you're right. We can't discount it."

CHAPTER TWELVE
Thursday, 3:00 PM

EMERSON COULD SEE THEM. THEY WERE STANDING IN a clump at the edge of the football field: Marta, Jessie, Hunter, Sean, Nate, and Tyler. She would be there, too, if she were still one of them. But she wasn't. She was watching from the outskirts.

She tugged nervously at the peacoat she was wearing over her cheerleading uniform. All afternoon, she hadn't been able to stop thinking about this new Matt twist. Was it really possible he was behind everything? Just considering it made Emerson feel as if something was curdling inside her. He was Sydney's *dad*. She kept trying to imagine her own dad tormenting and hurting her. It was unfathomable. But Sydney's dad wasn't Emerson's dad. He had a trophy box of high school conquests. One of them being her.

A shudder ran through her. She'd trusted Matt once. She'd *slept* with him once. The idea that she could have misjudged him so completely terrified her. She and Tenley planned to sit down with Matt's stalker box later and take another shot at the darer's identity. But first, she had to get through practice.

Out on the field, she could hear Marta's laugh. Emerson took a calming breath, then strode across the field. Her plan was to walk right up to the group and pretend nothing was wrong. *Fake it.* That was how she'd become friends with them in the first place, when she moved to Echo Bay in ninth grade. She'd acted as if she belonged, and they'd believed she belonged.

Emerson dodged two runners who were circling the track. She could hear Nate talking by the goalpost. "I say we go all retro and dress up like the movie *Dazed and Confused.*"

"I want to do *Varsity Blues* if we're doing retro," Marta whined.

"As long as Jessie wears the whipped-cream bikini, I'm in." Tyler slung his arm around Jessie's shoulders with a grin.

Emerson's hands were trembling as she neared the group. She clasped them together and forced a smile onto her face. "Talking Halloween?" she asked brightly.

Everyone fell silent. Jessie wrinkled her nose as if she smelled something sour. Nate met her eyes, then looked away. Emerson dug her nails into her palm, willing away the tears that were threatening to surface. "Yeah," Marta said, finally. She dug the toes of her ballet flats into the grass, avoiding Emerson's gaze. "Trying to decide what to dress up as."

Common sense was screaming at Emerson to bolt, but she refused to admit defeat. "I like the *Varsity Blues* theme," she offered. She smiled in Marta's direction, but Marta kept her attention solidly on her shoes.

"You would like a whipped-cream bikini," Jessie snorted.

Emerson recoiled. She waited for someone to defend her, but no one said a word.

"Yo, Em!"

The shout made Emerson turn around. Trevor Mills, Winslow's linebacker, was jogging down the track. "Got something for you." He tossed a balled-up sheet of notebook paper at Emerson as he ran past.

A note.

Nerves shot through Emerson. She struggled to keep her hands steady as she opened the paper.

A message was written in black marker. No typewriter letters in sight. But Emerson barely had time to relax. Because the large scribbled words that stared up at her were as cruel as anything the darer would write. *Like guys with experience? Meet me at Sunset Point tonight, 8 pm, for a good time.*

Emerson took a step backward, right into the path of a passing runner. Their shoulders collided, and the impact knocked the note out of her hand. It fluttered down, landing faceup on the turf, its message visible to all.

Marta's jaw dropped. Nate shook his head. Emerson stood paralyzed as everyone stared mutely at Trevor's words. Then Jessie let out a giggle. "You think you'll go meet him, Em?" she asked mildly.

"I—" Emerson looked around the group, but no one would meet her eyes. "Of course I'm not going to meet him," she spat out. She took a step toward Jessie, and suddenly it wasn't just Jessie she was angry at, or Trevor, or even the darer. It was herself. She was sick of her own self-pity. She was sick of running in the opposite direction every time Jessie walked down the hall. When she moved to Echo Bay in ninth grade, she'd meticulously cultivated a new version of Em Cunningham. This Em would be a girl who commanded respect, a girl who didn't shrink into corners, but stood up tall. The meek, silent girl she'd lapsed into this week barely resembled her at all.

"And you know what, how dare you ask me that, Jessie? How dare you *talk* to me like that?" Emerson's eyes swept through the group again. Finally, they were looking at her. It fueled her on. "I'm done with everyone treating me like this." Her voice grew louder with each word. "Yes, I did something I shouldn't have, and I'm sorry if that upset or hurt any of you." Her gaze lingered on Marta. "But how many times have you all made mistakes in the past? Did I ever judge you for them? Did I ever turn my back on you? No. Because that's not what friends do."

She picked up Trevor's note. "Do you know what Caitlin would do if she were still here?" She tore the note into a dozen pieces. "*That's* what she'd do. And if this was any of you, that's what I'd do. A friend isn't just some accessory to flaunt while she's trendy." She narrowed her eyes in Jessie's direction. "Friends are the people you choose to love. And, yes, they might make mistakes sometimes, or upset you, or embarrass you, but always, they stand up for you."

Out of the corner of her eyes, she saw Coach walking onto the field, whistle in hand. "The next time any of you want a real friend, you know where to find me." Emerson walked away without waiting for a response. It didn't matter how they reacted; she'd had to say it. She refused to be silent any longer.

Across the field, Coach blew her whistle, the sound piercing the air. Emerson jogged toward her all alone.

— — — — — —

Heading home, THANK GOD, Emerson texted Tenley as she got into her car after practice. *My house for box recon?*

Tenley's response came quickly. *Meet u there.*

Emerson couldn't help but think about Caitlin as she drove home. Cait had always been different from the others. She was the kind of friend who stayed up all night with you after a breakup even though she had a math test the next day. The kind of friend who skipped a party to bring you magazines and rom coms when you had the flu. In eighteen years, Emerson had had only one friend like that. Well, one friend and one boyfriend.

She glanced over at her phone as she pulled into her driveway. She ached to call Josh and talk to him, tell him what she'd said to Jessie and the others. But she couldn't. Josh was safer without her. She refused to drag him back into this, no matter how much she missed him.

Tenley was waiting for her on the front porch. They were quiet as they took the stairs to Emerson's bedroom. Matt's trophy box was right where she'd left it. Emerson lifted it onto her bed, and they both climbed up after it. "We don't mention this to Sydney until we have to," Tenley said. Emerson nodded her agreement.

Tenley was the first to reach in. She pulled out a silk C-cup bra, holding it between her fingers. "God, this is sick," she said. "He's like some kind of collector."

"I couldn't bring myself to look through the whole box," Emerson admitted. "But from what I gathered, these are all from high school girls. His conquests," she added with a shudder. She pulled out a pom-pom she'd once left in Matt's truck. She flung it at her trash can, watching in satisfaction as it sank inside.

"Ew," Tenley muttered as she tossed a pair of neon underwear and a book of love poems onto the bed. Emerson pulled out a napkin from Pat-a-Pancake, a lacy thong, and several handwritten notes. Suddenly Tenley let out a low whistle. "Houston, we have a match."

Emerson whipped her head up. Tenley was clutching a piece of blue stationery in her hands. "'Matt,'" Tenley read off the stationery. "'Please don't call me anymore. I'm sorry.'" She tossed the note to Emerson. It was signed *Kyla*. "It sounds a lot like a breakup note," Tenley said.

"Which would make it true. Kyla and Matt were together once." Emerson buried her head in her hands. "Could it really have been him all along?"

"Did you ever see a typewriter at his place?" Tenley asked tightly. She began rooting through the box again, her movements jerky.

Emerson closed her eyes, picturing Matt's apartment. "No, there was a laptop, kind of an old one, but that was it." She kept her eyes closed, thinking it through. "Maybe he kept the typewriter hidden—"

"Holy. Shit."

At the sound of Tenley's voice, Emerson's eyes flew open. Tenley was holding up a skirt. It was red and pleated and high-waisted in

126

an out-of-style kind of way. Emerson's jaw dropped. She'd noticed the red swatch of fabric folded at the bottom of the box, but she'd never dug it out. Now that it was in full view, though, there was no doubt what it was. A Winslow cheerleading skirt, from at least two uniform changes ago. Tenley had pulled out its tag. A name was written on it in permanent marker. *Meryl.*

"You don't think...?" Emerson said. She knew of only one Meryl who had attended Winslow: Meryl Bauer, Calum's older sister and the first Lost Girl. Meryl had died out by the Phantom Rock ten years ago, when they were in second grade.

"I don't know." Tenley grabbed Emerson's laptop off her desk. Emerson scooted closer as Tenley clicked open Winslow's online yearbook.

"Try eleven years ago," Emerson said tightly.

A minute later, Tenley had the photo of Winslow Academy's cheerleading team from that year open on the screen. Emerson leaned in, scanning the names. There, second on the list, was the name she was looking for: *Meryl Bauer.*

Emerson pulled back shakily. Not only had Matt dated Emerson and Kyla, but he'd dated the very first Lost Girl, too.

"Whoa." Tenley had zoomed in on the team's photo until Meryl Bauer's blond-haired, blue-eyed beauty filled the whole screen. "Calum clearly got the short end of the Bauer family stick. Meryl was *hot.*"

Emerson glared in Tenley's direction. "Not helping."

"Sorry." Tenley returned her attention to the box. "Let's see if there's anything else in there."

Emerson felt itchy all over as she and Tenley went carefully through the rest of the box. If Matt was the darer, then what they'd had together had meant nothing. Less than nothing. It had just been a magic trick, a sleight of hand—his way of sucking Emerson into his game. She thought of their one night together at the Seagull Inn, how carefully Matt had pulled her onto the bed, as if she were a porcelain doll. At the time, she'd thought it was sweet, protective even. Now she wondered if it had all just been strategy.

There was nothing else useful in the box, and Emerson wasted no time in shoving it back under her bed. "It makes sense in a lot of ways, doesn't it?" Tenley asked slowly.

Tenley slid off the bed and began pacing the room. "We already knew the darer had to be someone older, someone who was involved with the Lost Girl charade, someone who's been sending notes for a long time...."

"Matt," Emerson whispered. She flopped back on her bed. "It really could be Matt."

Tenley was silent for a minute, the only sound the plodding of her shoes against the carpet. "What I don't get is the kidnapper. We *know* she's involved somehow. The darer sent Sydney her ring! And it was the darer who framed Jack Hudson. But if it's been Matt all along, where does that leave the kidnapper? It has to be someone connected to him—pretty closely."

"Tracey." Emerson bolted upright in bed. The thought had slipped out before she'd fully formulated it.

"Sydney's *mom*?" Tenley abruptly stopped pacing. "No." She gave Emerson a sharp look. "It's not possible. Matt's clearly a creep, but her mom...She and Sydney are really close."

128

"You're right." Emerson's voice cracked, and she coughed to clear it. "Of course you're right." Her cheeks were flaming at having suggested it. She'd seen Tracey with her own eyes. She looked kind and happy, like a woman who'd fallen back in love with her ex-husband.

Unless... it was all part of an act.

"Except, it *could* fit, couldn't it? Just in theory?" The words kept tumbling out; she couldn't seem to stop them. "Matt didn't just cheat; he went after *high school* girls. What if Tracey found out, and it broke her? What if she kidnapped Caitlin as some kind of sick revenge, and Matt was forced to cover her tracks?"

"The scorned woman gone mad..." Suddenly Tenley froze. "In fact... maybe Matt's not involved at all. Think about it. If Tracey found out what a scumbag her husband was, maybe she decided to go after the girls he'd dated as *revenge*. Then we would have been right all along: The kidnapper really is the darer."

"But why protect Matt from discovery, then? And why bring Caitlin into it?" Emerson's head was spinning. "I get targeting Matt's girlfriends, but how would kidnapping some random girl punish Matt?"

"It wouldn't." Tenley shook her head forcefully, as if to banish the thought from her mind. "It can't be Sydney's mom. Because even if we could find a reason to explain Caitlin's involvement, there would be no way Tracey would bring her own daughter into this."

Emerson looked down. Tenley might be wrong about that. The darer was twisted and hell-bent on revenge. If it was Tracey, Sydney would be the ultimate leverage—the final straw in Tracey's revenge. Take his lovers one by one, then take his daughter. But where *did* Caitlin fit in? And what about Tenley? "You're right." Emerson practically yelled the words, hating herself for even having the suspicion. "If it's anyone, it's Matt. We already know he's twisted."

"Maybe he was working with a different woman," Tenley offered. "Or a high school girl—one of his conquests. Maybe she's the one who kidnapped Cait. Or they could have done it together. Crazy does love crazy."

Emerson jumped up, adrenaline surging through her. If the darer had been Matt all along, if he'd not only tortured her and killed her best friend, but made her think he *cared* about her while doing it...

"Enough!" She practically shouted the word. "We've been victims for too long. If Matt really is the mastermind behind this, then we have our name. Which means we can finally, *finally* end this." She met Tenley's eyes. In them, she saw the same fury she felt burning in her own. "It's time we stop being the puppets and start pulling the strings."

CHAPTER THIRTEEN
Friday, 4:00 PM

EVERYONE WAS SMILING. THAT WAS THE FIRST THING
Sydney noticed when she stepped into the cavernous, brick-walled
room housing RISD's Prospective Students Fair. Everywhere she
looked, from the RISD representatives fawning over pamphlets
to the eager students rushing from booth to booth, everyone was
wearing wide, toothy *like-me!* smiles. A mother-daughter pair
pushed past her, bickering over dining-plan options. Nearby,
a dad cooed over a RISD photo book with his son. Sydney felt a
pang of longing. Her own mom was stuck at work. And it wasn't
as if she could ask her dad to go, even if she'd wanted to. Not
when he was suddenly at the top of Tenley and Emerson's Most
Wanted list.

She stopped at the first booth and picked up a pamphlet
about RISD's class offerings. Her gaze went immediately to the

photography ones. She couldn't believe how close she'd come to losing this chance.

No! There would be no thinking about that here. RISD was supposed to be her escape.

But as she moved from booth to booth, admiring class syllabi and peppering professors with her most intelligent questions, those same thoughts kept creeping back in. Tenley and Emerson really believed her dad could be responsible for everything. It wasn't just the possibility that scared her, it was *why* they thought it. She knew her dad had cheated on her mom; it was the reason they'd divorced. She also knew he'd been seeing Emerson lately. But to find out there had been more... The worst was how young they'd all been. *Her* age—long before she was her age.

She thought about what Emerson had said about there being a trophy box. How could her mom not know? Had she turned a blind eye? Or had he just been that good at hiding it? Sydney stared unseeingly at a video screen flashing facts about RISD's top professors. Even if her dad was that sneaky, even if he'd kept everyone in the dark all this time... that still didn't make him their stalker.

Right?

She moved on to a booth featuring RISD student projects. She had to stop thinking like this. Her dad was a scumbag, yes. A high school girl addict, apparently. A class-A creep, definitely. But a murderer? A torturer? *Her* torturer? Of course not.

She picked up an amazing photograph of the beach after a storm: trash piled so high it looked like a sculpture. LUCY CANDOR, SOPHOMORE, the label on the bottom read. If Sydney played her cards right, soon it would be her photographs at this table. And then her dad and the darer would be nothing more than blips in her past. She dropped the photo. It was time to do what she'd come to do.

An hour later Sydney had spoken to four professors, including the head photography professor. It was the most schmoozing she'd ever done in her life. But it was worth it, because she'd shown the head of the photography program a copy of her portfolio, and he'd called her photographs "quite unique."

Now, Sydney kept hearing that word in her head. *Unique unique unique unique.* She pulled out her phone and dialed her mom's cell to leave her a message. The voice mail picked up after just one ring. "Mom," she said breathlessly. "Guess what. The head of the photography program just called my photos unique!"

"Sydney?"

At the sound of her name, Sydney ended the call and spun around. Standing before her with a RISD information packet tucked under his arm was Joey Bakersfield. Except it wasn't the Joey she remembered.

This Joey was no longer hidden behind chin-length hair and a huge hoodie sweatshirt that drowned him in fabric. Instead, he had a short, buzzed haircut that showed off his chocolate-brown eyes and sharp jawline. He wore a school uniform of khakis and a well-fitted blazer that called attention to his surprisingly broad shoulders. He looked taller, too, probably because he wasn't hunched over his ever-present notebook. In fact, that ratty green notebook was nowhere to be seen.

"Wow!" she managed to croak. "You look different! Good

different," she corrected hastily. Joey's lips curved up a little. She couldn't help but notice how nice they were without a mask of hair to hide them: heart-shaped and full. She let out a nervous cough. "What are you doing here?"

"Danford's college counselor suggested I come. He thinks RISD's drawing classes could be a good fit for me." Even his voice sounded different. It was still soft, but it was clearer now, so different from the mumble he'd adopted at Winslow. "I'm sorry I haven't e-mailed you back yet. I've been meaning to, but we've had exams at school and..." He trailed off as, across the room, a petite, doe-eyed girl waved to him. She had a pixie haircut and milky skin. The way she glided across the room toward them screamed ballerina. "You coming to the party tonight, Joe?" ballerina-girl asked.

Joe? Party? Sydney blinked in surprise as she watched the girl give Joey a friendly smile. Apparently more than just Joey's appearance had changed. "Fencer's calling it the Pre-Octo Bash. 'Octo drinks for everyone,'" she quoted, rolling her eyes.

"Uh...as in eight drinks?" Joey asked.

"I guess. I didn't have the heart to tell him it didn't make sense." She turned to Sydney, flashing her the same friendly smile. "I'm Brie," she offered.

"Sorry," Joey said hastily. He looked flustered for a second, the old Joey creeping back in. He quickly cleared his throat, composing himself. "This is Sydney. She goes to Winslow. Brie and I take Animation together at Danford."

"Hey," Sydney said. She dropped her eyes. She'd never been good at meeting new people, new girls in particular. But Brie didn't seem to notice.

"You should come to the party with us, Sydney." She winked at her. "See how much better Danford does it than Winslow."

"Oh, um, thanks," Sydney said shyly, "but I won't be in Boston tonight. I'm catching a train back to Echo Bay after this."

"Well, considering the party starts in"—Brie glanced at her watch—"four minutes, that shouldn't be a problem. Fencer's house isn't far from the train station." She ran a hand through her short hair. "You can have your Octo drinks and catch a later train. Fencer always has a theme for his parties," Brie added. "It should be an Octo-wonderland."

"With octuplets?" Sydney couldn't resist asking.

"And octopi," Brie agreed solemnly.

"And octogenarians," Sydney added. "What's a party without eighty-year-olds?" Brie laughed, and Sydney felt a tiny thrill. She couldn't believe how relaxed she felt. At Winslow, she had a set place. But here, she could be whomever she felt like. She wondered if that was all it had taken for Joey to become Joe.

"Don't forget doctors," Joey put in, his new, steady voice still taking her by surprise. Sydney gave him a confused look. Next to her, Brie did the same. "You know, *doctors*," Joey said, his face flushing a little.

Sydney groaned. "Remind me to never play Scrabble against you."

"Or Pictionary," Brie chimed in. "This boy can *draw*." She smiled over at Sydney. "So you coming? I promise it will be Scrabble-free."

Sydney glanced at Joey. His forehead was wrinkled as if in concentration. "You should come," he said suddenly. "I'll walk you to the station after." He coughed, his face flushing again. "That way,

I can answer your e-mail in person." Sydney hesitated. Back home, all that waited for her was a Matt Morgan manhunt. "All right," she said with a grin. "Octo-party it is."

- - - - - -

"Whoa," Sydney said as the elevator spit her and Joey out on the top floor of Danford's tallest building. Up ahead, wide glass doors led to a huge roof deck. A glass railing provided a flawless view of Danford's manicured campus below. Several tall heat lamps were scattered about, casting a warm glow over the whole place. "Are all of Danford's parties like this?"

"All of Fencer's are." Joey grabbed two beers off the glass bar and handed one to Sydney. She took it gratefully, downing a big sip. Echo Bay Sydney wasn't a huge drinker, but if Joey could become *Joe*, surely she could enjoy a beer. She smiled over at him. Back at the RISD fair, when Brie said she had to run a few errands before the party, Sydney had been nervous to be left alone with Joey. But as they'd trekked through the city back to Danford, there hadn't been a single lull in their conversation. In fact, Sydney couldn't remember the last time she'd had so much in common with someone. Not only was Joey applying to all the same art schools as she was, he was also applying for their scholarships and financial aid. "So, basically, you're my competition," Sydney had mused.

Joey had wiggled his eyebrows in response. "Better watch out, photo girl," he'd said. "Cartoon boy is swooping in."

"Joe!" A huge guy came over and pounded Joey on the arm. He

was wearing what once was probably a Danford blazer, but was now plastered in so many bumper stickers it looked more like a billboard. "About time you got here."

"Hey, Fencer." Joey nodded in Sydney's direction. "This is Sydney. She went to my old school. Fencer and I are on the swim team together," he informed Sydney.

Swim team? Sydney raised her eyebrows. This new Joey was full of surprises.

"*Hola*, blue eyes." Fencer threw his arm around Sydney's shoulders. "We're about to play Kings. You in?"

Sydney took another swig of her drink. She could feel the beer sloshing its way through her, slowing her pulse and unclenching her muscles.

Joey—*Joe*—gave her a questioning look. She shrugged. "All right," he said. "Looks like we're in."

Several rounds of Kings later, the rooftop felt more like a carousel, the glass railing spinning around Sydney. "My turn!" Brie called out. She made a big show of drawing a card. "Yes!" she squealed, waving it through the air. "I get to make a rule." She stroked an imaginary beard as she looked slowly around the group. Sydney swigged more beer, trying to ignore the incessant spinning. "Okay," Brie said, finally. "The next person to draw a four...has to kiss someone. And I'm talking a real kiss," she clarified. "No on-the-cheek bullshit."

Sydney finished off her beer as the game continued around the circle. The air felt thicker than usual, wrapping her in fog.

"Your turn." Brie nudged her in the side. Sydney nodded, trying to shake off the fog.

She pawed heavily at the deck, extracting a card. "Four of hearts," she read.

"We've got one!" Brie howled. She thrust her beer into the air. "Go ahead." She winked at Sydney. "Kiss away."

"Kiss! Kiss! Kiss!" Fencer chanted. Next to him, a slim guy who'd tied the sleeves of his blazer around his head leaned forward, puckering up. Sydney looked helplessly at Joey.

"Sorry," he mouthed.

"Better choose someone before you're an octogenarian, Sydney," Brie said, giggling.

"Kiss! Kiss! Kiss!" Fencer yelled.

The fog wrapped around Sydney, making the world feel underwater. Her eyes landed on Joey's lips. *Nice*, she thought again. And then suddenly she was there, pressing her lips against his. They were as full as they looked, and warm, and he didn't pull away, just kissed her back, his hand wrapping around her arm. And even through the haze she could feel it: a warmth, blazing from her stomach all the way to her toes. A minute passed, or ten, she couldn't tell. She pulled him closer, the kiss deepening, the warmth spreading. . . .

"Go, Joe!" someone screamed.

Just like that, reality set back in. She pulled back, the roof spinning faster than ever. She could feel eyes boring into her from every side. "Joe's the man!" someone else hooted.

"I—I have to go," she mumbled. She rose unsteadily to her feet. The thoughts she'd kept at bay all day suddenly lifted to life: big, sweeping gales of thoughts, her very own Octo-storm. *The darer. Her dad. Kyla.*

She fought her way across the crowded rooftop. What had

she been thinking, abandoning her life like this? Joey might have shed his past and started over, but she had almost a full year left at Winslow. Almost a full year left with the darer if this didn't stop soon. She stumbled onto the elevator and pulled out her nearly dead phone. She had one new text from Tenley, whom she hadn't spoken to since the tree house. *We need to talk, Syd. U can't avoid me forever!*

"Wait!" Joey slipped into the elevator right before the door closed. "What just happened? Are you okay?"

The elevator jolted as it descended, making Sydney stumble. Joey reached out to steady her. "Come on. Let's sit down." He put his hand on the small of her back and guided her out of the elevator, toward a bench outside. Sydney sank gratefully onto it. It was quiet in front of the ivy-covered building, the noise of the party as distant as rain clouds. Now that she was away from the crowd, the spinning in her head slowed.

"What's going on?" Joey asked.

Sydney clasped and unclasped her hands. "Things have just been tough at home lately." She sneaked a peek at him out of the corner of her eyes. He was watching her steadily. "You're lucky you got out when you did."

"It's the Echo Bay Kool-Aid, isn't it?" he asked. Sydney sneaked another peek. He was leaning forward, his elbows propped up on his knees. "I swear, it's like no one has their own mind there. Zombie town."

"The zombies are after my dad now." Sydney hadn't meant to say it, but now the words hung suspended between them, impossible to ignore.

She waited for Joey to jump down her throat with questions,

but he said nothing, just sat there watching her. She thought of the reason he was at Danford in the first place. Before her dad, before all of this, it had been him.

"People are accusing him of something horrible," she continued. She chose her words carefully, knowing just how close to home they must hit. "And, believe me, he *has* done horrible stuff. But I don't know. My gut is telling me that this thing...it isn't him." Sydney slumped down with a sigh. "Maybe my gut's the problem. I think it might have multiple personalities."

"No way," Joey said immediately. "Your gut is all you have, Sydney." He turned toward her, his expression fierce. "You've got to trust your instincts. When you don't...that's when you get lost."

Sydney closed her eyes. When they'd accused Joey of being the darer, had she really believed it could be him? Or had she just followed along blindly like everyone else? She wanted to believe that she was different, but the heat in her cheeks told her otherwise. She had never actually stopped and wondered if what they were doing felt right.

She opened her eyes. Joey was still watching her, a concerned expression on his face. "You're right," she said slowly. "Thanks."

Her dad was a million and one things, but he wasn't the darer. She felt it deep down in her gut, in that place that went beyond thinking, beyond logic.

Now she just had to prove it.

CHAPTER FOURTEEN
Saturday, 9:25 PM

FROM THE NEDDLES ISLAND BRIDGE, CALUM'S HOUSE looked as if it belonged in a painting. The windows glimmered with light, casting a deep glow across the sloping, leaf-scattered yard. On every side, the ocean rose to meet the grass, waves black and thrashing: a water-fence that grew and shrank, grew and shrank. The house itself brimmed with revelers. From a distance, they looked like bright splotches, dotting the deck and moving between windows.

Tenley felt a dart of satisfaction as she drove through the iron gates, which had been propped open for the night. For two days now, she and Emerson had been secretly following Matt Morgan around, on the hunt for any proof of foul play. But Matt's life had turned out to be annoyingly boring. No rendezvous or illicit meet-ups. Just firehouse and home, plus a few stops at a therapist's office.

There were still things that didn't quite fit, too. How did Matt connect to the kidnapper, for one? And where did Caitlin and Tenley, not to mention Sydney, work into Matt's motives? And, to top it all off, where was all the money coming from? Their darer had deep pockets—deep enough to rig their cars with surveillance and pay off Gerry Hackensack, the previous fire chief. Matt Morgan was the local fire chief; it was a noble job, but not a high-paying one. So who was funding him?

They couldn't actually *do* anything until they had more information. Emerson kept hoping Delancey's key would bring them answers. But the purple door—if that's even what it opened—still eluded them.

She might have failed in darer-land, but at least she'd succeeded here. The party was packed.

Calum's voice greeted her as she stepped inside the house's marble-floored entryway. "Rule number three," he boomed. "No going in the basement!" His voice was so loud that it echoed off the windowed walls and rattled the crystal chandeliers that dangled in every room. Tenley looked around, searching for its owner. But Calum was nowhere to be found. Instead, her eyes landed on a large intercom jutting out from the wall. A green light was flashing at the top of it.

"Obey those three rules," the voice continued, exploding out of the intercom's speaker, "and you can partake in all the debauchery you please!"

"You've got to be kidding," Tenley growled. She pushed her way through throngs of people, hunting for Calum's white-blond head. She finally spotted him in the kitchen, talking to Abby Wilkins.

Tenley strode over and grabbed his arm. "Can I borrow Calum for a second, Abby? We have some party logistics to discuss."

Holding tightly to Calum's arm, she yanked him into the pantry off the kitchen. The shelves were packed with canned food, enough to feed an army. For a second it distracted her. "Is there an apocalypse coming that I should know about?"

"Octo-storm," Calum replied solemnly. "Though we're always stocked at the Bauer household. My dad says that preparation is akin to—"

"Forget I asked." Tenley put her hands on her hips, glowering up at Calum. "*Rules*? Over an intercom? That was not in my party-planning guide, Calum!"

"I took artistic liberty," Calum replied. "This house is my dad's baby. It's important that no one swing on the chandeliers—they're all antiques—or go in the basement, where my dad has an office, or use the bedrooms for, well, you know, *romantic* relations. The intercom was the most efficient way to spread the word."

Tenley swallowed back a groan. "Here. I have something for you." She pulled a small, gift-wrapped box out of her purse and handed it to Calum. "Happy birthday. It's a thumb drive," she added before he could bother to unwrap it. "You know, for all your computer stuff."

Calum's jaw came unhinged as he stared at the box. "I... uh...wow."

"You don't have to look so surprised," Tenley huffed. She started back to the kitchen, and Calum followed. She scanned hopefully for Tim, but she didn't see him anywhere.

"Right," Calum said quickly. "I just..." He shook his head,

sticking the box in his pocket. "Never mind. Thank you, Tenley," he said, his voice turning formal.

"You're welcome." Tenley's cheeks warmed. "Now time to forget the rules, Calum, and have what we common folk like to call *fun*." She grabbed a beer off the counter and passed it to him.

Calum glanced past her as he took it. She turned around to find Sydney making her way through the crowd, looking as if she'd rather be mucking a horse stall than attending this party. Tenley bounced nervously on the balls of her feet. Sydney had been avoiding Tenley and Emerson ever since their fight in the tree house on Thursday. But finally, Tenley and Emerson had agreed: Sydney *had* to know what they'd found in her dad's trophy box, whether she wanted to hear it or not. So a few hours earlier, Tenley had sent Sydney a text, detailing their finds. She hadn't heard back.

Tenley had assumed she wouldn't be seeing Sydney tonight, considering her aversion to all things Winslow. Not even Emerson was coming to the party, claiming she needed a break from the whole human species. But here Sydney was. By the way Calum was gazing at her, Tenley had to assume he'd talked her into coming.

Tenley shifted nervously as Sydney made her way toward them. For the first time, she noticed that there was a guy with her. He had buzzed hair and chiseled features, and he wore a Red Sox T-shirt that showed off defined arms. Tenley rocked backward in surprise when she recognized him. "What's Joey Bakersfield doing here?"

"I don't know." Calum frowned, his eyebrows knitting together. *He's nervous to see Sydney*, Tenley realized.

"The big one-eight," Sydney said when she reached the kitchen. "Feeling one year wiser yet?"

"Still waiting on that." Calum gave Sydney a small smile. "I'm glad you came."

"Look who's in town," Sydney said, gesturing at Joey. She kept her attention firmly on Calum as she spoke.

"Good to see you, Joey." Calum extended his hand for the most awkward handshake Tenley had ever witnessed. "You're at Danford now, right?"

Joey nodded. "Yup." An uncomfortable silence fell over the group. It was made even more pronounced by the laughter and voices walling them in.

"Calum went to Danford for a while!" Tenley jumped in. She smiled in Sydney's direction, but Sydney ignored her. "Have you heard of any crazy senior pranks yet, Joey?" Tenley persisted, remembering Calum's story.

Joey scrunched up his forehead. "Senior pranks?"

"Yeah, there were wild ones when you were there, right, Calum?" Tenley nudged him in the side with a pointed look. "You helped some seniors make strawberry jelly squirt out of showerheads or something?"

"Yeah, the pranks can get pretty intense." Calum sneaked a peek at Sydney before focusing back on Joey. "But you're new. I'm sure you'll hear all about them once you acclimate."

"You'll have to tell us what the next one is," Tenley continued.

Crash!

The sound of breaking glass made them all jump. Tenley turned around to find a gorgeous stained glass lamp lying in a million shattered pieces on the floor. "Sorry!" Lizzy Helman squealed, swaying unsteadily on her feet.

Calum sighed. "I better..."

"We'll help," Sydney supplied quickly. By the way she grabbed Joey's arm, it was clear the *we* did not include Tenley.

Tenley turned in a slow circle. All around her people were laughing and drinking. Nearby, Missy Henderson and Hannah Welsh were cuddled in the corner of a couch, heads bent together. If Tenley squinted, it could be her and Caitlin there instead, so close it was hard to tell where one ended and the other began. She looked away, her chest squeezing.

She moved farther into the house. She'd hoped this party would lure out the darer, so what better time to start the hunt than now? No one was talking to her anyway. But when she neared the dining room, she faltered. Tim was in there, laughing with his friends. He looked up, his eyes meeting hers. He gave her the tiniest of smiles, and suddenly hope wafted through Tenley, silencing all thoughts of the darer. Tim had changed his mind. He was going to come over. He—

He turned away.

Tenley sank onto a white leather barstool in the kitchen, tears pricking at her eyes. She knew she should be out there, searching for the darer, but suddenly she couldn't muster the energy. As much as she despised their stalker, what if he or she had been right all along? What if her whole life was nothing more than a game?

For years she'd held her cards close to her chest. She'd waited her turn and planned out her strategy, and then gone in for the win. But she didn't want to play anymore. She just wanted Tim. Class-cutting, cold-weather-surfing, hemp-wearing, hairbrush-lacking Tim.

She slid off the stool, feeling jittery all over. The darer could wait. This couldn't.

She squared her shoulders as she stalked to the dining room, but her insides liquefied with every step. She stopped next to the table and cleared her throat. All three boys turned to look at her, but it was Tim's gaze she felt, warming her skin. "Can we talk for a minute?" she asked him.

The pause that followed felt like an eternity. In the ensuing silence, Tenley could feel her pulse throbbing in her neck. "You guys mind?" Tim asked his friends gruffly. He was wearing a dark blue sweater that matched his eyes, and Tenley was filled with the urge to press herself against it.

"Go." Sam waved him on. "We need more beer anyway."

Tenley's heart beat in time with her footsteps as she and Tim wound through the crowd, looking for a place to talk. "This way," Tenley suggested. A long hallway led away from the party, toward the back of the house. An Oriental rug carpeted the floor, and gilded framed paintings lined the walls. The hallway emerged into an empty entertainment room. Tenley went over to the couch, and Tim followed. His leg brushed against hers as they sat down, sending a tingle up her spine.

"I have something I want to say," she told him. "And I don't want you to interrupt until I'm finished. Understood?"

Tim nodded. His wavy blond hair was flattened against his head, as if he'd recently taken off a hat. He'd replaced his broken hemp necklace with a new one, and it looked too perfect on him, as if it needed to be dunked in the ocean several dozen times. He reached up now to fiddle with it, waiting for her to speak.

She swallowed hard. No more games.

"What I did to Jessie…do you know I didn't even regret it at first? I've done things like that my whole life, Tim. Selfish, scheming things. I was so used to it that I didn't *feel* it, you know? What it did to other people." She fidgeted with the zipper on her red moto jacket. She hadn't planned this speech, but the words kept coming, more honest than anything she'd said in a long time. What she'd done to Jessie—and Calum and Tricia and Joey and so many others—she couldn't blame that on a dare. She'd made the choices herself.

"Caitlin was the only one who knew how to save me from myself," she continued. "She was my conscience, I guess. But she's gone now and I don't want to be this person anymore." Her voice broke, but she kept going. "I'm different with you, Tim. Better." She put her hand on his knee, and he didn't pull away. His eyes met hers, and they reminded her a little of Caitlin, how kind they were. "I've played games for long enough. I just—I can't do it anymore." She paused. "I want to be with you, Tim. I want to make this work."

He was so close that she could feel his breath on her face: tiny gusts of warm air. He smelled like sunscreen and ocean. "You done?" His voice was low and husky. It made something flare to life in her chest. She couldn't wait any longer.

She answered by kissing him. For one long, horrible second, he resisted. Then his hand was in her hair and he was kissing her back.

His lips brushed her neck as he lowered her back on the couch, and she could feel herself getting lost in his touch. The party and even her thoughts receded, until there was only Tim. The way he touched her hair and slid his mouth down her collarbone. The weight of him on top of her, warm and solid. His breath in her ear and her hands under his sweater, skimming the taut skin beneath.

She wanted to stay there forever, tucked safely together, where nothing else could touch her. "You keep surprising me, Tenley," Tim whispered, and she kissed him harder, until there was no couch, no air, no party. Just them.

The lights in the room shut off.

Tim pulled back. "What the hell?" he murmured.

It was pitch-black. Tenley couldn't see a thing. Blood rushed to her head, a deafening sound. It all returned at once: Someone out there wanted her dead.

Tim was too heavy. She pushed him away and scrambled off the couch, bumping unsteadily into a table. "Tenley?" She could see Tim's outline in the darkness, rising from the couch. "What's wrong?"

Before Tenley could reply, the lights switched back on.

"Is someone back here?" Calum emerged in the doorway. "Oh! Sorry." Calum's eyes widened as they flitted from Tenley to Tim. Tenley let out a shaky breath. It was just Calum.

No sooner had the thought crossed her mind than a sound rose from her purse. A sharp, shrill beep.

Tenley barely registered reaching for her phone. But suddenly it was in her hands, a new text open on its screen.

Stealing your dead BFF's boy? Tsk, tsk, Ten. Let your punishment begin.

Tenley's heart was pounding as she quickly deleted the text. She tried to focus on what Calum was saying. "...didn't mean to scare you. I didn't realize a party would turn the back of my house into make-out central. I found a couple in the sunroom, too, and another one in the basement, even though I *expressly* forbade it."

"I…" She meant to apologize, but her head was spinning too fast to formulate words. The darer must have seen her go off with Tim. Which meant that whoever it was, was either at the party or spying on it.

"You okay, Ten?" Tim came up behind her and wrapped his arms around her waist.

This was what she'd wanted: to lure her tormentor out of hiding. But now here she was, without Emerson to back her, without Sydney to even *acknowledge* her, and she suddenly felt very, very alone. Her legs quivered, and she pressed her weight against Tim.

"I'm not feeling great all of a sudden." She looked up. Tim's dark blue eyes were narrowed in concern.

"Maybe it's the beer," Calum offered. "It's making me feel a little nauseated as well."

"You do look pale," Tim told her. "Do you want to go home?"

Tenley glanced back down at her phone, which was still clutched tightly in her fist. She should go back out to the party. She should do whatever it took to find this darer.

Let your punishment begin.

"Yes," she heard herself whisper. "I want to go home."

- - - - - - -

The morning sun probed at Tenley through a crack in her curtains, streaking light across her eyelids. She buried her face in her pillow, but it wasn't the sun that kept her from falling back to sleep. It was the memory of last night's text. Even after she left the party, she couldn't escape the feeling of being watched. It followed her as Tim walked her to her car. It followed her on the drive and all the way to her bedroom and kept her tossing and turning through the night. She felt like a little kid again, terrified of the monster in her closet. Except this time, the monster was real.

She gave up on sleep and dragged herself out of bed with a groan. She switched on the TV as she got dressed. Maya Louis, Miss-Massachusetts-turned-North-Shore-weather-woman, was standing in front of a digital map wearing knee-high boots and a short, pleated skirt. "I hope you've all enjoyed this final bit of calm weather," she was saying. "Because it's time to start gearing up for Octo-storm. The full mass of the blizzard isn't anticipated until Wednesday, but in the meantime, expect high winds and light snowfall."

Tenley reached for her phone as images of last November's blizzard flashed across the screen. *Anything?* she texted Emerson. She'd called Emerson as soon as she got home last night to tell her about the text. Emerson, on the other hand, hadn't heard anything from the darer in days.

Emerson's response came quickly. *Radio silence.*

Tenley stuck her phone in her pocket and headed downstairs. The house was eerily quiet.

Sahara had the morning off, and her mom and Lanson had finally been cleared to visit Guinness—parents only. Tenley blasted music as she ate breakfast, trying to fill the void. But when the wind beat a sudden pattern against the roof, she jumped so high she nearly fell out of her seat. Maya the weather woman was right: Octo-storm was gearing up.

She grabbed her phone. *Want to meet up to strategize?* she texted Emerson.

Finishing up English paper, Emerson replied. *Call u after.*

She tried Tim next. *Sorry, Ten*, he texted back. *Waves too crazy to miss today.*

Nervous energy flooded through Tenley. She used to love being home alone, but suddenly every noise seemed like an invasion. Another blast of wind rattled the shutters, making her pulse race. That was it. She had to get out of there.

Tenley hurried to her car and started on a route at random. Emerson still hadn't found anything useful online about a purple door, but maybe the best way to find it was just to drive around town and look. It was worth a shot; right now that door—and Delancey's key—was their best bet at solving this mystery.

Forty-five minutes later Tenley had seen what had to be every type of door in existence—rounded, rectangular, wooden, painted, metal—but not one had been purple. She took a sharp left off Ocean Drive. Her phone had remained dormant since she got in her car, and she had no interest in returning to an empty house. At least out here, she was *doing* something.

A few streets later she was in Matt Morgan's neighborhood. If she couldn't hunt down the purple door, a Matt stakeout would have to do. She parked a few blocks away from his apartment, where he wouldn't spot her car. There was a small side street that wound to his home, and she started down it on foot. Two rows of beach shacks formed a barricade on either side of the road, trapping the icy wind between them. She clamped a hand over her knit cap to prevent it from flying away. In the summer, this alley would be overflowing with tourists taking a shortcut to the beach. But today it was empty, not a person in sight. It made the street seem strangely still, as if the whole town had drifted off to sleep.

The sound of footsteps rang out behind her. Her heart skipped a beat as she glanced over her shoulder, but no one was there. Just the wind playing tricks on her ears. Still, she picked up her pace.

She was halfway down the street when her phone beeped with a text. "About time, Em," she muttered. She paused, digging her phone out of her purse. But the name on the screen wasn't Emerson's.

Blocked.

Footsteps suddenly reached her ears again. She whirled around, but once more she saw no one. Her breath came out in short, cold bursts. She started walking again, faster, as she clicked open the darer's text.

Let your punishment begin.

Tenley's mind collapsed in fear. Her mouth opened, but before she could scream, something slammed into her head from behind. Pain exploded through her, making spots dance in her vision. She had time for only one thought. *Caught.*

Then everything went black.

CHAPTER FIFTEEN
Sunday, 11:33 Am

EMERSON'S COMPUTER BLURRED BEFORE HER EYES. This English essay was worth 30 percent of her grade, but every time she tried to muster up the brainpower to write a conclusion, other thoughts crept in. Like the fact that she'd missed last night's party, and Marta still hadn't called to ask why. Or the fact that her ex might be a murderous stalker. Or how all she wanted right now was to hear Josh's voice. And did she mention that her ex might be a murderous stalker?

"We're leaving, Emerson!" her mom called up from downstairs. Sunday was errands day in the Cunningham household. "You sure you can't come?"

"Still working!" she yelled back. She heard the low drone of voices, then the front door slammed shut. Her parents had spent all morning pressing her about the identity of the man in the video. It hadn't been easy to hold her ground, but she'd done it. Lying to her parents was hard enough, but it was their disappointment that cut right through her. No matter how many mistakes she'd made over the years, she'd always been able to look at her parents and see her purest self reflected in their eyes. But this morning, they'd looked at her as if she were a stranger.

Emerson dropped her forehead onto her desk. Between her parents, Matt, and her social life, her head was a minefield. And waiting for the darer wasn't helping matters. It had been three whole days since she'd heard anything, three whole days of bated breath and jumping unnecessarily every time her phone rang. Three whole days of silence—which meant it had to be coming soon. And whatever it was, after three days, it was going to be big.

When the doorbell rang at 12:03 PM, Emerson was almost expecting it. Time became elastic, stretching and bending as she walked to the door. Everything was magnified: her breath in her ears, her footsteps on the stairs. Her mind screamed for her to flee, but her body kept moving numbly forward. Three whole days, tapering down to a single moment.

She pulled the door open. There was no one outside.

She stepped onto the porch and scanned the periphery. The yard was still, and so was the street. The only movement came from a large gust of wind. Emerson blew out a breath. She should know by now: The darer was like a shadow, quick and twisting, able to disappear into nothingness.

A soft, flapping noise drew her attention to the corner of the porch. A sheet of paper had been taped to the railing. Her mouth went dry as she walked toward it.

Typewriter font graced the top of the paper.

Go to 566 Seaview Ave and light Kyla's
breakup letter on fire. Hurry, or mommy
and daddy see this.

A photo was taped underneath. It was dark and grainy, like a still taken off video surveillance. But it was clear enough. The image showed Emerson standing on an X-shaped pile of rose petals in the Bones, wearing nothing but her underwear. Her hair was mussed, and there was a frantic expression in her eyes. It made her look wild: an animal that couldn't be tamed.

If her parents were holding on to any last remnant of the little girl they remembered, this photo would crush it. Emerson fought the urge to scream. How did the darer always manage to go straight for her jugular? Anger coursed through her as she looked back at the note.

566 Seaview Ave

Matt's apartment.

She'd told Matt once how much her parents' opinions meant to her. He of all people would know what this would do to her. Her mind was suddenly a hazard zone, explosions popping one after another. It made sense that Matt would want her to destroy the breakup letter Kyla had written; it was the only solid evidence linking them together. But why make her get rid of it in *his* apartment?

Emerson leaned against the porch railing. *Of course.* It was simple, really. If the deed happened at Matt's apartment, he could be absolutely sure she followed through. And he could be the one to wipe away all signs of the crime.

It was the last bit of proof she needed. Matt was involved.

Still...there were pieces that didn't fit. How had Matt, who used a half-broken ten-year-old computer, set up and accessed hidden surveillance in the Bones? More and more, it seemed that Matt was working with someone else—a woman who was filthy rich and tech-savvy.

Emerson crumpled the note in her fist. Her parents couldn't see that photo. Once again, the darer had pulled her strings, and she had no choice but to obey.

She had Kyla's letter and a pack of matches in her car before she had time to lose her nerve. She dialed Tenley's number as she sped toward Matt's apartment. The answering machine picked up. "Call me, Ten," she said tersely. "I think I have proof that Matt's involved."

She tried Sydney next, but her voice mail picked up, too. "Syd, it's Emerson." Emerson took a sharp turn toward Matt's street, eliciting a series of angry honks. "Call me as soon as you get this, okay?"

She was already pulling onto Matt's street as she ended the call. She abandoned her car in the first parking spot she found and raced the rest of the way on foot. Fear and anticipation wormed through her in equal parts. In some ways, the waiting had almost been worse. Silence could scream louder than words. At least now, following a note, she stood a chance. The darer had to slip up only once, and the game would be theirs.

She was panting by the time she reached the beach bungalow where Matt rented the second floor. She'd brought her house key, left over from their time hooking up, but she didn't need it. The front door was already unlocked.

Upstairs, the apartment was empty. She looked at the ceiling, but it was bare. That didn't mean there wasn't a camera on her somewhere. She turned in a quick circle, taking a sweep of the apartment. It looked the same as always: neat, but not exactly clean, with a thin layer of dust on top of the TV and gathering in the corners. There was an odd, sharp smell to the place, too, and it made Emerson wonder how long it had been since the apartment had been scrubbed.

Hurry, or mommy and daddy see this.

Emerson started for the kitchen sink, but it was piled high with dishes. She jogged to the bathroom instead. She could light it there, in the sink, where she could douse the flames with water before the fire had a chance to spread. She flicked a match, watching the flame leap to life.

Immediately, she could tell something was wrong. The flame should have nibbled gently at the letter, eating its way slowly through Kyla's words. Instead, it blew up to ten times its size, consuming the page in a single bite. Within seconds the whole sink was on fire, heat pouring off the flames as they surged up and out and down, submerging the porcelain fixture in orange.

Emerson jumped away as a flame bit at her finger, leaving a red mark behind. Her legs bumped hard against the bathtub, and she grabbed onto the shower curtain to catch her balance. But instead of steadying her, her hands slipped, unable to catch a grip. She crashed onto the floor. Pain reverberated up her spine, but all she could focus on were her palms. They were wet, coated in a greasy sheen.

She scrambled back up and touched a finger to the mirror, then the wall. Everything was wet, layered in the same slimy grease. She inhaled deeply. *Of course.* That strange, sharp scent she'd noticed! The bathroom had been doused in gasoline.

She'd been set up.

The fire was spreading, sliding over the floor and along the walls, the air so hot it pricked at her skin. She leaped over a stray flame, throwing herself into the living room. She raced toward the front door. Behind her, the bathroom was a wall of orange, fingers of fire stretching toward the living room. Smoke swirled around her, thickening the air.

Her escape was close, only two more steps. She hurled herself forward, heat and smoke at her back. She could already smell freedom—air wispy and clean—when she heard it.

A scream.

She froze, one foot in the hallway, one still in the apartment.

The scream came again, faint but unmistakably female. She spun in a circle, hoping it was coming from downstairs, from out in the street—anywhere but here.

But all hope was squelched as she heard the scream once more. It was coming from behind her. It was inside the apartment.

Every inch of Emerson's body screamed for her to leave. But someone was *in* there. Someone who wasn't Matt. There wasn't time to call the firehouse; there wasn't time to call anyone. The flames were in the living room now, taking the couch and the walls, skittering across the floor. The air was patchy, swirling clouds of black and gray.

It was instinct that drove her inside, instinct that silenced the warnings. She raced across the living room just seconds before the rug went up in flames.

"Help!" The shout was accompanied by banging this time. It was coming from the bedroom. Emerson pressed her sleeve over her mouth, trying to block out the smoke as she fought her way toward the sound. Still, tendrils seeped in, and she was hacking by the time she reached the door. The handle was hot to the touch, so she used her other sleeve to twist it open. Inside the bedroom, the smoke was thinner. She dove inside, sucking down big swallows of air.

The banging grew louder. Emerson looked around frantically, searching for its source.

Her eyes landed on the closet door. She sprinted toward it. The door had been locked from the outside and she quickly unlocked it, yanking it open.

Out fell a rumpled Tenley. Her eyes were wide and disoriented, and a streak of dried blood ran down the side of her face. She careened forward, landing on her knees.

"What are you doing here?" Emerson cried, helping her to her feet.

"I—I don't know!" Tenley leaned heavily against Emerson. "I came to stake out Matt's apartment, but then I got a text and then—I don't know. I woke up in the closet."

A plume of smoke rushed up Emerson's nostrils, punctuating

Tenley's words. The room was rapidly filling with smoke, thick black waves of it. In the living room, flames popped and crackled, inching closer to the bedroom door.

"We have to get out of here," Emerson coughed. She shoved her sleeve against her mouth as she narrowly avoided a loose flame. "If we stay away from the rug, we can—"

A loud boom drowned out the rest of her sentence. The fire had reached Matt's grandfather clock, and as flames had clawed their way up the wood, the whole structure had tipped forward, landing in front of the bedroom door.

"No!" Emerson cried. They were blocked in, inside a box of fire and smoke. "The window!" She rushed toward it, Tenley at her side. On the other side of the window, something caught her eye. "Oh my god, Tenley," she whispered. "Look."

The house across the street had a shed in its backyard. At street level, the house blocked the shed from sight, but two stories up, they had a perfect view of it. The shed was tan and windowless—and it had a bright purple door.

"No. Way," Tenley breathed.

Emerson went to open the window. But before she could reach it, a massive flame tore across the ceiling, sending the overhead light crashing down. She jumped backward with a scream. Heat seared at her skin. She could taste the smoke in her throat, burning its way through her chest and down to her lungs.

Smoke swirled around her. Another crash thundered nearby, but all Emerson could see was color: gray laced with orange and specks of hot, flashing blue. It was almost beautiful, like the sky during a storm.

"We have to get out of here!" Tenley's voice seemed to reach her from far away. "Em! Come on!" Clammy fingers grabbed at Emerson's wrist. They yanked hard, wrenching Emerson out of her fog.

"Window," she croaked. Each syllable burned at her throat. The smoke was so thick she could barely see her own hands, but she could feel Tenley at her side as they pushed their way forward. Through the cloud of gray. Over the sparking lamp.

"Watch out!" Tenley shoved Emerson hard. She stumbled forward with a cry. A flame ripped through where she'd stood only a second before.

"Thanks," she gasped. She was struggling to breathe now, but through the wall of smoke she saw it again: the window. She grabbed Tenley's hand and dove for it. The bottom of the window was hot, so she shoved her sleeve under it. Tenley did the same. Together, they hoisted it up.

Cool, fresh air poured into the room. Emerson gulped it down, letting it fill up her lungs. It cleared her head and sharpened her vision. "We're going to have to climb."

"How?" Tenley whispered.

Emerson looked down. There was no fire escape, just a two-story drop to the grass.

Behind them, Matt's bed caught fire, sending a fresh plume of smoke rushing into the air.

Emerson's eyes flew to a tree near the window. It wasn't very far away, but the closest branch looked thin and flimsy. If it held, the tree would be the perfect escape route. If it didn't... Emerson scrambled onto the windowsill. They didn't have a choice.

Carefully, she scooted onto the edge. She could feel the heat pressing in on her back. Soon, the flames would reach the window. She stretched out her arms and launched herself forward.

"Emerson!" Tenley's scream faded behind her.

For a second there was only air. Her arms grasped at emptiness as she catapulted through the sky. Then her hands slammed into the branch. The bark tore at her skin and the branch wobbled dangerously, but it held.

"Now you!" she shouted to Tenley. She was trembling all over as she clung to the tree, lowering herself to the next branch to make room for Tenley.

Tenley climbed onto the windowsill. Behind her, the fire crept forward, flames skimming her back. Sirens sounded in the distance. They drew closer, but not close enough. "Are you sure—"

"Now!" Emerson screamed.

Tenley threw herself forward. For a second she, too, was freefalling. It made her look so small, like a doll tossed on the wind. . . .

She latched onto the branch. It wobbled and creaked, but Tenley was light, and it held her weight. "Got it," she choked out.

They climbed quickly to the ground and broke into a run. They'd just made it to the street when a boom sounded from behind. Emerson spun around, her heart in her throat.

Matt's entire house was engulfed in flames.

CHAPTER SIXTEEN
Sunday, 2:48 PM

SYDNEY'S PHONE HAD DISAPPEARED. IT WASN'T IN
her backpack or her purse or, as far as she could tell, anywhere in the
apartment. She thought back to when she'd used it last. It was when
she'd texted her mom from the party. Had she lost it at Calum's
house?

She used the landline to try Calum's number. Voice mail. She
left a quick message, asking if he'd found her ancient clunker of a
phone. "Have you seen my phone, Mom?" she hollered, resuming
her search of the apartment.

"No, have you tried calling it?" her mom shouted back from her
bedroom. She had the whole day off work, which meant Operation
Ten Loads of Laundry was already in effect.

"It's dead," Sydney replied. "And, considering its ancient, ane-
mic battery, probably has been for ten—"

The apartment buzzer cut off the end of her sentence. Her mom emerged from her bedroom holding an armful of clean towels. "Are you expecting anyone?" she asked, peeking over the pile.

Sydney shook her head. "No one."

"Maybe it's your dad. Speaking of phones, he hasn't answered his all morning. Can you grab it?"

Sydney moved toward the intercom. Her mom's words echoed in her head. *He hasn't answered his all morning.* She stopped short in front of the intercom's video screen, dread pooling in her stomach.

It meant nothing. Absence did not make him guilty.

And neither did the mementos Tenley and Emerson had found in his so-called trophy box.

She jabbed at the intercom. The video screen flickered to life. Two uniformed cops stood outside her building. A stout, broad-faced woman and a pale, bald man.

The dread solidified into a tomb.

"Is this the home of Sydney Morgan?" the female cop barked. All Sydney could manage was a nod.

"Who is it?" Her mom came up behind her, halting at the sight of the cops.

"We were hoping to talk to you about a local fire," the female cop continued. She flashed a badge at the screen. "May we come in?"

Sydney's mom buzzed them in wordlessly. "What's going on?" she whispered as the cops disappeared from view. She dropped the towels onto the kitchen table, her face pale.

Sydney could only shrug. Her voice was lost in her throat. This had *darer* written all over it. A knock sounded on the door.

The cops were named Funley and Herman. Officer Funley, the woman, was clearly in charge. "There was a fire at 566 Seaview Avenue," she began.

Sydney went slack.

"Is Matt—?" her mom squeaked.

"The resident wasn't home at the time," Officer Herman jumped in, shooting Funley an irritated look. His thick mustache looked incongruous next to his bald head. "He's fine, ma'am," he added in a softer voice.

Sydney leaned against the back of the couch, emotions feuding for space inside her. *Relief. Fear. Disappointment.* She looked away, ashamed by the last one.

"Then what's this about?" her mom asked.

"An anonymous source placed Sydney Morgan at the scene right before the fire started," Officer Funley said briskly.

"*What?*" Sydney balked. A pit formed in her stomach. "I've been home all day!"

"I can vouch for that," her mom jumped in.

Officer Funley pulled a small evidence bag out of the satchel she was holding. A slightly charred cell phone was visible through the clear plastic. Sydney's eyes widened when she saw its case: neon orange, with a large *S* on the front. "We also found this on the premises," she said briskly. "The case led us to wonder if it belonged to Sydney."

"It does," her mom said. "But I'm sure there's an explanation for it. As I said, Sydney's been here all day."

The floor seemed to dip under Sydney's feet. "I must have lost my phone at the party last night. Or—" She could feel sweat pooling under her arms. "Someone could have stolen it."

"Two Winslow girls from Sydney's grade were trapped inside the house when the fire began," Officer Funley continued.

"Who?" Sydney interrupted. The walls were dipping now, too, making her feel as if she were underwater.

"It appears that neither sustained life-threatening injuries," Officer Funley continued, ignoring Sydney's question. "Thanks to their quick thinking. But both are in the hospital, and—"

"Why are they in the hospital?" Sydney asked frantically. Panic made her sweat even more. She could feel a bead rolling down her temple. "Are they okay? Will they be out soon?" She could tell how guilty the questions made her sound, but she had to know.

"They'll be fine," Officer Herman assured her. Her mom's hand found hers, and Sydney held on limply. It had to be Tenley and Emerson. But what had they been doing at her dad's apartment? She could think of only one answer. The darer had set this all up. But if that was true... and it happened at her dad's home... was it proof that Tenley and Emerson were right? Was her dad really behind this?

"Let's try again." Officer Funley fixed her laser-sharp gaze on Sydney. "Think hard, Sydney. Were you at your dad's place at any point today?"

"The more honest you are now, the better it will be for you in the long run," Officer Herman offered. "Especially with your history of arson..." He trailed off pointedly.

Sydney shook her head helplessly. "I swear I wasn't there."

Officer Funley sighed. "Would you mind if we looked around the apartment, then? If you have nothing to hide?"

"Of course we have nothing to hide," Sydney's mom said sharply.

"Great." Officer Funley smiled tightly. "Then, with your permission, we'll take a look around."

As the officers disappeared into Sydney's bedroom, she sank onto the couch. Her mom stormed over to the kitchen and grabbed the phone. "Still no answer," she said a minute later. "Where is your dad?"

Sydney was wondering the very same thing. Her mom picked the phone back up and dialed again. *This can't be happening.* But even as the thought crossed her mind, Sydney could hear the cops moving through her bedroom, proof that it was.

This wasn't just a scare—this was a *crime*. If Sydney was convicted of arson, she'd be forced back into rehab, or worse, juvie. Would her own dad do that to her?

Her mom dropped onto the couch next to her. Her eyes, so like Sydney's own, were filled with tears. "Syd—"

"I didn't do this," Sydney cut in. She grabbed her mom's shoulders. "You have to believe me."

Officer Funley emerged from Sydney's room before her mom could reply. "I'd like to ask you a question, Sydney." She stalked over to the couch, her arms crossed against her chest. "Why is a search for 'homemade explosives' open on your computer?"

"Sydney?" Her mom's voice was raspy. "What's she talking about?"

Sydney drew in a breath. She'd spent hours researching online last night, trying to determine how someone might have thrown an explosive from the cliffs with that long rock bridge in the way. She must have forgotten to close the page. "I…" Sydney looked frantically between her mom and Funley. There was only one way to explain it. The truth bubbled up inside her, begging for release. And why *should* she stay quiet any longer? She'd listened to the darer. She'd played by the rules. And look what it got her: cops in her apartment.

"Someone's after me!" It exploded out of her. Saying those words, hearing them in her own voice, made her feel stronger than she had in months. "Someone's been texting me and threatening me, and I think whoever it is made a bomb. I think it's the same person who killed Kyla Kern! That's why I was Googling explosives. I was researching, trying to figure it out." The longer she spoke, the better it felt. She was finally telling the truth. Whoever the darer was—her dad or not—the cops could help her. But as she looked between her mom and Officer Funley, their expressions were like one-two punches to the gut.

They didn't believe her.

"It's true!" She straightened up, shoving her hair out of her eyes. "Someone has been texting me, threatening to kill me if I told! Plug in my phone. If it's still working, you can check. You'll see—all the blocked texts. Whoever's been sending them must have planted my phone at the fire and placed that anonymous call!" She pointed at a charger in the wall, and Officer Funley went to it with a sigh. A minute later Sydney's phone powered on. "Look in my texts," Sydney repeated firmly. She watched as Officer Funley tapped impatiently at her phone. The officer was silent as she scrolled through Sydney's in-box. Sydney held her breath, waiting.

"I don't see any blocked numbers." Officer Funley yanked the phone off the charger. "And, frankly, I don't appreciate stalling tactics, Sydney."

"What?" The breath Sydney had been holding came out hard and fast. "That's not possible."

Officer Funley held up the phone and scrolled quickly through her texts. Further and further back. There were no threats, no blocked numbers. They must have all been erased before her phone was planted. Sydney buried her face in her hands, tears burning at her eyes. The darer beat them every single time.

"Did I hear someone say Kyla Kern?" Officer Herman emerged from Sydney's room. A necklace was gripped in his gloved fingers. "Because I found this sticking out of Sydney's backpack."

The room blackened around the edges. All Sydney could see were the four gold swirly letters dangling from the end of the chain. *KYLA*.

"It's not what you think," she choked out.

"Then, please," Officer Funley said calmly, "tell me what it is."

Sydney stared mutely at her. She thought of the clown they'd found in the ocean, four words scrawled across its face. *This is no joke.* But that was just it, wasn't it? It *was* a joke, and the darer was the only one laughing. Sydney opened her mouth, then shut it again. There was nothing left to say.

She'd been framed.

— — — — — —

By the time the cops left, Sydney could barely think straight. Her mom was scurrying around like some kind of cartoon character, cleaning at warp speed. Sydney knew she should help, but the thought couldn't seem to work its way from her head to her muscles. She remained immobile on the couch, her mind frozen on the same two thoughts.

The darer had framed her.

Was the darer her *dad*?

The shrill beep of the apartment's buzzer made her jump. "Can you get that, Syd?" her mom asked wearily. Sydney dragged herself to her feet. Her limbs felt weighted as she made her way to the video monitor for a second time. The image on the cheap screen was fuzzy, and it took her a second to place the stoop-shouldered man outside. "It's Dad." One by one, she could feel her nerves waking up, blood rushing from limb to limb.

"Finally," her mom sighed. "Buzz him up."

"I'll just go down and let him in. I need some fresh air anyway." Sydney was out of the apartment before her mom could protest. The questions she had to confront her dad with were not ones she wanted her mom to hear.

"Sydney!" Her dad's shoulders sagged with relief when she opened the door. Immediately, the wind whipped inside, lifting the hood on her sweatshirt. Her dad stepped into the building and closed the door behind him, shutting out the growing storm. "It's so good to see you in one piece. When Officer Funley called and said there were two high school girls in my burning house…God, I was so scared it was you." Sydney was shocked to see tears in his eyes. He grabbed her shoulders and pulled her into a rough hug. Sydney's arms hung awkwardly at her side as her dad clutched her, but he didn't seem to notice. "I'm sorry the cops were here, Syd."

"I didn't start the fire," Sydney said sharply.

"I never thought you did." Her dad pulled back and ran a hand through his thick hair. "I'm just sorry I wasn't here to tell the officers that myself."

Sydney stared blankly at this distraught man, searching for signs of a twisted killer. But in his concern, all she saw was a dad. A dad who used to take her to catch butterflies and jump waves. Who taught her how to throw a ball, and laughed when she threw it right into his chest. Sydney squeezed her hands into fists. "Where *were* you, Dad? Why didn't you answer any of Mom's calls?"

Her dad looked around furtively, and in that second, Sydney's blood froze. "Where were you?" she repeated, tenser this time.

Her dad pulled something out of his pocket. It was a small box, not so different from the one that had held Tenley's lock of hair. Sydney's muscles spasmed. She took a step back, ready to flee.

Her dad opened the lid.

Sydney blinked. A gorgeous diamond ring glittered inside. "I was in Boston," her dad said. "Buying this for your mom."

"You're proposing?"

"Reproposing, technically. But, yes, I'm going to ask your mom to marry me again. A new ring for a new start." He touched Sydney's shoulder. "If I have your permission, that is."

"My permission?" Sydney repeated dully. All at once, the old memories of her dad popped: *Bam! Bam! Bam!* In their place rose new memories, hovering large and glossy above her. *Her dad with Emerson. Her dad keeping Meryl Bauer's skirt as if it were some kind of prize. Her dad receiving a breakup note from Kyla Kern.*

She'd been trying so hard to listen to her gut—to hold on to the belief that her dad was innocent. But it was becoming harder and harder to remember why.

"I know the truth, Dad," she said slowly. "I know about all of them. Not just Emerson, but Meryl, Kyla, your whole high school girl trophy box." She glared up at her dad, and the ring box slipped from his grip, landing with a light bounce on the Berber carpet. He knelt clumsily to retrieve it.

"I—" he began.

"I'm not done," Sydney said tightly. If she stopped, even for a second, she wasn't sure she'd be able to start again. "As I said, I know about the girls, Dad, and I do mean *girls*. But what I don't know is just how far it went." She took a deep breath, then forced out the question. "Did you kill Meryl Bauer? Or Kyla Kern? Did they have to pay for breaking your heart?"

"What?" Her dad bolted up, the ring box gripped tightly in his fist. "You think I *hurt* someone, Sydney? And what are you even talking about? Meryl and Kyla weren't murdered. It's this town—the curse—that killed them. How could you think I..." He trailed off, tears choking up his words. "I know I've made huge mistakes. Believe me, Syd, I've lived in shame for years. But I'm done with that now," he added forcefully. "I'm getting help. I've been going to therapy sessions nearly every day, and I've been working hard to make amends with your mom. I want to be with my family—with your mom and you. To be the father you deserve." A tear worked its way down his cheek. "How could you think I *killed* someone, Syd?"

Answers fought for space on her tongue. "You dated almost

every Lost Girl, Dad. Meryl, Kyla, and Emerson—Caitlin's best friend. I've heard theories that their deaths weren't such accidents. And here you are, connected to *each* of them."

"I didn't date Kyla," her dad said, shaking his head. "I did try. I tried with several girls over the years. But Kyla wasn't interested."

"But that letter in your box," Sydney protested.

"You mean the one where she told me to stop calling? That was her rejecting me." He smiled ruefully through his tears. "She was a strong girl. I still remember how I found out that she'd died. I was in San Francisco at a fire chief–training seminar. Bob Hart called to tell me."

"You were in California the weekend she died?" Sydney whispered. "Fall Festival weekend?"

Her dad nodded. "Other side of the country from Echo Bay. Lots of witnesses to prove it, if you'd like." She could tell he'd meant it as a joke, but it fell flat.

"When Bob told me…" Another tear rolled down her dad's cheek. "I had to pretend it meant nothing to me. But the truth was, it made me feel like *I* was the one who was cursed. First Meryl, then Kyla. It was almost like I was being punished for my indiscretions. It was enough to shake some sense into me for a long time. I didn't slip again until recently, with Emerson—" He broke off, shaking his head. "And now it seems like I'm being punished for that, too."

Sydney leaned against the wall, fighting to think straight. Her dad couldn't have killed Kyla. And if the darer was responsible for Kyla's death, then he *couldn't* be the darer. Relief surged through her, followed by something else. A thought. It was something her dad had said: *punished for my indiscretions.*

It was what the darer was doing, wasn't it? Seizing onto their worst mistakes, their deepest flaws, then making them pay for them.

Was that what had happened to the others, too? What secret had the darer lorded over Kyla? And Delancey?

"Listen, Syd." Her dad's voice drew her out of her thoughts. "I'm going to keep this ring hidden for now, until you're ready. We'll do this on your time frame. I want us to be a family again, but for that to happen the right way, we all need to want it."

Sydney looked up at her dad. The old images were reappearing, faded but there, like a photograph left out in the sun. *Her dad telling her that she deserved to go to Winslow, that he'd find a way to make it happen. Her dad dropping her off on her first day, hugging her so tightly she could hardly breathe.* "Thank you," she whispered.

Her dad nodded. "Now I'm going to go apologize to your mom that my phone was off. You coming?"

The thought of being cramped in her apartment right then made Sydney want to bang her head against the wall. Besides, it sounded as if her parents could use some time alone. "You go ahead. I'm going to drop by the hospital to see how Tenley and Emerson are doing."

Her dad paused. She could tell he had more questions—what Emerson and Tenley had been doing in his house in the first place, for one—but after a few seconds, he shook his head. "Be careful" was all he said.

The wind drummed a steady rhythm against the roof of her car as she pulled out onto the street. The temperature had dropped drastically since the day before, and she switched on the heat, the familiar rattle of the system soothing in the face of the wind.

She braked at a red light and looked over at the beach. The wind powered the waves, sending them tall and white-tipped toward the sky. The sun was setting earlier and earlier lately, and it was already dusk outside. The water was a steely blue in the dimming light. The ocean used to be so soothing to her. Now, when she looked at the waves, all she felt was fear.

Flash.

Sydney bolted forward so fast that her forehead nearly banged against the windshield. She could swear she'd just seen it: five ghostly tendrils of light flashing across the darkening sky.

She held absolutely still, not wanting to break the spell. And then it was there again, like silent fireworks: five lights glowing over the waves. The ghost lights.

Sydney whipped her car around, making her tires squeal loudly. If the lights were fake, that meant someone was up on Dead Man's Falls right now, fabricating them. She sped to an inlet down the street. She'd never make it all the way to Dead Man's Falls in time, but she had a direct view from there. She grabbed a camera she'd left in her car and zoomed all the way in. Dead Man's Falls came into focus in the viewfinder. Tall, craggy rocks. A sharp, sudden cliff. And a man.

She gasped.

The man turned away—too fast for her to catch on camera. He was climbing up the cliffs now, higher and higher, and soon he melted out of sight. But it didn't matter, because she'd gotten a glimpse.

He was tall and pale, with broad shoulders and curly blond hair. Sydney had never seen him in person before, but she'd seen him in pictures. She'd seen him on the news.

It was Sam Bauer, Calum's dad.

CHAPTER SEVENTEEN
Sunday, 5:30 PM

NIGHT HAD FALLEN IN ECHO BAY. THE DARKNESS turned the wind menacing: invisible mouths howling into the night. "Octo-storm is coming," Emerson said grimly. After half a day in the hospital, Tenley knew she should be home right now, recuperating in bed. If her mom realized she'd sneaked out, she could only imagine the screech that would fill their house. But when they were trapped in Matt's room, they'd *finally* seen a purple door. They had to check it out.

They hit a bump in the road, and Tenley grimaced. It wasn't just her leg that ached anymore; after the fire and their escape out the window, her whole body hurt. She was crisscrossed with scrapes, bruises, and burns. But at least she was alive. She sped the rest of the way, pulling over on Matt's block. On the other side of the street stood the house his apartment was in. Or what was left of it. The roof had caved in and the windows had been blown away, leaving gaping holes rimmed with soot. The once pretty yellow facade was now charred and black.

"Come on," she said fiercely, pushing away the memory of being trapped in Matt's closet. The smoke had crept into her lungs, racking her body with coughs as she screamed for help. If Emerson hadn't heard her... She refused to complete that train of thought.

Outside, the air had taken on that pure, crisp scent that always preceded a big storm. The street was eerily quiet. Most of the homes were summer rentals, abandoned until warmer months. They stopped in front of a small, beat-up house. The windows were dark, the furniture on the porch covered in plastic. "A rental," Tenley breathed. "We're in luck." They hurried into the backyard. There, hidden from the street, was the purple-doored shed.

Emerson removed Delancey's key from her pocket. Tenley dug her nails into her jeans as she waited for Emerson to insert it into the lock. With a soft click, the door to the shed opened.

"It worked," Emerson said wonderingly.

Right away, Tenley could hear it. A soft, steady whirring. Emerson stepped inside first. Fear grasped at Tenley, but she refused to give it a stronghold. She stepped into the shed and shut the door behind her.

It was a square, windowless space, filled with computers. They were packed densely together on two long tables, leaving only a thin aisle of walking space between them, just large enough for a single metal stool. They whirred softly in unison, making the room feel as if it were breathing. Screen savers of Echo Bay vistas flashed on their screens.

Tenley's gaze traveled to the walls. All four of them were plastered with photos. She let out a cry as her eyes darted from one section to the next. There were photos of her, of Emerson, of Sydney and Caitlin and Tricia and Delancey. Tacked up with the photos were notes—notes typed on a typewriter.

On the back wall hung a list of their names. A thick red marker had been used to cross off *Caitlin*, *Tricia*, and *Delancey*.

Tenley clutched her stomach. She felt like she might heave at any second. "It's the darer's headquarters." She squeezed her way over to the wall that featured pictures of her. There she was with Caitlin. With Tim. In her bedroom. Photo after photo, taken when she wasn't looking. An icy chill spread through her. In the middle of the photos, two typewritten notes had been tacked up. The first held a single word, typed in all caps. IMPLANTS.

Bile rose in Tenley's throat. It was the secret the darer had tortured her with when the game first started. That secret had blackmailed Tenley into doing everything the darer wanted. Fury sparked inside her as she turned to the other note. This one included three words. The only witness.

"What does *that* mean?" Tenley muttered. She looked over at Emerson, who was studying her own photo shrine. Two typewritten notes hung among her photos as well. Tenley moved closer to read them.

AFFAIR, read the first one. Like Tenley's implants, it was the secret the darer had lorded over Emerson. Her second note was just as curious. Just like her.

Tenley moved on to Caitlin's section. Photos of her friend assaulted her. She bit down on her lip, refusing to cry. There were notes here as well. PILLS, and Replaced her. Nearby was Sydney's section. Her notes said PYRO and Spawn.

Delancey's followed the same pattern. NUDE PHOTOS, the first note read. Tenley furrowed her brow. Why did Delancey, Purity Club cofounder herself, have *nude photos*? Tenley shook her head. She'd never know now, and the truth was, it didn't matter. The point was that Delancey, like everyone, had a secret, and the darer had used it to pull her strings—turn her into a puppet. She forced herself to concentrate on Delancey's second note. Found out about Tricia.

"*Of course*," Tenley murmured. She raced over to Tricia's section. Her first note—her secret—said: BULIMIC. Her second read: Insecure—easy target.

"These second notes, they're the *reasons*." Tenley looked over at Emerson. Her friend's sickly green coloring told her she'd figured out the same thing.

"They're why the darer chose us all," Emerson breathed.

Tenley looked back at her shrine. The only witness. "The only witness to *what*?"

Emerson shook her head, her eyes on her own note. Just like her. "*Who* am I just like?"

"Maybe one of the Lost Girls? It would make sense if this really is all connected...." Tenley trailed off. Her eyes were glued to a small desk in the corner of the shed. Its desktop was empty, but for the first time she saw something sticking out from underneath it. She moved toward it as if in a dream.

Boxy and black. Old and shiny. A typewriter.

"Em, are you seeing—?"

"*Oh my god.*" Emerson's gasp cut Tenley off. But when Tenley spun around, Emerson wasn't looking at the typewriter. She was looking at one of the computers. The screen saver was gone, and in its place was a video image of a bedroom. Tenley's bedroom. "There's a hidden camera in your bedroom!" Emerson cried.

Tenley moved woodenly to a second computer. The screen saver vanished, replaced by a video of Emerson's bedroom. "Yours too." She moved to the next computer. "And here's Sydney's car. And her apartment."

They went through the rest of the computers in a daze. There was surveillance everywhere: in half the rooms in their houses, in Tenley's pool house and gazebo, inside each of their cars, in the Winslow cafeteria and auditorium, inside Pat-a-Pancake and the Crooked Cat Diner and Dr. Filstone's office, outside on Art Walk, even in the Echo Bay police station. "This is why it's felt like there are eyes everywhere," Tenley whispered.

"It's because there are."

Tenley fought the urge to scream. How many times had the darer been watching when she thought she was alone? It made her feel as if someone had ripped open her chest and left her standing exposed, heart bloodred and pumping for all to see.

"This is it." Emerson's voice drew Tenley back to the present. "This is our lead. Finally. Think of all the data stored on computers. Technology always leaves a trail somewhere, right? We should call the police right now. Get them to come down here. There *has* to be an answer on one of these computers."

Emerson was still talking, the words tumbling frantically out, but Tenley had stopped listening. Her eyes were on the line of computers instead. The screens had gone black. All at once, an identical message flashed on each of them. "Em," Tenley whispered. She pointed soundlessly to the message.

FILES TRANSFERRED TO BACKUP SERVER. MEMORY WIPE COMPLETE.

"No!" It was more cry than word. Emerson launched herself at the computer, desperately shaking the mouse. The screen remained black.

Tenley stood immobilized as Emerson rushed uselessly from computer to computer. A realization was dawning on her slowly, like an old lightbulb flickering on. "We have to get out of here," she breathed. Emerson looked up, tears shining in her hazel eyes. "This must be some kind of security measure. Which means the darer knows we're here."

"We need proof. Something!" Emerson whirled around, her expression wild. She began taking photos of the walls with her phone, one after another, the clicking sound echoing through the silent shed.

The silent shed. It took Tenley a second to process it. The computers had stopped whirring.

"Now," Tenley hissed.

Emerson froze. From the way her eyes widened, Tenley could tell she, too, had registered the silence.

They both broke into a run. The wind lifted goose bumps on Tenley's neck as they raced back to the car. Tenley had just locked the doors and started the ignition when her phone let out a shrill ring. She slammed down on the gas pedal, speeding away from the shed. The phone rang on.

Time seemed to slow as Emerson fumbled through Tenley's bag. Finally, she extracted the ringing phone. "Unknown number," she whispered.

Tenley's heart banged loudly against her ribs. "Answer on speakerphone."

She took a sharp left as Emerson jabbed at the phone. "Hello?" Emerson answered.

The speakerphone crackled silently in response.

"Who is this?" Tenley shouted.

"It's me." There was another crackle, then Sydney's voice blasted through the speakerphone. Tenley's breath came out in a long whoosh. "I'm calling from my home phone," Sydney continued. "The cops have my cell—it's a long story. Are you guys okay? Are you out of the hospital?"

"We're fine," Emerson said hurriedly. "Out of the hospital. But you won't believe where we just were."

"You won't believe what I just *saw*!" Sydney cut in. "The ghost lights went off. I used my camera to get a good look at the cliff, and I saw someone up there. It was Sam Bauer."

"Calum's *dad*?" In Tenley's surprise, she jerked the wheel, making the car skid across the road. She quickly straightened it out, her pulse racing.

"He must be the darer," Sydney continued. "Think about it. He definitely has the resources. Not just the money, which obviously he has plenty of, but he's also a tech *genius*. He's consulted for

185

the government! I called Calum after I saw his dad, to try to poke around a little, and he told me he was at a techie awards ceremony, waiting for the guest of honor to show up: *his dad*. If anyone could set up surveillance to stalk us, it would be Sam Bauer."

"Well, whoever is sending us these dares, we just left his surveillance shed," Tenley told her. She quickly filled Sydney in on everything they'd found.

"That proves it," Sydney breathed. Her voice dimmed on the speakerphone, then grew louder again. "My dad can barely use a computer, let alone set up *surveillance*. It's Sam we want. He must have set up my dad."

"Spawn!" Emerson said suddenly. "That's what Sydney's second note said, right? The reason the darer chose her? It's because your Matt's *kid*, Sydney. Sam must really hate your dad. I wonder if that's why he set up his shed across the street from his house."

"Wait." Tenley pressed too hard on the gas, making Emerson fly back in her seat. "Think about the darer's reason for choosing Emerson. *Just like her*. Meryl Bauer dated Matt, according to his trophy box, right? Maybe Sydney's in the game because she's Matt's daughter, and Emerson's in the game because she dated Matt. You're *just like Meryl*, Em." She glanced over at Emerson. Tenley's own horror was reflected back on her friend's face.

"We need to go to the police," Emerson said tightly.

"With *what*?" Tenley shook her head in frustration. "That shed proves we have a stalker, but it's like you said: without the computer memory, there's nothing to connect it to Sam."

"Maybe he left fingerprints behind?" Even through the speakerphone, Tenley could hear the doubt penetrating Sydney's voice. Their darer was nothing if not meticulous.

"We have to at least try," Emerson said angrily. "We'll show the cops my pictures of the shed and tell them we're sure it belongs to Sam."

"And if they don't believe us?" Tenley shot back. She took another turn, speeding toward Emerson's house. "I was *just* at the station being questioned about drugging Jessie. My credibility is shot."

"So is mine," Sydney groaned. "The cops accused me of starting the fire at my dad's place."

"If they don't believe us, and they take their time hunting down Sam..." Tenley trailed off, the words sticking in her throat.

"Then Sam will have plenty of time to hunt us down instead," Emerson finished.

"And punish us for disobeying," Sydney added.

Tenley pounded her fists against the steering wheel. "We need a visible lead—something that will give the cops no other option but to look into Sam."

"The backup server!" Emerson burst out. "That's what the computers said before they were wiped, right? 'Files transferred to backup server.' If we could find that server, it would *have* to lead to Sam!"

"Especially," Tenley said slowly, "if it was in Sam's office."

"I've been in Sam's office before with Calum." Sydney's voice filtered loudly over the phone. "There were lots of computers and printers in there. Maybe it's on one of them?"

"You've been in Calum's basement?" Tenley asked.

"No." Sydney sounded confused. "The office was upstairs."

"Not this one. At Calum's party, he said no one could go in the basement, because his dad has some office down there." Tenley paused. "Why would Sam care so much about keeping people out of his basement office, but not his upstairs office?"

"Maybe because his basement office houses his stalker server." Emerson drummed her fingers against the window in a restless pattern. "If we could find the server and call the police while we're there, they'd *have* to come check it out." Emerson blew out an angry breath. "But there's no way we're getting into the Bauers' house."

"Maybe there is," Sydney said. "Calum and his dad are at an awards ceremony all night, remember?"

"Yeah, I also remember that Neddles Island is barricaded like Fort Knox," Tenley replied.

"Except that I know the code to the gate," Sydney shot back.

Sydney's words made Tenley's breath catch in her throat. "What did you just say?"

"I know the code," Sydney repeated hurriedly. "Calum gave it to me a while ago, when I went over his house. That time I saw his dad's upstairs office. It's his mom's name: Cassandra."

"It's risky," Emerson said.

"Doing nothing is even riskier," Tenley argued. "If we go to the cops without a real lead, then we're just sitting ducks once again. This is our chance to finally end this." Out of the corner of her eyes, Tenley saw Emerson nod.

The car's tires screeched as Tenley made a U-turn toward

Neddles Island. "I'll meet you there," Sydney said on the other end of the line.

"No." Tenley gripped the wheel tightly, making the color flee from her knuckles. "We're closer. And of all of us, you're on the thinnest ice with the police. You stay at your place. We need someone to be our check-in call."

She took a deep breath as she slammed on the gas pedal and accelerated toward Neddles Island.

- - - - - - -

There was an eerie perfection to the inside of the Bauer mansion. All the surfaces gleamed, the chandeliers glittered, and there wasn't a single item out of place: no strewn couch cushions or dirty dishes in sight. Any evidence of last night's party was gone. It made it seem as if no one lived there at all.

There had been a moment of panic on the bridge when Tenley had punched in *Cassandra* and the gate hadn't opened. "He changed the password," Tenley had moaned. "*Of course* he did."

Emerson had tried to convince her it was a sign, but Tenley had refused to give up. She'd tried *Calum*, then *Bauer*. Finally, on the fourth try, she'd gotten it: *Meryl*. After that, getting into the house had been easy; apparently when your home was gated, it wasn't necessary to lock the door. Now Tenley moved quietly through the house, wishing Emerson was with her. But someone needed to keep watch from the car.

She pulled her sweater over her hand before opening the door to the basement. She didn't plan on leaving any fingerprints behind.

The room loomed below her: a dark descent. She gripped the banister tightly and started down.

In the basement, it was too dark to see anything. Tenley's breathing became shallow as she felt around for a light switch. Once she found it, the dim overhead light flickered on.

There were no computers, no high-tech equipment, no office paraphernalia at all.

Tenley looked around, confused. The room was filled with workout equipment. There was a treadmill, a rowing machine, a punching bag, and several racks of weights. The disappointment was crushing. Sam Bauer's private office was a *home gym*?

She had just started picking her way toward the back of the room when a distant noise stopped her.

A car. She could hear the rattle of the Bauers' one-lane bridge as the car trundled over it. She froze, listening hard. The car came to a stop. There was a pause, then the whine of the iron gate as it swung open. Tenley grabbed frantically for her phone. Where was Emerson? She was supposed to be keeping watch! Why hadn't she warned her?

She had no missed calls or texts. *Update???* she texted Emerson. She didn't have time to wait for an answer. She could hear footsteps making their way down the driveway. They were hard, stomping footsteps—footsteps that definitely didn't belong to Emerson. They drew rapidly closer, until they were climbing the deck to the house.

Tenley's eyes flew to the basement door. It was hanging wide open. She heard footsteps upstairs advance inside. There was no time to make a run for it, or even to close the door. She had to hide.

Her gaze landed on a closet in the corner of the room. It was her best shot.

She sprinted for it, clicking the door shut softly behind her. It was dark inside the closet, only a sliver of light stretching under the crack. A strange smell permeated the space, making Tenley wrinkle up her nose.

She could hear the footsteps working their way across the house upstairs. Slowly, her eyes adjusted to the darkness. The outline of coats and linens flickered in her vision. Her heart plunged as she noticed a small, furry form. She covered her mouth, trapping her scream inside. It was just a stuffed bear.

Above, the footsteps moved steadily toward the basement. If only she'd thought to turn off its light! But it was too late now. She slunk backward, trying to will herself into nothingness.

Her foot tangled with something on the ground. She grabbed wildly for the clothing rod, but she missed. Her phone slipped from her grip as she stumbled backward. She landed hard against the back wall. Pain shot down her arm and up her leg, but she was too numb to react to it, because the footsteps were louder, they were closer. They were *right above*. She was just about to grab a coat to hide under when she felt a strange buckling in the wall.

She twisted around. The wall looked normal. She shoved her palms against it and pushed. Nothing. The footsteps paused at the top of the basement stairs. "Hello?" The voice that reached the closet was muffled and unfamiliar, but there was no doubt: It was a man's voice. "Someone down there?"

Tenley didn't have time to think. She rammed her shoulder into the wall. Pain pulsed through her as it shifted under her weight, revealing a crack where it didn't quite meet the carpeted floor.

Hope flowed through Tenley. She was in the basement; maybe behind the wall was the backyard! She dug her fingers into the crack and pulled. The space between the floor and the wall widened. There was that strange smell again, a little stronger now.

She could hear the footsteps moving down the stairs, growing louder every second. Adrenaline surged through her. She tugged harder, using her feet to gain momentum. The wall shuddered, then widened even more. The smell sharpened, a foul tickle in her nose. She hesitated for only an instant. Then she grabbed her phone and squeezed through the opening, into a well of blackness.

She pushed the wall back into place behind her as best as she could. It muted all sounds, making it difficult to hear where the footsteps were. She pushed blindly forward, the floor soft beneath her feet. Around her, the darkness seemed to wake, blackness so thick it came alive, twisting into shapes in the corner of her vision. She fumbled with her phone. Finally, she got the flashlight app on. She shone it over the space. Its thin beam was enough to see that she wasn't outside.

She was in a room. The walls and ceiling were painted a deep red, and the floor was covered in matching red carpet. The room was windowless, but a window had been painted in white on the far wall, with real red curtains draped over it.

The realization hit her like a slap.

She was in a red basement. Red walls, red carpet, red curtains. Exactly like the room Caitlin had described from her kidnapping.

There was only a single piece of furniture in the room: an old bookshelf. She moved toward it as if in a dream. She could hear nothing but her own movements. Her heartbeat. Her ragged breaths. Her stumbling footsteps. Sitting on the middle shelf was a beautiful toy: a steel circus train. It was *the* train. The one Caitlin had remembered from her kidnapping. The one she'd drawn so meticulously in her journal.

They were right. It was Sam Bauer all along. Not just the dares, but the kidnapping, too. He'd held Caitlin captive in this hidden room, drugged her, and made her fear for her life.... Tenley hunched over, about to be sick.

Footsteps. The sound, dulled by the wall, crept closer.

Tenley straightened up. She had to get proof before it was too late. She aimed her phone at the train and snapped a photo. The flash was much too bright, but she kept going, photographing the walls and the curtains. The flash lit on something in the back corner. A lumpy pile of sheets.

Something crawled under Tenley's skin, a warning. *Don't go there.* But her limbs were deaf to the command. She crept toward the sheets, her body moving as if of its own accord. And then she was there, only inches away. She held her phone up, shining the light over it. The material jutted out at sharp angles. It wasn't a pile at all. It was a single sheet, with something hidden underneath it.

It all felt surreal. This hidden room with its red walls and its *off* smell: It was the stuff of stories, of nightmares. But then the sheet was in her hands and what she was staring down at was all too real.

It was a skeleton, slumped in a seated position against the

wall. Tenley leaned over and vomited. Still, she couldn't drag her eyes away. The skeleton was wearing a long yellow dress, and had a pretty linen napkin spread over its lap. An empty plate and fork sat next to it, as if it had just sat down for a meal. Even decomposed like that, Tenley could guess the body had once belonged to a woman.

She sagged to her knees, retching again. How long had this woman rotted away down here while life cycled on above, school and work and parties and love and meals? The room twisted around Tenley, a cesspool of red. She could hear her breath coming out high and heavy, and she wondered vaguely if she was hyperventilating, if soon she, too, would succumb to this room: another corpse to rot inside a cell of red.

A creak rang out behind Tenley. Someone had opened the closet door. She switched off her phone, using the darkness as a mask. The footsteps rang out again, directly behind the wall this time. Tenley pressed her hand into her mouth, trying to silence her breathing. If she didn't move, didn't even exist, maybe he would turn around.

Another step. Scenarios flashed through her mind. Sam drugging her as he'd drugged Caitlin. Sam propping her body up next to the woman's. She'd be lost down here forever, and she'd never see her mom again, or Tim or Winslow or Emerson or Sydney. She'd never again take the walk to Great Harbor Beach or curl up in her bed or speed down Ocean Drive with the wind blowing through her hair. Her life, which had once seemed so big, suddenly shrank to bug-sized, small enough to squash.

The footsteps inched closer, so close she could hear the rustle of shoelaces. Tenley squeezed her eyes shut, not wanting Sam to be the last thing she saw.

Ding! The noise, sharp and high, drifted down from above.

The footsteps paused. The noise came through again, clearer this time. *Ding-dong!*

It was the doorbell.

CHAPTER EIGHTEEN
Sunday, 6:45 PM

EMERSON JAMMED HER THUMB AGAINST THE DOORBELL for the second time. "Come on," she begged under her breath. *"Answer."* When the SUV had rattled onto Neddles bridge a few minutes earlier, right past the bushes she was parked behind, there hadn't been time to think, or plan, or even to text Tenley. She'd acted on instinct, leaping out of the car and slipping through the gate before it shut.

She'd stayed in the shadows, pressed up against the gate's iron bars as Sam Bauer emerged from the car. He was bigger in person than she'd expected: tall and broad, with thick arms that made him look more wrestler than techie. His coloring was darker than Calum's, but he had the same wild blond curls, impossible to miss. He'd stormed toward his house, muttering to himself. As soon as he'd disappeared inside, Emerson had raced across the front yard and rung the doorbell. She didn't have a plan. All she knew was that she had to give Tenley time to escape.

Now Emerson shrank back at the sound of footsteps stomping up a flight of stairs, from somewhere deep inside the house. Sam must have gone straight for the basement. She half-expected him to appear dragging Tenley behind him, but when the door finally swung open, he was alone.

"Can I help you?" He looked curiously down at her. He was even larger up close. She waited for some sign of recognition—*hey, here's the girl I've been stalking!*—but she found none.

"Is Calum home?" she asked quickly. It was the only excuse she could think of on the spot. She wondered if Tenley was still in the basement somewhere. She had to have heard the doorbell. If she distracted Sam long enough, she hoped it would give Tenley time to sneak out. "We're doing a school project together and I think he has my notes—"

"How did you get through the gate?" Sam interrupted. He had a steady way of talking, with little inflection, making it impossible to gage his emotions.

"The gate?" The intensity of Sam's gaze was making it difficult to think straight. "It, um...was open."

"It closes automatically." A wrinkle formed between Sam's eyebrows. There was something unnerving about his focus, as if he could see through skin and bone, straight to the lies forming inside her head.

Emerson broke into a sweat. "I—it was open," she repeated helplessly. Her voice was much too squeaky. There might as well have been a neon sign above her head, flashing *liar*.

Sam shook his head, but his gaze never left her face. "Well,

Calum's not home." His tone made it clear the conversation was over. "I'd appreciate it if you would vacate the premises, before I'm forced to report you for trespassing." He went to close the door.

"Wait!" Behind Sam, Emerson caught a flash of chestnut hair. She craned her neck. It was Tenley! She was tiptoeing through the living room, slowly making her way toward the back door in the kitchen. Her hair was mussed, and there was a wild look in her eyes. *Stall*, Tenley mouthed.

"I, uh, don't have his number!" Emerson blurted out. "Can you give it to me?" She pulled out her phone and made a big show of opening up a new contact. "Calum," she said loudly, taking her time typing in his name. "Okay." She flashed Sam a quivering smile. Behind him, Tenley crept closer to the back door. "What's his number?"

"Nine seven eight," Sam recited impatiently. "Two eight one—"

"Wait, was that two *nine* one? Or two *eight* one?" Emerson cringed inwardly. But it was working. Tenley was almost at the door.

"Two eight one," Sam snapped. "One five three—"

The last number was drowned out by a loud creak.

A muscle twitched in Sam's jaw. Slowly, he turned around. Tenley stood immobile on the creaky floorboard by the back door. "Run!" Tenley yelled, making a leap for the door. Sam's hand shot out behind him, clamping down on Emerson's arm. She tried to yank away, but his grip was strong. His fingers dug down so hard she could feel them pressing against bone. They rubbed against one of her bruises from the fire, making her wince. "Your friend isn't going anywhere," he informed Tenley. "So I suggest you don't, either." Tenley froze, only an inch from the back door.

Sam pulled Emerson into the entryway with a hard tug. The movement knocked her phone out of her hands. It landed on the marble floor with a clatter, just out of reach. "No one move," Sam said calmly, "and we can discuss this like adults." He kept a tight grip on Emerson's arm as he lifted a large black remote control off the glass entryway table. He pushed a button and a strange series of clicks sounded throughout the house. He smiled. Instead of softening his face, it distorted it, like an angry black splotch in the center of a painting.

He freed Emerson's arm, and she lunged immediately for the door. In the back of the house, she could hear Tenley doing the same. "What the hell?" she heard Tenley cry. Emerson pulled desperately at the handle, but the door didn't budge.

She spun back around to find Sam watching her. His eyes were eerily void of emotion. It made him strangely un-lifelike, like a walking cadaver. "Smart house remote control," he explained. In the kitchen, Tenley kept clawing at the locked door, to no avail. Sam pushed another button on the remote, and it momentarily glowed red. "We're in panic mode now. No one gets in, and no one gets out."

He gestured toward the living room. A white leather couch was the focal point. It was flanked by matching leather armchairs, and a chrome-and-glass coffee table. Something about how crisp and spotless it was unsettled Emerson. The house was too clean, too perfect. Like Sam, it was almost un-lifelike. "Take a seat," Sam said. He didn't lift his voice, but the command in his words was clear. It wasn't a question.

Emerson moved woodenly toward the couch. There were floor-to-ceiling windows behind it, which made the outside feel tantalizingly close, as if she could just reach out and touch the cold night air. She turned away. The windows were at her back as she sank into the plush leather cushions. Tenley sat next to her, close enough that their knees knocked together. A full-length mirror hung on the wall opposite them, next to a fireplace. As Emerson stared at their reflection in it, an odd detachment settled over her. It was as if a veil had suddenly dropped over her eyes. She could still see through it—could see her wide-eyed reflection, could see Tenley's hand grabbing hers, nails digging into skin—but it was all distant, like watching a movie screen. She couldn't feel a thing.

Sam paced past the mirror, momentarily blotting out their reflection. "I suggest you tell me what's going on while I still have some patience." His voice had taken on a soft, soothing quality. It was a dad's voice now, a voice that belonged to bedtime stories and good nights. But there was that same deadness in his eyes as he stopped in front of them, and the veins in his hand bulged from gripping the remote so tightly. They were tells: This wasn't the voice of a dad, or the teller of bedtime stories. This voice belonged to a monster.

Sam's gaze traveled from Tenley to Emerson. His expression hardened, and suddenly Emerson saw it: He knew. He knew they knew, and he had no plans to let them go. Tenley stiffened next to her. She saw it, too. "Someone better speak." Again, Sam didn't lift his voice, but the threat flashed in his eyes, unspoken.

Emerson's mouth felt as if it were filled with sand. She couldn't open her lips to formulate a word.

"I was in your basement!" Tenley blurted out. Her face was set in concentration, as if she was calculating each word. "Just like you were in our houses and our cars." Tenley's voice broke, but she didn't stop. "Just like you were in our *bedrooms*."

Sam cocked his head. Through her veil, Emerson could see his sculpted cheekbones, his thick blond eyebrows. Tenley's nails dug into her hand, so hard it should hurt, but it was all so distant: dreamlike. "What are you talking about?" Sam asked slowly.

"You know exactly what I'm talking about." Tenley's voice broke again. Her shoulder shuddered against Emerson. "I saw everything downstairs. I saw the red room and the train and"—the last word rode out on a sob—"the body."

That word. *Body.*

It pushed through the veil, sending pins and needles down Emerson's arms. Her eyes flew to Tenley. "Body?" she choked out. "Was it…?"

"Dead," Tenley spat out. "A woman." Tears filled her eyes, but she jutted her chin out in defiance as she turned back to Sam.

Emerson sagged against the couch. The word was in her head now, working its way through all her defenses. A body. In Sam's basement. Sam had killed someone. Sam would kill them.

The veil splintered away, and all at once she could feel everything: the sharp prick of Tenley's nails on her hand, the tugging in her lungs as she drew in more air, the terror flattening her insides. And beneath it all, a single purpose, rising, solidifying.

Stop him.

"I know who you are," Tenley continued. Tears were streaming down her face, but she kept talking. "And I know what that red room is. I know it's where you held Caitlin."

Time seemed to skip forward and backward. It was all a circle, one tragedy bleeding into another: Caitlin and the Lost Girls and now them. It all came back to this house. *Stop him.* She could hear the words this time. They came in Caitlin's voice, whispered softly in her ear.

She blinked, her vision refocusing. She dragged her eyes over the room. Other than the furniture, the decor was sparse. A large modern painting hung on one wall, and a thin silver vase filled with fresh flowers stood on the mantel. Her eyes traveled down to the fireplace. A set of wrought-iron fireplace tools stood next to it. A shovel. A broom. Tongs. Her eyes locked on the last tool: a poker. Its point was long and sharp. A perfect weapon.

"And I have proof of the room," Tenley was saying. "Photos." Emerson could feel her trembling as she pulled her phone out of her pocket and pressed several buttons. "And now my friend has the photos," Tenley rushed on. "If you want me to get them back—keep them from going to the police—you better let us go right now." As she spoke, her finger kept moving over her phone. Emerson watched as she dialed three numbers. Nine. One. One.

Sam laughed. A low bark of a sound. "Like I said, the house is in full panic mode." He enunciated each word carefully, as if talking to a child. "All cell and Internet service is cut off. Any message you send will bounce right back to you."

The poker seemed to shimmer in its holder. *Stop him.* It wasn't Caitlin's voice anymore; it was her own.

Tenley was saying something next to her, but it faded to white noise. Sam was preoccupied with Tenley. This was her chance. She lunged off the couch and wrapped her hand around the poker. In a single thrust, she had it pointed at Sam. It sliced through the air, driving straight into his shoulder.

There was euphoria in fighting back. As the poker tore through suit jacket and flesh, as blood spilled and Sam screamed, the euphoria flooded Emerson's veins like a drug. It filled her with power.

Tenley was off the couch now, halfway toward the fireplace tools. Emerson jabbed again, but Sam was quicker this time. He jumped out of the way, hugging the remote to his chest. Blood darkened his suit jacket and drained color from his face. "You're going to regret that." His voice, so silky and smooth before, came out rough. He moved toward her, and he was someone else altogether now, not a person at all, but just parts: mouth and hands and eyes, cobbled together to form a beast.

Emerson could hear Tenley behind her, lifting another iron tool. "We're armed," Emerson said shakily. "And you're not. Let us go."

Sam approached her. Everything sharpened. The bitter smell of blood. The high, stringy sound of Tenley's breathing. The feel of her muscles, tightening. Instinct took over as Sam moved even closer. She stabbed at him, aiming the poker at his stomach.

Sam dodged the attempt, making Emerson stumble forward. She'd barely had time to catch her balance when his foot slammed into her back. She went careening forward. She landed hard on her knees, losing her grip on the poker. It skittered across the floor, out of her reach.

Her knees were screaming in pain, but she forced them to move, to crawl toward it. She was getting close when there was a crash from behind, followed by a high-pitched scream.

"Tenley!" Emerson twisted around. Sam had Tenley pinned against the wall, the iron fireplace shovel pressed up against her neck. She looked so small next to him, fragile as a doll. One twist and she'd break in half. "Don't do anything rash," Sam warned Emerson, "or I'll smash her head in." The eerie calmness had returned to his voice, and it sent ice through Emerson's veins.

Her eyes darted to the poker. Just a few more inches and she'd be there. She could grab it and run, smash a window, and save herself. She edged toward it. A whimper from Tenley stopped her. She looked back. Sam had pushed the shovel deeper into Tenley's neck. Tenley's eyes bulged wide, and an awful scratchy noise came out when she tried to scream. She was struggling, kicking, and twisting, but Sam was stronger. He pushed the shovel even harder, making tears roll down Tenley's face. His free hand went to Tenley's chin. "It would be so easy," he said softly. He loosened the shovel just enough to tilt Tenley's head forward. "This wall is concrete. One hard smash against it"—he gently pressed Tenley's head back to demonstrate—"and, *crack*, game over."

Sam turned to look at Emerson. "Touch that poker again and I'll do it." His voice was a purr. The curve of his lips told Emerson that he'd enjoy it, too. Shame burned at her cheeks, stronger even than her fear. How could she have thought of leaving Tenley? She rose unsteadily and stepped away from the poker.

"Good girl." Sam kept Tenley pinned against the wall as, with his free hand, he pushed a button on his remote. There was a whirring sound, and suddenly the full-length mirror next to the fireplace slid to the right, revealing a narrow doorway. Behind it was a windowless steel box of a room. "In," Sam ordered.

Emerson's eyes met Tenley's. "You escape," Tenley squeaked. The request made Sam smile wider, and Emerson had no doubt: He'd do it. He'd kill her.

She walked into the room.

Sam grabbed Tenley's shoulders and threw her in behind Emerson. Tenley collided with the back wall, yelping out in pain. Emerson looked around wildly, but there was no escape. Just the narrow doorway, on which Sam now stood, the iron shovel resting in his palms.

"This is my panic room," he told them. "Which means it's time for you to panic." He pushed his remote again, and the door slid shut in front of him, leaving only steel walls behind.

"You okay, Ten?" Emerson turned anxiously to her friend.

Tenley pushed herself off the wall with a grimace. "Yeah." She turned in a slow circle, examining the room. Emerson did the same. The place was truly a steel box. Even the ceiling was steel, with high hat lights embedded in it. There was no furniture, no windows. Just two large vents in the walls and a single black speaker protruding from the ceiling. "What is this place?" Tenley whispered.

Static burst out of the speaker, making Emerson falter. "I'm glad you asked." Sam Bauer's voice flooded through the speaker. "As I said, this is my panic room. I had it specially designed. It has only two vents in it, as you can see. They're computerized, which means that, with a touch of a button, I can suck all the air out of the room."

"He wouldn't. . . ." Tenley whispered, but Emerson knew she was wrong. Sam Bauer the dad might not and Sam Bauer the tech genius might not, but this changeling of a man, this monster-Sam, would. Fear coursed through her, making her feel faint. She looked up at the speaker, her thoughts reeling. This was all a game to Sam. Which meant they had to keep playing.

"Why did you do it?" she blurted out. It was their best hope: get him talking. *Buy time*, she mouthed to Tenley. "Why did you kidnap Caitlin?"

There was a pause, then Sam's velvety voice filled the room. "You're mixed up. I didn't kidnap Caitlin. My wife did. All I did was clean up her mess." His voice dropped a notch. "That's all I ever did."

So it *had* been a woman who kidnapped Caitlin. Emerson drew in a long breath. She didn't think Sam had closed the vents yet, but already the air seemed to be thinning.

"Why?" Tenley jumped in. "Why not just turn your wife in?"

Sam's scoff came through the speaker. "Because it would overshadow everything I'd ever worked for. After everything I'd accomplished, my legacy would be nothing more than that of a kidnapper's husband."

Phone? Emerson mouthed to Tenley. Her own was lying somewhere on the house's entryway floor. Tenley pulled her phone out of her pocket and passed it to her. Still no service. *Keep talking*, Emerson mouthed. She clicked open the video recorder on Tenley's phone. They might not be able to send anyone the recording while the house was in panic mode, but at least somewhere, proof would exist. She lifted the phone toward the speaker, her finger dangling over the recording button.

Tenley gave her a shaky nod. "Why did your wife kidnap Caitlin?" she asked loudly.

"She—you know what, that's enough questions," Sam declared.

"Don't you want to talk about it, though?" Emerson burst out. If Sam kept talking, they were safe. If he stopped... "How long have you kept this all buried inside?" She fought to keep her voice steady. "Don't you want to *tell* someone? Every secret you've ever had to hoard. How you did it? How you got away with it? So much brilliance, and no one could ever know about it." She cringed but forced herself to keep going. "Before long, we'll both be dead. We're the perfect people to tell, because we'll never be able to say a word."

There was a long pause. Tenley moved closer, burying her head in Emerson's arm. Neither of them moved as they waited for an answer. Emerson tried to breathe, enjoy the air while there still was some, but her body wouldn't obey.

Sam broke the silence with a sigh. The sound streamed through the speaker. "It all goes back to Meryl." Emerson's finger landed on the record button. The red recording light lit up. "For so long Meryl was the perfect daughter. Our beautiful little girl. Then she met *him*." His voice dipped on the last word. "The married man. The one who ruined her forever."

Emerson flinched. He was talking about Matt. "When I found out about her affair, I could never look at her the same again. My baby girl was gone." Emerson closed her eyes, her own parents' words echoing in his. Her fingers tightened around the phone. If she died in here, the last conversation she had with her parents would be a fight.

"What does Meryl have to do with Caitlin?" she pressed, desperate to keep him talking.

"I'm getting to it," Sam snapped. His voice faded out, and then grew louder. He was pacing. "Meryl died in that boating accident soon after I learned of her affair," Sam continued. "It seemed like fate. She'd brought such shame on our family, and she paid the ultimate price for it."

The words pricked at Emerson's heart. She held the phone steady. She refused to miss any of this.

"If only my wife had seen it that way, too. Then we'd still be together today. But Meryl's death broke her. She was devastated, barely able to get out of bed. I kept thinking time would heal her, but with each year she got worse. She seemed to forget she had a husband and son. She was wasting away, and I knew I had to do something to save her. When Nicole Mayor happened to die four years later, on the anniversary of Meryl's death, my path became illuminated. It was the perfect coincidence. I could convince my wife that Meryl had died as part of something bigger than herself; I could memorialize Meryl, make sure her death was never forgotten."

Tenley snapped her head up, her eyes wide as they met Emerson's. "So I created the Lost Girl myth," Sam went on. "I invented the curse. I started flashing two lights up on the cliffs and planted the seed that they were ghost lights. It was nothing short of genius. But there was a kink in my plan. I was *too* right; Meryl became too immortalized. Her memory, her story, her picture, they were everywhere. And instead of making my wife feel better, it just worsened her condition. The constant reminder of her daughter's death was too much for her."

Emerson's own shock was reflected back at her on Tenley's face. They'd been right. All these years, all these deaths...it was all connected. "What about Kyla?" she asked. "Was she part of it, too?"

Sam continued talking as if he hadn't heard her. "Cassandra couldn't take it," he said. "Eventually she just broke. She kept saying she wanted a new daughter: a perfect, pure daughter. I said we could adopt, but she insisted that wasn't fast enough. Then one day, I came home to find Caitlin Thomas in our basement, half-drugged out of her mind. 'She can be our fresh start,' Cassandra kept saying."

"Caitlin replaced Meryl," Emerson whispered. It was what Caitlin's note had said in the shed, her reason for being dragged into the game: *Replaced her.*

"My wife was unstable," Sam went on. "She didn't know what she was doing. Even after I returned Caitlin to her home, I knew I couldn't rely on Cassandra to keep it a secret." For the first time, Emerson heard a note of remorse in Sam's voice. "It wasn't just my life I was worried about. If anyone found out what Cassandra did, she'd go to jail. And Cassandra wasn't suited for that. It would break her even further. So I had no choice. Once again, I was forced to fix my family's mistakes."

"So you killed your wife, and pinned the kidnapping on Jack Hudson." The statement came from Tenley. Emerson held the recorder up, waiting for Sam to confirm it.

"It was easier than I thought it would be," Sam said. "I told them Cassandra drowned herself in the same spot Meryl died. The press ate it up. Everyone believed a grieving mom could be driven to end her own life. The ocean was deep enough there that no one ever questioned why her body wasn't found. No one ever guessed that she was in my basement all along."

"The body," Tenley gasped. "It's Cassandra."

"Of course," Sam replied smoothly. "It was the perfect solution."

A strangled cry escaped Emerson. Black spots swam in her vision, and she grabbed Tenley's hand to steady herself. Tenley's skin was cold and clammy, but her grip was firm: a reminder she wasn't alone. "Why Jack Hudson?" Emerson choked out. "Why frame him?"

Emerson could hear Sam sighing through the speakers. "Jack had dated Cassandra before she met me. He was always jealous we ended up together, and when he somehow found out about Meryl's affair, he tried to use it to blackmail me. He knew what it would do to our family's reputation. So, instead, I set him up to take the fall for my wife. Full circle, I like to think."

"But what about Kyla?" Tenley pressed. She was still gripping Emerson's hand, her nails digging grooves into her skin. "How does she fit into this? And what about us, and all the—?"

"Enough." Sam turned the word into a command. "I've answered too many of your questions already. Time's up."

No. It couldn't be over. The walls spun around Emerson, a kaleidoscope of steel. "Wait!" She threw herself at the wall where the mirror had opened and pounded against it. Next to her, Tenley did the same. Their reflections were warped in the steel: strange, funhouse versions of themselves. "Come back!" Emerson screamed. "We have more questions!"

"We want to know why you came after us!" Tenley shrieked.

The only response was a low buzzing. Emerson spun around. The slats on both vents were moving. A second later they emitted a strange sucking noise. Emerson slid to the floor, her heart beating out a protest against her rib cage. It was happening. The vents were draining the air out of the room.

Already she felt light-headed. Tenley slid down next to her. Emerson wrapped her arm around her friend's shoulders. *This is how we'll be when they find us*, she wanted to say. But she didn't want to waste her breath. So instead she just leaned against Tenley, their shoulders rising and falling in unison as they swallowed down the dwindling air.

"Freeze!"

The voice came from so far away, Emerson wasn't sure it was real. But by the way Tenley straightened up, she could tell she'd heard it, too. It was punctuated by the shriek of glass shattering. "Police!" the voice yelled.

They both leaped to their feet at once. "In here!" Emerson screamed, hammering against the door. "We're trapped behind the mirror!" She was growing dizzier, her vision darkening at the edges. But she refused to give in. She pounded harder, ignoring the compression in her lungs. "Please, help us!"

Everything was going fuzzy. Emerson heard a wheezing, and it took her a second to realize it was coming from her. Her pounding grew limper, her voice hoarser. "Help!"

"Is someone behind the wall?" The voice was male, but it didn't belong to Sam.

"Yes!" Emerson sagged against Tenley, pounding harder.

Footsteps raced toward them, the sound flickering in and out. There was a crash and a scream and voices. . . . Everything was growing fuzzier, sounds blurring together. She gasped for air. All she could focus on was the pain building in her chest. She fell to her knees, unable to hold herself up any longer.

Whirring.

Emerson fought to lift her head. Like a mirage, the door slid open.

∎ — ∎ — ∎ — ∎ — ∎ — ∎

Huddled under a blanket on the leather couch, Emerson couldn't stop taking deep breaths. The air slid into her lungs, fresh and cool. "Look, Em," Tenley whispered. She nodded toward the wall of windows behind them, one of which was shattered to pieces: the police's entry point. Past it, red and blue lights cast patterns across the grass. Under the light, it was easy to see Sam Bauer being led to a police car in handcuffs.

Emerson turned back to the two cops who had pulled them out of Sam's panic room. One was pale and bald, with a thin sheen of sweat on his forehead, and the other looked as if he lived on doughnuts. Right now, Emerson could kiss them both. "How did you know to come find us?" she asked.

"Matthew Morgan, the fire chief," the doughnut eater answered.

Emerson leaned forward too fast. The movement made her dizzy all over again. "What do you mean?" she asked cautiously. A cold breeze blew in through the broken window, caressing her arms.

"Seems his daughter, Sydney, grew concerned when she couldn't get through to either of your cell phones." The bald cop disappeared into the kitchen and returned with cups of water. Outside, an ambulance siren cut through the night, the sound drawing closer for the second time that day. "Sydney told her dad her suspicions," Doughnut Eater continued. "And Matthew came to the house to check it out. But he said that when he got here, nothing was working: the buzzer, the gate, the phones. It was as if it were all frozen. So he put a call in to us. Good thing, too. It looks like this was a real hostage situation."

"It was more than that." Emerson thrust Tenley's cell phone at the cop. Now that her head was clearing, she recognized him as one of the ones from the fire at Matt's apartment earlier that day. She collapsed back on the couch, suddenly bone tired.

"It's all on the video," Tenley finished for her. "Sam Bauer admitted to killing his wife, and pinning Caitlin Thomas's kidnapping on Jack Hudson."

"Well, you can relax now, girls," the cop said. "We have Sam in custody."

Emerson twisted around to look out the window. As the sound of the ambulance wailed closer, she watched Sam being shoved into the police car. A second siren filled the air, and then the car was gone, speeding off Neddles Island. Emerson squeezed her eyes shut, relief working its way into every cell of her body.

Sam Bauer was gone. The game was over at last.

CHAPTER NINETEEN
Tuesday, 12:05 PM

"STILL NO SIGN OF CALUM?" EMERSON ASKED. SHE dropped her phone onto the cafeteria table next to Tenley's. Their identical gold cases flashed up at Sydney as she shook her head. "He's definitely not at school," Sydney said. "And his phone keeps going straight to voice mail."

It had been two days since Sam Bauer was arrested. Sydney had tried calling Calum a dozen times since, but she still hadn't reached him. According to the police, Calum was staying with family while a forensics team searched Neddles Island. But that didn't explain why he wasn't answering his phone.

"I can only imagine...." Sydney trailed off, unable to finish the sentence. Sam Bauer's arrest might be the end of their nightmare, but it was the beginning of Calum's. His dad was the only family he had left, and now it looked as if he'd be spending the rest of his life in jail. There would be a trial, of course, but the evidence was overwhelming, and there would be no bail set before then.

Sunday night, Tenley and Emerson had spent hours at the police station, giving their statements to the police. When they were asked why they'd gone to Sam's house in the first place, they both realized it was finally time to tell the truth.

Sydney had been called down to the station soon after, and together they explained everything: how they'd been stalked and threatened ever since Labor Day weekend; how Caitlin and Tricia and Delancey had been part of it, too; how they finally found Sam's shed and figured out he was their stalker. They were too frightened to go to the cops without proof, for fear Sam would kill them as he'd killed the others. So Tenley and Emerson had gone to the Bauers' mansion, instead, in the hope of obtaining definitive proof.

When the cops asked why Sam had targeted them specifically, Emerson answered carefully. "I think we all remind him of his daughter in one way or another." The cops moved on easily to why they were at Matthew Morgan's house when the fire started. This time it was Tenley who answered, explaining that their stalker—Sam—had sent them an anonymous text demanding they sneak into the fire chief's home. It had been his first attempt to kill them together; the panic room in his house his second. It was the truth, at least as much as they could tell, and getting it out had felt even better than Sydney had expected.

"Has your dad heard anything new from the cops?" Tenley asked now. Her voice was weary, but the tense look that had taken residence on her face lately had started to fade.

"Sam still isn't admitting to the dares," Sydney said, shaking her head. "Or the fire. But two witnesses placed his car in the vicinity of the fire. And there's enough evidence to put him away for life, whether or not he talks anymore. Honestly, maybe it's better he doesn't." She looked down. "It's not just our secrets Sam holds. It's my dad's, too."

Sydney looked out the window. Snow had started to fall, dusting the world in white. Octo-storm was nearing the coast, expected to hit later that night. Every news channel was blasting warnings in between their Sam Bauer coverage: Stock up and stay safe. There was talk of downed phone lines, no school, widespread power outages. But all Sydney could think of was how white it would all be, untouched and pristine. Big snows always felt like a cleansing.

"It wasn't your dad's fault, Sydney." Emerson touched a hand to Sydney's shoulder. In skinny jeans and a leather jacket, her hair combed into a glossy ponytail, she looked the most put-together she had in weeks. "Sam might blame your dad for his family unraveling, but we all know that's crazy. Sam was a ticking time bomb. Something else would have set him off eventually." Emerson's voice grew fiercer with each word. "It wasn't your dad's fault, and it wasn't Meryl's fault, and it wasn't Caitlin's fault, and it definitely wasn't our fault. All of this—every single, horrible moment—is on Sam."

Sydney looked up. Emerson was watching her steadily, a concerned look in her eyes. Just a few weeks ago Sydney couldn't have imagined looking at Emerson without feeling resentment, let alone being grateful to her. But Sam had trapped them all in his twisted web, and it didn't matter how they'd felt before; it didn't matter who they'd been before. They were tangled together now, their lives threaded through with shared memories and shared fears. "Thanks," Sydney said softly.

"And hopefully no one but the police and our families will ever know the truth about what happened," Tenley added. "According to my stepdad's lawyers, the identity of all of Sam's victims will remain private, since, other than Emerson, we were all minors."

Sydney blew out a long, slow breath. The realization was like a release. After months of being caged, they were finally free.

"Em?" Sydney looked up to see Marta standing over their table. "Can I talk to you?"

Emerson looked nervous as she followed Marta to an empty table nearby. Soon Marta was talking fast, her hands flying through the air, punctuating her words. Her voice floated over to their table: "So sorry...I miss you..."

Sydney blinked, embarrassed by the tears suddenly pricking at her eyes. Her whole life she'd convinced herself that she didn't want close girlfriends, that she didn't need the drama or petty fights, the endless sleepovers and shopping trips. But as she watched Emerson hug Marta, she wondered if, at some point, things had changed. If, at some point, she had changed.

"I haven't gotten to really thank you, Syd." Tenley's voice drew her back to their table.

Sydney scrunched up her forehead. "For what?"

"For listening to your gut last night. For telling your dad. You know"—Tenley gave her a small smile—"for generally saving our asses."

Sydney smiled back at her. "Well, I couldn't let anything happen to the great Tenley Reed, now could I?"

Tenley shook her head. "If someone had told me last year..."

"I know." A laugh bubbled up in Sydney. "Believe me, I know."

- - - - - - -

Later that afternoon, Sydney stepped into Winslow's parking lot to find her dad's truck waiting for her. "You really didn't have to pick me up," Sydney said as she climbed into the passenger seat. "Or drive me this morning. I drive home early when I have last period free all the time, and I've always been just fine." It came out sharper than she'd intended it to, and her dad frowned.

"I know I haven't been much in the dad department, Syd, but I'm trying now. After everything that happened Sunday, you can't blame me if I want to chauffeur my daughter around a bit."

"I'm sorry," she said softly. The truth was that when she'd needed him on Sunday, he'd come through for her. "I didn't mean for it to come out like that."

Her dad nodded, keeping his eyes on the road. "It's a process. For all of us." He turned into her apartment building's lot. "Are you going to be okay alone? Your mom's not going to be home from work until late. If you want, I could hang out for a bit, until my shift starts...?" He left the question hanging in the air between them.

"It's okay," she assured him. "Honestly, I'm pretty exhausted. I think I might take a nap."

"If you're sure." Her dad's voice was cheerful, but his face fell a little.

"I am. But...maybe another time?" The words took effort to say, but the look on her dad's face made her happy she'd forced them out.

"Another time," he agreed.

"A process," Sydney reminded herself as she headed into her apartment a few minutes later. Definitely a process.

She grabbed the landline from the kitchen and flopped down on the couch. She might not be a suspect in the fire at her dad's place anymore, but her cell phone was still sealed in an evidence bag at the police station. She'd found Calum's cell phone number, though, and after trying it at least a dozen times the past few days, she knew it by heart. She dialed it now, but once again it went straight to voice mail.

"Hey, Calum, it's Sydney. Again. I'm sure you're probably taking refuge somewhere from all the reporters, but just know that I'm here if you need me." She paused. She had no idea what Calum knew: about her dad's involvement in this, or hers. "No matter what, you're my friend. Okay, Calum? Call me." She left him her home number and hung up.

She'd told her dad the truth: She was exhausted. But as she curled up on the couch, she couldn't seem to turn off her brain. Even after Sam's arrest, there were still things about Kyla's death she didn't understand. Had Sam really thrown an explosive from up on the cliffs? And if so, *how*, with that rock ledge in the way? And even more important, what was his motivation for killing Kyla? This wasn't some one-off kill-and-run. If Sam did it, he'd taken the time to really plan it out. He obviously had the resources to pay off Hackensack, and the intelligence to pull it off, but *why* go through with it? Emerson told Sydney she'd asked about it when they were locked in the panic room, but Sam had never answered.

Sydney turned over, burying her face in a pillow. There were other holes, too. As she lay there, they crept out from the crevices of her mind, where she'd tried so hard to banish them. Why had Sam decided to stalk them? If he wanted them gone, why not just kill them flat out, as he had Cassandra and Jack Hudson? When she'd brought it up, Tenley had said there was no explaining insanity. And maybe that was true. Maybe there was no *why*.

Sydney rolled over again. Maybe answers were overrated. With Sam in jail, they were safe. How much more did they need to know than that?

Before long, her thoughts were fading into white noise. She'd just drifted off when a ringing jolted her back awake. Panic was a reflex, clutching instantly at her chest. But as the fog of sleep cleared, she remembered: Sam was in jail. It was over.

She reached for the phone. Calum's name flashed on the caller ID. Guilt replaced the panic. At least it was over for her. She pressed the phone to her ear. "I'm so glad you called."

"Hi, Syd." Sydney started at the sound of Calum's voice. It was flat and bruised, nothing like his usual tone.

"How are you?" she asked softly. It was a feeble question given the circumstances, and she grasped for something more. "I've been so worried, Calum. Where have you been staying?"

"I've been at my aunt and uncle's house. And, thanks to the Calum-sized shadow my uncle's lab skeleton is casting on the curtains, I still am, as far as any reporters know."

"Brilliant," Sydney said. It came as no surprise; Calum had

inherited his dad's off-the-charts IQ. She paused. She couldn't tell from Calum's tone whether he knew about her involvement in his dad's case. She opened her mouth to bring it up, but she couldn't bring herself to do it over the phone. "So where's the real live Calum?" she asked instead.

"I'm home." Calum paused. Sydney thought she heard a sniffle, but she couldn't be sure. "The police cleared my house, finally, and since I'm eighteen, there's no reason not to come back. Who wouldn't want fourteen bedrooms to themselves?" It was clearly supposed to be a joke, but this time Sydney was sure: A sniffle followed.

Her heart tugged. She'd never heard Calum cry. She'd never heard him be anything but joking and nerdy. It made her realize how little she really knew him. He'd been there for her time and again, but she'd never really looked past his computer-game-loving, SAT-acing, valedictorian facade to the depths underneath. "You shouldn't be alone, Calum."

"I'm fine." His voice broke, exposing the lie. "Honestly, it's better being here alone than having my aunt and uncle tiptoeing around me. They were acting as if I were being held together by chewing gum."

Sydney closed her eyes. She knew that feeling. After she returned home from rehab, people tiptoed around her for weeks. It had made her recovery even tougher. It's impossible to piece yourself back together when everyone's waiting for you to break.

She opened her eyes. Outside, the snow was falling a lot harder, but there should still be some time before the roads got really bad. "I'm coming over," she declared. "And you might want to put in some earplugs, because I'm a stomper, not a tiptoer."

"Syd—"

"See you soon." She hung up before Calum could protest.

Her mom would be at work for another hour, so she left her a quick message, telling her where she was going. "I'll be home before it gets worse out," she promised. Then she jogged to her car and pulled into the street, her headlights slicing twin paths of light through the wall of white.

CHAPTER TWENTY
Tuesday, 2:35 PM

"YOU'RE SURE YOU'RE FEELING OKAY? YOU DON'T
need anything?" Concerned wrinkles marred Tim's forehead as he
rested his hands on Tenley's shoulders.

Tenley smiled up at him. Tim didn't know about what happened at Sam's house, but he did know about the fire—or at least
the darer-free details she'd told him—and he kept popping up
outside her classes, making sure she was feeling all right. "I'm fine.
Really." It was only half a lie. Bruises and scrapes crisscrossed her
body, the burn on her leg still hurt, and there was a steady pressure in her head, a headache that wouldn't quite go away. But the
darer was gone. It was like a salve, rubbing away all her pain. She
looked into Tim's deep blue eyes. "Better than fine, actually, now
that school's over. I have the perfect cure-all evening planned for
tonight."

"Oh yeah?" Tim threaded his arm around her waist and pulled

her to him. She pressed her forehead against his chest, listening to the steady thumping under his shirt.

"Mmm-hmm. I plan to wait out the storm in my bed with a movie marathon and a big bowl of popcorn."

"I love popcorn," Tim replied. "And movie marathons."

Tenley lifted her head. A playful smirk tugged at Tim's lips. "Are you digging for an invite, Timothy Holland?"

"Me? Never."

Tenley cocked an eyebrow. "Well, you are officially invited to wait out the storm at Casa Reed. Just in case you're interested."

"I could probably be convinced."

Tenley lifted onto her toes and kissed him, not caring anymore who saw or who knew. The pressure of his lips sent a tingle through her whole body. "That do the trick?"

Tim looked thoughtful. "I could use a little more convincing."

Tenley was midconvincing when an announcement blasted over the loudspeaker. "Tenley Reed, please report to Principal Howard's office."

Tim pulled back. "What's that about?"

Tenley's first instinct was *darer*, but she quickly dismissed it. There was no more darer. "Guess I better go find out." She squeezed his hand. "Meet at my house in a bit?"

Tim smiled. "I believe I am officially convinced."

Tenley tried to banish any nerves as she headed to the principal's office. It was probably something to do with the fire. But then why hadn't Emerson been called in, too?

"Miss Reed?" Mary, the principal's secretary, looked up when

Tenley entered the office. Tenley nodded. "Principal Howard will be with you in a moment. You can take a seat while you wait."

"Is she expecting anyone else?" Tenley glanced around, but the office was empty, as was the hallway behind it.

"Just you," Mary replied. "She said it wouldn't take long."

The loudspeaker crackled on as Tenley sat down. "Good afternoon, Winslow." Mary was speaking briskly into the microphone. The slight delay made her words ring through the office twice. "This is an announcement that school will be closed tomorrow due to the pending storm. I repeat, Winslow Academy will be closed tomorrow."

Tenley heard the distant roar of cheers from the hallway. She closed her eyes, imagining a whole free day, with no darer to shadow her every move. "Miss Reed?" Mary's voice cut across the room. Tenley snapped her eyes open. "The principal will see you now."

Principal Howard had run Winslow for as long as Tenley could remember. She was a thick woman, with a neat bob of blond hair and kind brown eyes that could harden when necessary. "Miss Reed," she said warmly, gesturing for Tenley to sit. "I'm sorry to call you in at the end of the day, but I came upon something I thought might interest you." She placed a puffy pink photo album on her desk. It was tattered and dirt-stained. "I thought it would be best if I gave it to you myself."

Tenley picked up the album. Six dainty letters were painted across its cover. *Tenley*. "Where did you get this?"

"It was the strangest thing." Principal Howard ran a hand through her straight blond hair. Each strand fell right back into place, as if it had never been disturbed. "Do you know about the construction being done over at the lower school?"

Tenley nodded. She'd seen the mass of construction trucks over at the lower school's sports field. The grass was being replaced with the same fancy turf the upper school had.

"The whole field has to be dug up so the turf can be properly installed, and while digging, one of the construction workers found the album. Said it looked as if it had been buried years ago." She tapped a finger against her desk. "Maybe as part of your eighth-grade time capsule?"

Tenley shook her head mutely. She didn't attend Winslow in eighth grade; she was on the other side of the country in Nevada by then. She cradled the album in her hands. She remembered exactly when she'd started taking it to school. It was in the weeks after her dad's death. She'd taken it to every class with her. Until it went missing.

"Maybe you left it outside by mistake," Principal Howard suggested. "And over time it got buried."

Tenley stood up abruptly, clutching the album to her chest. Dirt clumped off it, slipping under her fingernails. She would never have been that careless with this album. It had been her most prized possession, filled with her favorite photos of her dad. She mumbled something to Principal Howard—thank you, maybe—but she had no recollection of it as she hurried out to the parking lot.

She scrambled into her car. Snow painted the windows white, blocking out the world. "The clouds have landed," her dad used to say after a snowstorm, right before pulling out the family sled. He used to love the first snow of the season. He claimed it was sacrilegious not to sled it. Tenley still remembered the thrill of soaring down a snowy hill, her dad behind her on the sled. The speed would turn her stomach and quicken her pulse, but if she ever got scared, if it ever got to be too much, all she had to do was lean back, and her dad would be there, tall and steady behind her.

She opened the album. The cover might be dirty, but the pictures inside had been perfectly preserved in their plastic slip covers. Tenley smiled at the first one: a photo of her dad lifting baby-her over his head. As she turned the pages, she grew from a swaddled baby to a teetering toddler to a Winslow lower school student. Her dad's hair thinned and his midsection thickened, but his smile, so wide and crinkly-eyed, remained the same.

She paused on a page of terribly taken photos. The first was an off-center shot of her dad smiling on a boat, the second a close-up of his hands on the rudder. A laugh escaped Tenley. She remembered that day so clearly. It was long before her dad got sick. They'd gone out for a sunset boat ride during Fall Festival weekend, just the two of them, and she'd bossily insisted on taking all the photos herself. They'd stayed out on the water for hours, talking and laughing as night fell around them.

The last few pictures from the boat ride were mostly black, her dad's face a blur of white in the camera's flash. She smiled down at the page, wishing so much that she could talk to him now. There was an ache in her throat as she turned the page. Her dad's face was a little less fuzzy in the next photo. Tenley paused. There was a strange reflection on the water behind her dad. What was that?

Her eyes skipped to the next photo. In the edge of the frame was a faint image. Tenley frowned. She'd never noticed that before. She flipped on the car's overhead light to get a better look.

It was the corner of a life raft. Clinging desperately to the raft was the shadowy figure of a boy. He had white-blond curls that caught the light from the camera's flash. Wait a minute. Those curls looked familiar. Was that a young *Calum*?

Tenley had been in second grade when that photo was taken. Part of the reason she remembered it so clearly was because of the news story that broke later that night. Meryl Bauer had taken a boat out on her own, only to crash into the Phantom Rock and die, becoming the very first Lost Girl. Tenley could still see her dad glued to the TV set, rare tears gathered in his eyes. "That's awful," he had whispered, pulling Tenley onto his lap. "And to think we were also out on the ocean tonight."

Tenley fiddled absently with the album page. Had she and her dad been out on the water right around the time Meryl died? And if so...could this photo mean Calum had, too? Had Calum been on the boat with Meryl that night? Why had she never heard that before?

"Oh my god." Tenley bolted upright in her seat. *The only witness.* It was the note in Sam's surveillance shed—his reason for dragging Tenley into the game. At the time, Tenley had wondered what she could possibly have witnessed to make Sam hate her so much.

What if this was it? What if something had happened on the water that night—something Sam didn't want anyone to know about? If Sam had found out about her photos, he could have stolen her album and buried it: insurance those photos would never get out. But if that were true, why wait so many years to target Tenley personally? And why mention nothing about it when he told her and Emerson about Meryl's death?

Tenley slammed the album down in the passenger seat. It didn't matter. Sam Bauer was in jail. He couldn't hurt her anymore. She was *done* with conspiracy theories. She quickly wiped the snow off her car windows and took off for home.

"Hello?" she called out as she walked into her house. She shook a light layer of snow off her coat. "Anyone home?"

"Tenley?" It was Sahara's voice that greeted her. The house-keeper peered out from the kitchen. "Your parents are stuck in traffic, behind an accident. They be home soon." Tenley smiled as she stuck a bag of popcorn in the microwave. That meant more time alone with Tim.

She was halfway up the stairs, photo album in one hand and buttery bowl of popcorn in the other, when the house suddenly went dark. Tenley stopped short, nearly missing a stair. A cold trickle of fear worked its way through her. She hugged the popcorn bowl to her chest, refusing to acknowledge it. It was just the storm. There was nothing to be afraid of anymore. "Sahara?" Tenley called out.

"Electricity went out!" Sahara called back. "I go look at backup generator."

Tenley felt her way carefully up to her bedroom. She pushed aside the curtains, letting in the dim afternoon light. Outside, the snow was thickening, and across the street, a power line was down. Tenley circled impatiently as she waited for the generator to turn on. But when Sahara stuck her head into her room a few minutes later, the house was still dark. "Something wrong with generator," she informed Tenley. "It not turning on." She handed Tenley a battery-powered flashlight. "Keep this with you."

Tenley took the flashlight. She was suddenly very glad not to be home alone. "Thanks, Sahara," she said softly.

Sahara gave her a surprised nod. "I be downstairs if you need me."

The house felt different without electricity. There was no whirring of computers, no humming of appliances. The silence was so heavy it seemed to take on a sound of its own. At least Tim would be over soon. They might not be able to watch movies without electricity, but she could think of other ways to pass the time. . . .

She flopped back on her bed, embracing the cool darkness. Just yesterday, the dark had felt like a threat. But there were no more shadows now, no more beasts lurking in the corners. There never had been. There had only been Sam, and he was gone. She smiled into the darkness. Life was back to normal at last.

CHAPTER TWENTY-ONE
Tuesday, 3:45 PM

ECHO BAY WAS GOING DARK. ONE BY ONE, LIGHTS flickered off along the bay, like reverse fireworks. *Pop*, blackness, *pop*, blackness. It gave the shoreline a backward feeling: dark houses against a light sky, a whole world inverted. The streets were slick with snow, keeping the traffic at a crawl. It was leaving Emerson with way too much time to think about what she was planning to do.

Yesterday, after they'd put the craziness of Sunday behind them, she'd spent a long time talking with her parents. It had been a good talk, and Emerson had climbed into bed that night feeling different—as if she'd pushed a button to start over. And she had, in a way. Sam was gone. She was mending her relationship with her parents. Even Marta was back in her life. It was exactly what she'd wished for. Except she couldn't feel a thing. Because where her heart once was, there was now a gaping hole. And the worst part was, she'd dug it herself.

Thoughts of Josh had occupied her brain for two days straight now. She'd finally texted him that morning, but she'd never heard back. And why should she? She was the one who'd pushed him away in the first place.

Now she drummed her fingers impatiently against the steering wheel as the long line of cars inched forward. There was one night she always went back to in her head whenever she thought of Josh. It was in the beginning of their New York summer, not long after they started dating. They'd gone to this hole-in-the-wall Italian restaurant, close enough to Little Italy to feel authentic, far enough away to be cheap. They'd sat there for hours nursing gnocchi (her) and spaghetti (him), talking about things that weren't important enough to remember. Except Josh kept interrupting her, and *that* she remembered.

She'd be midsentence, whatever she was saying long since gone to fuzz in her memory, and Josh would suddenly cut in with a "five!" Or an "eight!" Or a "twenty-six!" which was as high as he'd gotten before the restaurant pointedly cleared their table. It had started with some inane joke she'd made at the beginning of the night—*you just like dating a model, don't you?*—which had set him off on a mission to prove just how much more he liked about her.

He'd begun enumerating, listing reasons whenever they popped into his mind. The reasons weren't boring, either, because Josh didn't do boring. They were things like: "Number five: The way you say your *r*'s! It's almost as if you're about to roll them, like you're Spanish. But then you stop just short of it, and it leaves them with this nice, smooth sound. I like that you are an artist of *r*'s." Or:

"Number eighteen: Your cheese inclinations. It cracks me up that you hate all nice cheeses—you actually spit out that Brie!—but you love things like Cheez-Its and string cheese and *spray cheese*, which is basically the penny of cheeses." It went on like that for the whole meal. The waiter kept overhearing and giving them strange looks, and it was completely embarrassing—and one of the best nights of her life.

At last, traffic cleared and she pulled up to Josh's rental house. The lights were out—the whole street was dark—but she caught a flicker of movement behind the curtain. He was home. She was surprisingly calm as she climbed the steps to his front door. She'd learned her lesson with the darer. You could try running. You could try hiding. But sometimes all that was left was to fight.

Josh answered the door wearing flannel pants and an old Mets hoodie. His half Mohawk was rumpled and there was a crease on his cheek. "Emerson? What are you doing here?"

She strode past him into the house. A quilt hung off the couch and there was an imprint in the pillow, suggesting he'd been lying there recently. The lights were out, but Josh had set up a framework of candles around the room, and they made the whole place glow. "One. I love how rumpled you get when you sleep, because it makes me want to crawl into bed next to you. Two. I love how you say you're not a dog person but a walrus person, as if that's even a *thing*."

She hadn't planned ahead. She hadn't needed to. She couldn't name a single state capital and she'd probably fail a test on the presidents, but this she knew.

She turned around. Josh had closed the door and was now

leaning against it, watching her intently. "Three. I love your eyes, how they're always changing from brown to green and back, as if they're trying to match your mood. Four. I love the way you speak. Other people just *talk*, but with you, it's more like you're writing out loud. Five. I love your toes, even though they are long enough to be fingers, which, technically, is disgusting. Six. I love that when I think of you, I think of that night and you yelling out numbers in the Italian restaurant, loud enough to make half the place glare at us."

"All twenty-six times," Josh said softly.

She took a step toward him. Her arms felt awkward hanging at her side when they wanted to be reaching out for him. "You remember."

"Number fourteen," he recited. "I like how you love the smell of parking garages but hate the smell of Starbucks."

"Number seven," she shot back. "I love that you make things happen. You didn't just want to write a book, you *actually wrote* a book."

"I finished, you know. Last night." Josh ran a hand through his half Mohawk, making it stick out at all angles.

"You did?" Emerson knew he'd been struggling with the ending of his book for a while now. It was why he'd come to Echo Bay in the first place, to work through it. Josh went to the kitchen and grabbed a stack of paper off the counter. It was bound together by a thick rubber band. He looked almost shy as he passed it to her. *Almost Lost*, the top page read. *By Joshua Wright*. "Josh—" she began.

"Em—" he said at the same time.

She shook her head. "Me first." She ran her finger along the edge of the pages. Her skin was clammy all of a sudden. "Here it is, Josh: I really messed up." She looked up again, meeting his eyes. They looked golden in the low, flickering candlelight. "I messed up in New York, and I can give you a dozen psychoanalytical reasons why—I didn't believe I was good enough for you; I was terrified you'd end things, so I self-sabotaged it instead; my confidence was at an all-time low living with all those models—the list goes on, but none of that matters. What matters is that I did it, and I lied to you, and every time I think about how much I hurt you, I feel like I'm breaking in half."

Tears sprang to her eyes, but she didn't look away. Josh's face was twisted in a familiar look of concentration. He was listening. The rest came out in a long rush. "I don't think I can ever tell you how sorry I am. All I know is I can't lose you. Things don't feel right without you. *I* don't feel right without you. I know I don't deserve you after what I did. I probably never deserved you. But that doesn't change the fact that I'm in love with you, Josh. Forget twenty-six reasons; I could give you a thousand reasons why."

She cut off abruptly. She'd said it. She could feel her pulse thrumming in her neck as she waited for his reply.

There was a long pause. Emotions flitted across Josh's face, too quick for her to decipher. "Let's sit," he said finally. The couch was a small two-seater, and his knee brushed against hers as they sat down. It was nothing, a throwaway movement, but, still, it made hope swell inside her. "You really did mess up, Em," Josh said with a sigh.

"I know." Her eyes couldn't contain the tears anymore. They slid silently down her cheeks as she looked over at him. "I'd do anything to change it. But I can't. All I can do is tell you that it changed me. I'll never be that girl again. I'll never make that kind of mistake again. What you saw at the Bones wasn't that, I swear. It was a stupid dare, that's all. You have to believe me."

He was quiet again, watching her. "Turn the page," he said. She gave him a questioning look, and he nodded down at the manuscript, which she now had clutched in a death grip. Emerson slid the rubber band off the stack of pages. The cover came away in her hand. The next page had a single line of type on it.

For Emerson, the girl I never want to lose again.

"Logic keeps telling me to walk away." Josh shook his head. "But the thing is, I'm really freaking sick of missing you, Em."

Hope swelled higher, cresting in her chest. "What are you saying?"

"I'm saying that against all better judgment"—he reached out and took her hand—"I love you."

The moment came at Emerson in flashes. The candles painting shadows across the ceiling. The snowflakes being born into the world, sparkling and new as they touched down outside. Josh's hand warm against hers, and those three words, burning straight to her heart.

"I love you, too." It felt different to say this time, knowing the words were returned. Like shadows materializing, stepping into the light.

She wrapped her hand behind his head and drew him to her, so close that his face became just peaks and valleys. And then there was no space between them at all. He laid her back on the couch, and his warmth enveloped her, shuttered out the storm.

It took her a minute to hear her phone. The ringing worked its way between them, until, finally, reluctantly, she pulled away. "I should get that."

Away from Josh, the air was cold. Already the temperature in the house was dropping. "Is it your parents?" Josh asked. "I'm impressed you still have reception at all."

Emerson extracted her phone from her purse. She didn't recognize the number on the screen. Or, she realized, the phone's background photo of a glittering, turquoise pool. "Crap," she muttered.

"What's wrong?" Josh asked from the couch.

"My friend Tenley and I must have accidentally swapped phones at lunch." The unfamiliar number kept ringing. She pressed the phone to her ear. "Tenley's phone," she answered.

The phone crackled loudly. "Tenley?" The voice on the other end was fuzzy and a little distant. Reception cut out, then returned. "It's Joe Bakersfield."

"This is actually Emerson," she replied, but a burst of static cut her off, and Joey didn't seem to hear her.

"I hope it's okay I got your number from Winslow's phone book," Joey continued. His voice was threaded through with static.

"I'm not—" Emerson tried again, but Joey was still talking.

"I thought you might want to hear this. Remember how you said that Calum helped out with some big senior prank when he went to Danford? Well, I asked around and there are no senior pranks here. Here's the weird thing, though. Someone *did* put strawberry jelly in a showerhead two years ago, but not as part of some big, organized prank. It was just put in one showerhead—in this girl's room who was like deathly allergic to strawberries. Jenny Hearst. She was hospitalized because of it."

Emerson tensed. She didn't want this feeling again. She was *done* digging. And this call wasn't even for her! But the words formed in her mouth anyway. "Did they ever find out who did it?" From the couch, Josh gave her a curious look, and she held up a finger, indicating she needed a moment.

"No. I talked to my friend who works in the student-affairs office, and there's no official record of it. But she checked the school roster for me, and this is where it gets kind of creepy. The shower incident happened at the end of May our sophomore year, and by the start of the next school year, Jenny had already transferred schools. Apparently, there was one other name that dropped off the roster around the same time. Calum Bauer. He started back at Winslow right around then, at the beginning of our junior year."

Emerson sucked in a breath. The line crackled loudly. "Do you think...?"

"I don't know what to think. It could just be a coincidence. But something feels off about the whole thing. Sydney seems pretty close to him, so..." He trailed off, and the blank envy in his voice made Emerson blink in surprise. Apparently, Joey Bakersfield had a thing for Sydney. "I just thought she should know." The static grew stronger, almost drowning him out. "Her phone went straight to voice mail, though, so I tried you."

"Thanks, Joey." Emerson practically had to shout over the static, and she didn't bother trying to clear up her identity again. Her mind was already skipping ahead to what this might mean. "I'll make sure to tell Sydney." A heavy feeling welled in her stomach as she ended the call.

"What was that?" Josh asked.

"Nothing—" Emerson began. She stopped short. She wanted so badly to ignore it, to just crawl back onto the couch and wrap her arms around Josh. But that heavy feeling was still there, traveling from her stomach to her chest. "Actually, I'm not sure." She leaned against the kitchen counter and accessed the Internet on Tenley's phone. "Come on," she murmured, as it slowly loaded. Finally, a search bar opened on the screen.

Josh climbed off the couch and joined her at the counter. He looked over her shoulder as she typed *Jenny Hearst, Danford* into the search engine. "I'll explain in a minute," she said when Josh gave her a questioning look.

Several links popped up. One Jennifer Hearst was a doctor at Danford Medical in Louisiana. Another Jenny Hearst had won the Danford toddler pageant in Virginia. Halfway down the list, Emerson found a possible match. A Facebook page for a Jenny Hearst in Boston. She clicked on it. It took a full minute, but, finally, the page loaded.

Jenny Hearst's profile picture was a shot of Fenway Park. Most of the page was blocked, but a few public items were listed under her information. Her hometown of Newton, Massachusetts, and two schools: Danford Academy and Haleworth Prep, another fancy boarding school.

"Bingo," Emerson whispered. She knew Haleworth. Her freshman year at Winslow, a girl from her grade had transferred there. It was an all-girls school north of Boston, not far from Echo Bay. She quickly looked up the school number.

"Haleworth Prep," a fuzzy voice answered a minute later. "How may I direct your call?" The connection faltered, then returned.

"Can I be transferred to Jenny Hearst's room?" Emerson asked quickly.

"Transferring to 213. One moment please." Staticky music filled the line, then abruptly cut out. A girl's exasperated voice exploded through the phone. "Mom, I told you, I have enough flashlights and canned food to last me a year!"

"Uh, Jenny?" Emerson's voice squeaked a little, and she quickly cleared her throat. "My name is Emerson."

"Oh. Sorry." A laugh cut across the phone line. "That's embarrassing. I thought you were my mom calling for the twentieth time. Who did you say this is?"

"My name's Emerson. We've never met, but I was hoping to ask you about Danford Academy." The lie came out in one long stream. "I'm thinking of transferring there, and my friend gave me your name. I thought maybe you could tell me about your experience?"

There was a pause on the other end of the line. "Who's your friend?" Jenny asked finally.

"His name is Calum Bauer." Emerson cringed at the lie. "He said you might—"

Click.

The line went dead.

Emerson looked down at her phone. It still seemed to be working.

Maybe Haleworth had lost its phone lines? She quickly redialed the number. "Haleworth Prep," the same fuzzy voice answered.

Emerson's phone dropped away from her ear. If Haleworth's phones still worked, then Jenny Hearst had just hung up on her. As soon as she mentioned Calum's name.

She could feel the blood draining from her face. It could mean nothing at all.

Or it could mean something.

She dialed her own cell number, hoping Tenley would pick up, but after several rings, she got voice mail. She tried Sydney next, but her phone went straight to voice mail, and she remembered that Sydney's cell was still in an evidence bag at the police station. She quickly looked up the Morgans' landline number, but the call didn't go through. It looked as if all regular phone lines were down.

She stared blindly at the phone screen. Something was off. She felt it deep down, the same way she'd known when her last dare was coming. A gut instinct that demanded she listen.

There could be a simple explanation. Maybe it really was just an innocent prank gone wrong. But wouldn't someone have told Joey that? It was the shroud of mystery she kept returning to. No records...no public knowledge. It screamed *suspicious*. If they hadn't already nailed Sam, it would also scream *darer*.

She grabbed her car keys. There was only one person who could answer her questions.

"Whoa." Josh's hand clamped down on hers. His fingers were warm against her skin. "Where are you going in this weather, Em?"

She looked up at him. His half Mohawk was even more rumpled

now, and his nose was wrinkled up adorably with concern. She could lie, say she had to get home. But she was done with lying. "I have to get to Haleworth Prep before the roads close. It's not a far drive, only about twenty minutes." It was a crazy plan. She knew that. But after weeks of running from the darer, she was feeling crazy. Sometimes all that was left was to fight.

Josh studied her for a moment. She was worried he would try to stop her. But he just nodded. "Fine." He grabbed his keys off the table. "But we're taking my rental car. It has snow tires."

"You don't have to—" she began, but she fell silent when she saw the determined look on his face. Maybe he did have to. Maybe that's what you did when you loved someone. She lifted onto her toes and kissed the soft stubble on his cheek. "Thank you," she said instead.

Josh held up a hand. "Don't thank me yet. I have one condition." He tucked a loose strand of hair behind her ear. "Once we're in the car, you have to tell me what the *hell* is going on."

Emerson hesitated. She thought of Caitlin and Tricia and Delancey, of the darer and the Lost Girls, how it all spiraled backward, year after year, fear breeding lies breeding fear. And suddenly she found herself wanting to talk about it. To tell him. "Everything," she promised.

- - - - - - -

The windows at Haleworth Prep were all dark. It made the huge gothic building look menacing, all spike-tipped spires and blackened windows. Snow crept into Emerson's boots as she and Josh treaded toward the school's entrance. The grounds were silent around them. Even the birds had stopped chirping. It was as if the whole place had frozen solid.

Josh's hand found hers. "This is exactly how I pictured our third first date," he said.

Despite everything, Emerson laughed. "I do know how to have a good time, don't I?"

She'd told him everything on the car ride over: Caitlin and the dares and Tricia and how they'd thought it had ended, but it had only just begun. The more she talked, the easier it became, and soon the words were spilling out of her, more than she'd told the police, more than she'd ever told anyone. She'd explained how she'd been dragged into the game; how her secrets had been lorded over her, how no place, not even her home, had felt safe anymore. She'd told him how wrong they'd been: about Joey, and Tricia, and Abby, and Delancey. She'd told him about the surveillance shed and Sam Bauer's panic room, and how, that night, she really thought she might die. And, finally, she'd told him about Jenny, and the uneasy feeling Joey's story had left her with. When she was done, she felt the way she used to after a tough cheerleading practice, as if she'd sweat out any poison inside her.

Now they both grew quiet as they walked up to the building's entrance. The door was locked, a large buzzer next to it. Emerson jabbed at the buzzer several times, but nothing happened.

"The power's out," Josh murmured. "Maybe we should try the—"

The door swung open before he could finish his sentence. A girl hurried outside, bundled up in a thick ski jacket, a cigarette clutched in her gloved hand. Her eyes widened when she caught sight of Josh and Emerson. "You never saw me here," she snapped.

Emerson grabbed the door before it could slam shut. "Or you us," she replied.

Lucky, Josh mouthed as they slipped through the doorway. Inside, the main lights were out, but the building's emergency lights cast a dim glow over the hallways. Emerson took a quick look around. The floor was empty; everyone was in their rooms.

"Earlier when I asked for Jenny, the operator transferred me to two thirteen," Emerson whispered. "Her room number, I'm guessing?"

Josh led the way to the stairs. She followed him soundlessly up, her heart knocking loudly against her rib cage. She barely had time to prepare herself before they were standing in front of room 213. The door was shut, but the faint sound of pages turning drifted out from behind it.

Josh squeezed her shoulder. "You up for this?"

No, she wanted to scream. They should be cuddling on Josh's couch right now. But they'd come this far. "Let's do it," she croaked.

Josh rapped on the door.

Nothing.

He knocked again.

"Coming!" It was the same voice that had greeted Emerson on the phone: bubbly, but impatient. The door swung open to reveal a willowy girl with wavy brown hair and wide-set blue eyes. A wrinkle formed between the girl's eyebrows. "You're not check-in."

"Jenny Hearst?" Emerson asked. The girl gave a hesitant nod. Emerson tried to say more, but she found her mouth had stopped working. She and Josh had come up with a game plan during the drive, but now, standing face-to-face with Jenny, her mind went blank.

"I'm Josh," Josh jumped in. He stuck out his hand. Jenny looked wary as she shook it. "And this is Emerson," Josh continued. "You spoke on the phone before?"

Immediately, Jenny's countenance changed. Her shoulders stiffened. Her expression hardened. "I'm not sure why you're here," she said quietly, "but I'll get school security if you don't leave now." She went to close the door, but Emerson reached out to block it.

"Please! Wait! I—I was getting notes," Emerson blurted. It came out on instinct, a last-ditch attempt.

Jenny froze, her hand on the door. "What—what kind of notes?" she asked slowly.

"Threatening ones." Emerson forced the words out. Even now, talking about the dares in public felt like writing her own death sentence. But Jenny was paying attention. "They'd show up at my house, or on my phone, demanding I obey, or—or else. Like this horrible game I had no choice but to play."

Jenny's face had gone sheet white. "So he's still doing it."

Emerson could barely feel her own body anymore. "Who?" she whispered. The voice seemed to come from someone else. "Who did it to you?"

Jenny shook her head mutely. Emerson knew her expression well. She was terrified.

It made Emerson want to stop and walk away, leave this poor girl in peace. But she'd come too far. She had to know.

"Calum." Emerson was the one to say it: the name that had made Jenny hang up the phone. Now Jenny recoiled as if she'd been slapped. Emerson's blood ran cold. "Was it Calum who was sending you the notes?"

Jenny gave a single shaky nod.

The dorm room swam in Emerson's vision, and for a second she thought she might pass out. Josh took her arm, steadying her. "How did you figure out it was him?" she asked.

"We grew up together." Jenny's voice was so quiet Emerson had to strain to hear it. "Our dads used to be business partners. One night, I was at his house for dinner. I'd been getting the notes for almost a year at that point. They were destroying me, and I had no idea who was sending them, which only made it worse. I went to borrow a sweatshirt from his room, because the house was freezing, and—and I found one of the notes." Jenny's voice wobbled. "It gave me the courage to tell my mom. When she confronted Calum's dad, he offered to pay for the rest of my schooling if I transferred to Haleworth and kept the whole thing quiet." Her voice caught, and she cleared her throat.

"At first, we said no, but then there was this awful shower incident and..." She shook her head. "I just wanted it to stop. I really believed it was just me, though. Some kind of personal vendetta. I didn't—I never thought he'd do it to someone else."

Adrenaline surged through Emerson's veins, clearing away any last remnants of fog. "The notes Calum sent you, were they typed on a typewriter?" She was surprised by how steady her voice sounded when inside she felt like jelly. She inched closer to Josh, leaning against him.

"Yeah." Something pulsed in Jenny's neck. "It was his dad's old one."

Emerson couldn't stop the strangled sound that spilled out of her. Josh said something, but she didn't hear him. There had been holes—she'd known that. But she'd reasoned some away and refused to acknowledge others. But here was the truth, too bright and burning to ignore.

Cassandra Bauer might have been a kidnapper, and Sam Bauer might be a killer, but neither was the darer.

It was their son.

It was Calum.

CHAPTER TWENTY-TWO
Tuesday, 5 PM

"SO THAT'S EVERYTHING THAT HAPPENED?" CALUM took a long swig from his beer. It was his second since Sydney's arrival, but judging by the unfocused look in his eyes, it wasn't just his second of the night. Sydney wished she had gotten there earlier, but between the snow and an accident on the road, the fifteen-minute drive to Neddles Island had taken over an hour.

"That's it." Sydney fought to conceal the lie in her voice. It turned out Calum hadn't been allowed to see his dad yet, so when he asked her to tell him everything she knew about what happened, Sydney had planned to answer openly: the darer truth and all. But then she'd looked at Calum's bleary red eyes. She'd smelled the alcohol on his breath and seen the glossy sheen of sweat on his skin. And all she'd been able to think about was Guinness: how on his worst days, he wasn't himself anymore, but a brittle shell. One wrong touch, one cruel word, and he'd shatter to pieces. So Sydney had found herself editing—twisting the story into its most harmless form: Emerson and Tenley had come looking for Calum, and his dad must have snapped when he saw them, and locked them up in the panic room.

"I'm so sorry, Calum." She scooted closer to him on the couch. "No matter what he did, he's still your dad."

Calum twisted around, looking out the living room's wall of windows. The one the police had shattered was now boarded up with wood. Outside, the sun was setting, darkening the sky. The snowflakes grew thicker with each passing second, until they seemed to thread together, a quilt of snow, flapping in the wind. The sight lifted goose bumps on Sydney's arms despite the prickly heat flooding through the Bauer house.

"Good thing you've got a backup generator." Sydney squeezed Calum's hand, trying to elicit a response. But, still, he didn't look at her. The silence, so unlike him, made her squirm. She stood up, busying herself by going over to the landline. "Still no dial tone," she told Calum.

"Looks like no calls are getting in or out." Calum's voice was flat, but when he finally looked at her, she saw a glint of tears in his eyes.

"Oh, Calum." She went back to the couch and wrapped her arms around him. "Just tell me what I can do. Do you want a drinking buddy?" She said it jokingly, but once again, she got no response. "Calum?"

Slowly, he pulled back. A single tear had worked its way down to his chin. "My Syd." He pressed a hand to her cheek. His palm was warm against her skin, and there was a longing in his voice she'd never heard before. "We really could have had something. Or at least I believed that once."

Sydney blinked. His expression was pained, a swirl of regret and self-pity. It reminded her of how he'd looked after he tried to kiss her at homecoming. "The timing was bad, Calum—" she began, but he kept on talking as if he hadn't heard her.

"For a while I assumed it was Guinness's fault." He pressed his palm harder against her face, cupping her cheekbone. "That if I just got rid of him, you'd finally give me a chance. But it didn't happen as I predicted."

Sydney drew back. Her skin felt cold in the sudden absence of his hand. "What do you mean *got rid of him*?"

Calum gave her a sad smile. But when his eyes met hers, it wasn't pain or sadness she saw anymore. It was nothingness. Hardness. "My whole purpose of working at the Club's pool was to get to know you better, and I have to say: You took me by surprise, Syd. You really made me believe that you were different from the other girls. Real in a way that none of them are. But I should have known better."

Sydney moved off the couch. Something in Calum's voice wasn't right. It was too cold, too low. It wasn't *him*. "You're freaking me out a little, Calum. Maybe you've had too much to drink." She took a step away from the couch. The room suddenly felt much too hot.

"Don't be scared, Sydney." The words were soothing, but his tone was razor sharp. He pushed his sleeves up, revealing a small bandage on one of his arms. "You're finally getting to see the real me. Did you really think I was that oblivious? That *pathetic*?"

Sydney took another step backward. The heat was oppressive

now; sweat beaded on her temples and licked at her lips. "It sounds like you need some sleep, Calum. I'm going to get going, and I'll come back tomorr—"

Calum's laugh drowned out the rest of her sentence. It wasn't the sweet, honking laugh she was used to hearing from him. This laugh was harsh and bitter. "Look at the bridge, Syd. Look at all that snow. No one's going anywhere. And no one's coming, either. No little friends to save you." Calum nodded, looking pleased. "It's almost as if this storm were made just for me. Fate, you might say. Just like my sister's death."

"W-what are you talking about?" she stammered.

"You know exactly what I'm talking about. Meryl was a whore, thanks to your dad. She ruined everything our family could have been. And she died for it. Fate punishes those who deserve it, Sydney. And you, Tenley, and Emerson deserve it. Just like Caitlin did."

Sydney couldn't think straight. Calum's words jumbled up in her head, impossible to make sense of. When the realization finally came, it was like a crash. She felt it slam through every inch of her body. "It was you."

Calum applauded over his head. "Bravo, Sydney! Took you long enough."

"What about Meryl?" Sydney choked out.

A flicker of what could be remorse crossed Calum's face. "I didn't mean to do it. She was the one who took the boat out. She was on her way to a rendezvous with your dad; did you know that? I was just a kid. I had hidden belowdecks to play. It took me a few minutes to even realize the boat was moving. When I messed around with the controls, I thought I was playing captain. I didn't know—I didn't think—but then I heard the crack. I'd crashed the boat right into the Phantom Rock."

Calum frowned. "The jolt must have made her fall, because by the time I got on deck, she was already dead, sprawled out on the ground with her neck bent at the wrong angle. All I did was push her overboard. I had no alternative. She was the one doing something shameful. I was just a kid; I couldn't take the blame for that." Calum let out a long sigh. "Afterward, I took a life raft back to shore in the darkness. I only ever told one person what really happened that night."

"Your dad." Sydney dug her nails into the sides of her legs. "He didn't just create the Lost Girl myth for your mom. It was to cover for you, too."

"He didn't need to at first. I'd handled it; everyone believed Meryl had died in an innocent boat crash. No one would ever guess that her little brother had been the one to crash her boat—then dump her body overboard. But then Kyla Kern started poking around for an article for the school paper."

The room swam around Sydney. She reached for the wall to steady herself.

"When Nicole Mayor died, my dad thought we could use her death to solve everything: Kyla's questions and my mom's depression. All he had to do was create the Lost Girls myth, flash some ghost lights, trick the whole town into believing Echo Bay was cursed. No one dares question a curse. And for a while it worked; we were triumphant. But then Kyla started asking questions again.

I stole my dad's typewriter and tried to scare her off with notes and threatening phone calls, but she refused to stop."

"So you killed her." It was a statement, not a question. How had she not seen it before? She'd thought no human could fit in that small cave on the cliffs—the one with the perfect shot of the Phantom Rock—but she'd been wrong. A small, scrawny seventh grader could. "You threw an explosive at her Fall Festival float." Each word was like a noose, tightening around her neck.

"I waited until all her friends had gone swimming," Calum said magnanimously. "Kyla was afraid of the water. Did you know that about her? So as soon as her friends climbed off the float, I did it. I took care of her, just as my dad took care of my mom and Jack Hudson. Like my dad always says, 'The Bauer men handle their problems.'"

"But it was done after that," Sydney whispered. "Why didn't you stop?"

"It was never done." Calum closed his eyes, sinking back into the couch cushions. "After Kyla, my dad transferred me to Danford. But Danford was no better. Jenny Hearst was there, and all she ever talked about was Meryl. 'Meryl this, Meryl that; Meryl was like a big sister to me.' It left me on edge all the time. How could anyone condemn me for snapping? That was when I had the idea to send her notes like I did with Kyla."

Sydney was shaking all over. "So all of this—this whole *game*— it was all about Meryl?"

"The shameful sister," Calum hissed. "Our family was in ruins because of her! And all of you—you're all tied to our collapse in one way or another."

"All those reasons in the shed," Sydney murmured.

Calum smirked. "I don't know how Tenley and Emerson found my shed, but I have to admit even I was impressed when the security system went off and my surveillance showed they were the ones who'd triggered it. I'd chosen that spot specifically because of how remote it was: in the backyard of a dilapidated house on renter's row. No one would ever think to look for me there, not even my dad. Plus, it was the perfect vantage point to keep an eye on your Romeo of a father."

Calum crushed a couch cushion between his hands. "Your friends almost managed to throw me for a loop. After my security system went off, I knew I had to act quickly, but I was trapped at my dad's awards ceremony. Luckily, Tenley and Emerson made it all too easy in the end. When the security system went off at our house, my dad assumed it was a false alarm, but I persuaded him to let me accept the award on his behalf so he could go check it out. I knew exactly what would happen if he found intruders in our home. Too bad he wasn't successful." A twisted smile tugged at Calum's lips. "But I digress. You asked about the reasons in my shed, and, yes, Sydney, you're right: I chose you all for this game because of Meryl. You because you're the devil's spawn. Caitlin because she dared to squirrel away in our basement like some Meryl replacement."

"She was *kidnapped*—" Sydney spat out, but Calum talked right over her.

"Tenley was the most important. She and her dad were out on the water the night of my ill-fated boat ride. They didn't see me—I spied on them long enough to ensure that—but there were photos.

I had to hunt them down and bury them where no one could ever see them."

Sydney cowered against the wall, her heart pounding wildly. This couldn't be happening. But Calum kept talking, his voice insistent. "I thought that would be enough. I never planned to take things further than that. But then junior year, I transferred back to Winslow, and everywhere I went, I saw you or Caitlin and I just—I couldn't take it. Then Tenley moved back, and it was the last straw. I knew I had to punish you all, the same way I punished Kyla and Jenny."

"So you started the game," Sydney whispered. She was shaking all over now, and she pressed her hands against her legs, trying not to let it show.

Calum nodded. "I bided my time throughout the summer. I wanted my game to be perfect this round. In the end, it was Tenley herself who gave me the idea for my theme, thanks to that infantile game of truth or dare she played at her party. At first, I just targeted you, Caitlin, and Tenley, but then I learned about Matt Morgan's new affair." Calum slammed his fist into the couch, making Sydney jump. "After that, Emerson Cunningham joined the game. There was Tricia and Delancey, too, of course. But they were never important—necessary casualties."

"Why not just kill us?" Sydney hissed. "Why torture us first?"

"I wanted you all to feel what I've been forced to endure: a slow, gnawing fear, the kind that eats away at you. If anyone were ever to find out what my dad had been forced to do, or what I had been forced to do...the last of my family would be destroyed. Do you know what that kind of fear does to you? You didn't, of course. But thanks to my little game, now you do."

Calum tilted his head until he was looking straight at Sydney. "You were the only one who almost got out. At the homecoming dance, I was going to tell you everything. But then you rejected me—left me—just like all women do."

Calum stood up abruptly. "You deserved to be framed for the fire in your dad's apartment after that." He took one step toward her, then another. Sydney's eyes darted toward the window. The snow was a wall of white outside. Calum stuck his hand into his pocket. "I have something for you, Syd. I stole it back from Tenley." He lifted the sapphire ring from his pocket. The stone glittered in his palm.

A scream rose from Sydney, but before she could run, Calum grabbed her hand and shoved the ring onto her finger. "There." His nails dug into her skin. "My mom died in it, and now you will, too." And then his hand was on her neck, and he was squeezing, hard.

Spots danced before Sydney's eyes. She tried to kick him, scratch at him, *anything*, but Calum was bigger than she was, and much stronger. He pinned her hard against the wall, sending pinpricks of pain reverberating down her shoulder blades. "Please," she coughed. The spots grew bigger, flashes of light that drained all color from her vision. She struggled even harder, trying to wriggle out of his grip, but Calum just jammed his hand against her windpipe, cutting off more air.

"I didn't want to do this, Syd." His breath was hot on her cheek and he stank of beer. "I really was in love with you. But love is just another game, isn't it? How hard can we stomp on Calum's heart before there's nothing left? You thought you won, Syd, but you didn't. I always win."

"No!" The word came out in a choking rasp. "I do love you, Calum!" At the proclamation, his grip loosened, just a little. Air rushed down her throat, making her cough. The room spun around her, walls blurring into ceiling.

She could feel the lie building inside her. It hurt as she forced it out. "I was confused! You'd left me in a tailspin with all your notes, and I didn't know which way to turn. But it never changed how I felt about you."

He was watching her intently now, his forehead scrunched up in confusion. His grip loosened further. "You're the only one who ever really understood me," she rushed on. The words scraped out of her, painful. "I need you, Calum. I love you."

His grip relaxed. The room stopped spinning. Calum's eyes were heavy on her face. She lifted a hand to his cheek, pulling him to her. "I need you," she said again.

"Syd," Calum murmured, and then his lips were on hers. The kiss was hard and intense. His hand released her neck and slid into her hair. It was her chance.

She lifted her hand and slammed the sapphire ring against his face. It dug a gash into his cheek, and Calum leaped backward with a howl. That was all the space Sydney needed. She sprinted away, grabbing her car keys and racing toward the front door.

Outside, the cold slapped at her, an assault from every side. The sun was almost finished setting, and the snow was so thick she could barely see a step in front of her. She pushed blindly forward, the wind whipping her hair into her face. She had to get to the gate. Because of all the snow, she'd left her car parked on the other side, out on the street.

"Sydney..." Calum's voice lifted behind her, tossed left and right on the wind.

Sydney ran faster, toward what she could only hope was the gate. She'd made it several yards when her foot hit something hard and she went flying forward. She landed face-first in the snow, on top of her keys. Cold stung at her skin, rubbing her cheeks raw. She could feel the snow seeping into her clothes, until the cold wasn't just around her, but inside her, settling in her bones. Still, she dragged herself up and lurched forward again, hands out in front of her, searching for the gate. "Sydney?" Calum's voice floated toward her, a little louder this time. A laugh followed, distant and hollow.

Icy iron bars hit up against her fingers. *Yes.* She was shivering violently as she felt around for the door. Her hand closed around the knob. She pulled. Pulled again.

It was locked.

She sagged against the iron bars. She couldn't see the keypad anywhere, and the gate had to be at least eight feet tall and coated in slippery, wet snow. There was no way she was climbing over it.

"Sydney? Where are you?" Calum's voice reached across the darkness and the snow. "The gate's in panic mode; we're locked in. You'll never outrun me. I was a lifeguard, remember?"

Sydney pushed herself off the gate, squinting through the blur of white. Her gaze landed on the cliffs that bordered Neddles. They were the same ones that ran through Dead Man's Falls. She thought about how dark and twisty it had been up there. If there was ever a place she could lose Calum, it was up on those cliffs.

Sydney shoved her keys into her pocket and took off in the direction of the rocks. Drifts of snow were starting to pile up on them, making the climb treacherous. But she had no other option. She could hear Calum calling out in the distance: "Sydney... Sydney..."

She pulled herself up onto the rocks. Snow crept under her fingernails, sending a chill convulsing through her. Calum's voice rang out again. "You want to play, Sydney? Fine, I'll play. But remember: I always win."

She had to keep moving. She had to get away.

She crawled upward through the snow. Hand, foot, hand, foot, inching from rock to rock. She didn't dare look down, or take her eyes off the route. The snow was a tunnel around her. The wind beat at her back. The cold wetness soaked through her sweater and boots until she could no longer feel her limbs.

It had been Calum all along. It was dawning on her slowly, a spinning, twisting realization, the full impact of it dancing just out of her reach. How could she have missed it? How could she have been so blind? She'd *trusted* him. Maybe that was the problem. In the end, it was the people you trusted who had the power to break you.

She forced herself to keep going: up and up.

The cliffs were slick with snow, and she slipped as she climbed higher, slamming hard onto her knees. Pain reeled through her, but she refused to stop. In the distance, a round beam of light broke through the snow. *A flashlight.*

The killer was here.

She pushed herself further. One foot, then the next, then—*ice*.

Her foot slid out from under her. Suddenly she was careening forward, the edge of the cliff much too close. She cried out as she caught herself on a jagged rock. She stretched a toe out, searching for a safe pathway, but at every angle she was met with ice. This high up, it coated everything.

Behind her, the flashlight burned brighter. She was trapped.

She looked out over the cliff. The storm was colorless: stark white brushstrokes against a black sky. Down below she could hear the ocean roaring and crashing. She wrenched the sapphire ring off her finger. She was breathing hard as she threw it over the cliff.

She was nearly at the edge now. Just a few more inches and, like the ring, she, too, would fall into nothingness.

The icy crunch of footsteps rang out through the night.

There was nowhere left to run. Nowhere left to hide.

CHAPTER TWENTY-THREE
Tuesday, 5:50 PM

IT HAPPENED IN A BLUR OF SNOW AND FOG. THE flashlight beam tangled in the snow, illuminating the cliffs in bursts. *Burst*: a thick green sweater. *Burst*: a thin figure, shoulders hunched against the cold. *Burst*: Dark hair, threaded white with snow. "Sydney!" Tenley tried to scream her name, but her lips were too cold to move, and Sydney stood at the edge of the cliff, unaware.

It happened in a frozen web of terror. Tenley clambered upward, scraping and clawing at the snow, too numb to feel it anymore. Emerson slipped, bumping into her side, making her flashlight falter. The beam swept to their left and there was a flash of waves—seething and openmouthed—before Tenley yanked it back.

"Sydney!" Tenley tried again, but the frost was on her lips and clamping down her tongue. It turned her words into ice. Sydney stretched her arms out over empty black air. Finally, Tenley's voice came. It cracked through her icy lips and shattered the air.

It happened in screams.

Emerson slipped again, but Tenley flung herself toward Sydney, rock tearing through her jeans. "We're here, Sydney!" Her fingers grasped at Sydney's sweater, but it was icy on the rocks, and Tenley couldn't get a good grip. They both slid along the edge of the cliff.

"Hold on!" Emerson jumped onto the rock, colliding with Tenley. The impact sent all three of them tumbling away from the edge. They landed tangled together in a snowdrift. Emerson was on top of Tenley's injured leg, making it throb all over again.

"How did you guys get here?" Sydney panted. "The bridge is closed off!" She groaned as she pulled her arm out from under Tenley's back.

Tenley tried to stand up, but her leg gave way. She collapsed back into the snow, pain knifing through her. Gritting her teeth, she tried again. This time her leg held. "Tim stole his dad's boat to take us. It was—we almost—" She tried to shake the image out of her head: waves dwarfing the boat, tossing it on massive palms. "But we made it."

"Tim's waiting in the boat," Emerson added. She groaned as she stood up. There was a long scrape on her forehead. Her blood mixed with snowflakes, staining her skin pink. "We just have to climb back down, and we can all get out of here."

"The darer—it's Calum," Sydney gasped. Her face was so pale that she might have blended into the snow, if it weren't for the purple of her lips.

Tenley flinched. "We know. We sent Josh to tell the police before we left."

"I thought you were him—Calum," Sydney whimpered. "I thought he was going to—"

"Going to what?"

The low voice scraped against Tenley. Calum emerged from the snow, curls drenched in white, feet climbing steadily up the rocks. He wasn't wearing a jacket, but he showed no signs of cold. In fact, he looked perfectly at peace, as if he'd simply gone out for a night-time stroll. "I told you I'd catch you, Sydney. I just didn't realize I'd get all three of you at once." His teeth glowed under the beam of his flashlight when he smiled. "Happy belated birthday to me."

"There's three of us, Calum," Sydney hissed. "And one of you. What do you think you're going to do?"

Calum's hand disappeared into the pocket of his pants. It returned holding a slim knife. Silently, Calum unsheathed it, making the silver glint against the snow. "I brought this with me. If I've learned anything from the movies, it's that every villain needs a good backup plan." He cocked his head to the side. "Though, am I really the villain here? Or is it actually the slut?" His eyes lingered on Emerson. "Or perhaps the bitch?" His gaze traveled to Tenley and she grimaced involuntarily. "Or, the worst culprit of all." His eyes locked on Sydney. "The liar."

He lifted the knife, his eyes never leaving Sydney's face. "Stop him!" Tenley screamed. She switched off her flashlight. Emerson dove for Calum's flashlight at the same time. One-two: the lights snuffed out.

Calum lunged for Tenley, and she kicked hard with her good leg. His dark form buckled, and something slipped from his grip, landing softly in the snow. *The knife.* She dove for it, but his arms were longer, and he clutched it first. Tenley could hear him panting as he lunged at Sydney, the silver blade slicing through the air.

"No!" Tenley launched herself at him from behind. She landed on his back, clinging on like a piggyback ride as she gouged at his eyes. "Drop the knife!" she ordered. She could feel skin tearing away beneath her nails. Calum arched his back with a scream, bucking her off instead.

Emerson ran at him before Tenley even hit the snow. The knife swiped at Emerson's arm as she shoved Calum hard, sending him stumbling backward. Sydney came from the side, punching him in the face with a grunt. Tenley scrambled back to her feet. Her injured leg protested, but adrenaline surged through her, numbing the pain. Separate, Calum had been able to hurt them. But together, they were stronger. They were powerful.

Tenley rammed into Calum, her elbow smashing into his cheekbone with a painful crack. The knife swung wildly as he stabbed blindly at the air.

Emerson grabbed Calum's hair, yanking him backward. "Get the knife!" she yelled. As Sydney dove for the knife, Tenley kicked Calum right in the gut. Once, twice, three times. And then Calum was buckling over and Sydney was screaming, "I got it," and the knife was above her head, a trophy glinting in the moonlight.

"Not for long," Calum growled. He tore out of Emerson's grip. In the darkness he was nothing but a shadow, but Tenley didn't need to see his face to know the evil that was on it. This was the person responsible for Caitlin's and Delancey's deaths. The person who'd made them all fear for their lives again and again.

"Get him!" she howled. They ran at him from all sides, their combined weight enough to knock him off his feet. Tenley felt the slam as Calum collided with the snow. She was on top of him in an instant. She kneed him in the ribs with all her strength. "Stop," he croaked.

"That's enough, Tenley!" Tenley heard Sydney's scream, but she couldn't pull away. She flung herself at Calum, again and again, pounding, kicking. For their freedom. For their fear.

"Tenley, stop! We've got him!"

But she couldn't. She wouldn't.

For Caitlin. For Delancey.

She hit him again. His blood wet her fists, but still she didn't stop.

"Tenley! Tenley!"

Arms wrenched her back. "It's okay," someone was saying. "It's okay. I'm here now." The arms were around her, hugging her tight. Voices rang out nearby, loud and shouting, and suddenly light washed over the island, turning night into day.

"It's okay. It's okay." The voice was Tim's. The arms around her were Tim's. He pulled her away from the police and the firemen, away from Calum, face bloody and battered as a cop dragged him to his feet, away from Sydney collapsing against her dad, and Emerson crying into Josh's shoulder. "It's okay," Tim said again.

Sirens were blaring now, one after another, until the ground vibrated with their song. "Look at me, Tenley." Tim's voice was gruff, and she could hear the whisper of his heartbeat through his shirt. Slowly, she tilted her head up. In the flashing lights, Tim's face glowed red and blue. Gently, he cupped her chin in his hand. "I have you," he promised. "You're safe now."

EPILOGUE
Eight months later

"IT IS WITH GREAT PLEASURE THAT I STAND BEFORE this year's graduating class!" Principal Howard rested her hands on the lectern and stared out at the seniors and their families gathered before her. A soft breeze rustled the trees nearby, dusting the football field with flowers. "I know that for many of you, this has been a year of hardship and loss. But after darkness comes light, and I'd like to think that, for everyone, today is a bright day. You did it! When you leave this field today, you'll be ready for your future."

Sydney clasped her hands together, pressing her new ring into her palm. Her parents had given it to her the night before: a thin gold band dotted with tiny diamonds. "A grown-up ring for our grown-up girl," her dad had said, and Sydney hadn't even flinched.

Up on the podium, Principal Howard was still talking, but Sydney was only half-listening. She twisted around in her chair. The crowd was filled with people she knew, but it was Winslow itself that caught her attention. She still remembered the first time she saw the school. She'd been in second grade, and the building had seemed almost monstrous in size. She'd been so sure it would eat her alive. But here she was eleven years later, still in one piece.

A familiar name drew her focus back to the podium. "...like to honor the memory of Caitlin Thomas, Patricia Sutton, and Delancey Crane," Principal Howard said. "All were exemplary students and highly valued members of the student body. So on behalf of the senior class, I'd like to bestow the Thomas, Sutton, and Crane families with honorary degrees. Winslow wouldn't have been the same place without your daughters."

Sydney swallowed back tears as Caitlin's, Tricia's, and Delancey's parents went up to accept the honorary degrees. A few rows up, Emerson looked back at her. Her cheeks were wet, but there was a small, determined smile on her face. Sydney smiled back.

Of all the crazy things about this year, in some ways, this was the craziest: Someone could torch your whole existence, leaving only charred remains behind, and, still, new life could grow from the ashes.

She glanced at Tenley, who was sitting two rows behind her. She had a faraway look on her face, and Sydney wondered if it was Caitlin she was thinking about, or Calum. Just that morning, twin guilty verdicts had been delivered in the Bauer trials. Sydney had watched on TV as Calum and his dad were led away from the court in handcuffs. They were being sent to separate high-security prisons. In some ways it seemed fitting: She and Calum would leave Echo Bay on the same day.

"And now..." Up on the podium, Principal Howard broke into a smile. "I pronounce you all graduates of Winslow Academy!"

With a cheer, Sydney threw her cap into the air. She watched as it joined the others. They filled the sky, like a flock of birds flying to freedom.

"We are out of here!" Tenley came over to Sydney, her arms raised in triumph. "Sunny skies and outdoor parties, here I come!"

Sydney laughed. At the end of the summer, Tenley would be leaving for the University of California, San Diego. She swore she'd chosen UCSD because of its beach parties and sunny weather, but Sydney had a feeling the job Tim had accepted at a nearby surf school hadn't hurt.

Emerson made a face at Tenley as she joined them. "You are going to be so annoyingly tan by Thanksgiving break."

"And I plan to have a massive party to show it off." Tenley hooked her arm through Sydney's. "One that you will *not* get out of attending, Miss RISD."

"I can't believe you leave today, Syd." Emerson hooked her own arm through Sydney's free one so that they all stood linked: a single, solid chain. "I don't leave for New York and FIT until August. It's going to be really strange without you here."

"Things I never thought I'd hear Emerson Cunningham say," Sydney pointed out with a laugh. She looked down at the ground, where the caps had fallen in a haphazard pattern. "I can't believe I leave today, either."

She'd signed up for RISD's summer program the very day she received news of her scholarship. She'd been so sure she'd want to get away from Echo Bay as soon as possible. But now that the day was here, she wished everything could move in slow motion.

In so many ways, she hated Echo Bay. It was the place where

Calum had tortured and hurt them. It was the place where Caitlin and Tricia and Delancey had died. It was the place where she'd been watched and judged and baited and played. But it was also the place where she'd taken her first award-winning photo. It was the place where she'd jumped waves with her dad and had dozens of movie nights with her mom and, most recently, said good-bye to Guinness when he won his photography internship in Africa. It was the place where she'd kissed Joey for the very first time, and, as strange as it was, it was the place where she'd found her friends—Tenley and Emerson. She cleared her throat, embarrassed by the tears pricking at her eyes. "Thanksgiving," she declared. "I'll even come to your stupid party if I have to."

They were all quiet for a moment, and time seemed to stretch out before them, impossibly big. "Are you scared?" Emerson asked.

Sydney shook her head. "I'm a million and one things, but after this year, not much scares me anymore."

Emerson nodded. So did Tenley. They didn't need to speak to know they were all thinking the same thing.

"There's our graduate!" Sydney's mom ran over and threw her arms around her daughter. "This calls for a picture." Her engagement ring flashed in the sunlight as she handed her camera to Sydney's dad.

"Wait." Sydney smiled shyly at her dad. "You should be in the photo, too." He slung his arm around her shoulders. Their relationship might still be a work in progress, but it got easier every day. It was like her mom said: Change was hard, but it wasn't impossible.

"Ten Ten! There you are!" As Tenley's mom pranced over in a skintight minidress, and Emerson's parents wrapped her up in a hug, and cameras clicked and zoomed all around them, Sydney caught sight of a familiar face weaving through the crowd.

"Congrats, grad," Joey said when he reached her. He wrapped his arms around her waist and kissed her. Like always, it felt like coming home. "Ready to hit the road?" Joey tossed his car keys into the air. "RISD waits for no man. Or woman," he added graciously.

Sydney looked over her shoulder at her mom laughing with her dad, and Tenley tossing a tassel at Emerson, and suddenly she knew: She could drive a thousand miles, but there were some things she'd never leave behind.

She slipped her hand into Joey's. "I'm ready."

ACKNOWLEDGMENTS

It has been a pleasure to work with such a smart, creative, and inspiring publishing team on this series. Thank you to Lexa Hillyer, Lauren Oliver, Rhoda Belleza, Angela Velez, Tara Sonin, and Kamilla Benko at Paper Lantern Lit, Stephen Barbara at Foundry Literary + Media, and the whole team at Little, Brown, especially Elizabeth Bewley, Pam Gruber, and Lisa Moraleda.

Mom, Dad, and Lauren: To have a family who treats your dreams as their own is the most incredible of gifts. Thank you for believing in me and supporting me every step of the way.

Nathan: As a writer, I find it embarrassingly difficult to express just how much your faith, pride, encouragement, and love have meant to me over the years. So I'll just say this: Every day I'm married to you, I feel luckier than the last.

Finally, a huge, heartfelt thank-you to all the readers of this series! Knowing you were out there made me excited to sit down every day and write.

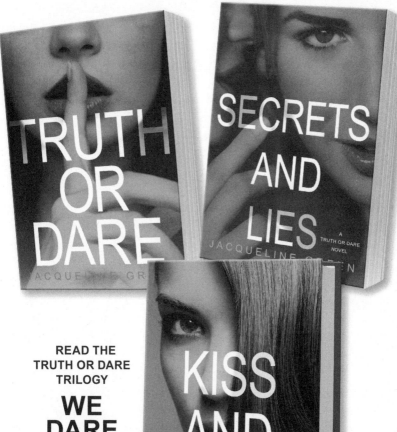